D0483581

Dear Readers,

Many years ago, [illegible], my father said to me, "Bill, it doesn't really matter what you do in life. What's important is to be the *best* William Johnstone you can be."

I've never forgotten those words. And now, many years and almost 200 books later, I like to think that I am still trying to be the best William Johnstone I can be. Whether it's Ben Raines in the Ashes series, or Frank Morgan, the last gunfighter, or Smoke Jensen, our intrepid Mountain Man, or John Barrone and his hard-working crew keeping America safe from terrorist lowlifes in the Code Name series, I want to make each new book better than the last and deliver powerful storytelling.

Equally important, I try to create the kinds of believable characters that we can all identify with, real people who face tough challenges. When one of my creations blasts an enemy into the middle of next week, you can be damn sure he had a good reason.

As a storyteller, my job is to entertain you, my readers, and to make sure that you get plenty of enjoyment from my books for your hard-earned money. This is not a job I take lightly. And I greatly appreciate your feedback—you are my gold, and your opinions *do* count. So please keep the letters and e-mails coming.

Respectfully yours,

William W. Johnstone

WILLIAM W. JOHNSTONE

THE LAST REBEL: SURVIVOR

PINNACLE BOOKS
Kensington Publishing Corp.
http://www/kensingtonbooks.com

PINNACLE BOOKS are published by

Kensington Publishing Corp.
850 Third Avenue
New York, NY 10022

Copyright © 2004 by William W. Johnstone

All rights reserved. No part of this book may be reproduced in any form or by any means without the prior written consent of the Publisher, excepting brief quotes used in reviews.

If you purchased this book without a cover, you should be aware that this book is stolen property. It was reported as "unsold and destroyed" to the Publisher and neither the Author nor the Publisher has received any payment for this "stripped book."

This novel is a work of fiction. Names, characters, places and incidents are either the product of the author's imagination, or are used fictitously. Any resemblance to actual persons, living or dead, or events is entirely coincidental.

All Kensington Titles, Imprints and Distributed Lines are available at special quantity discounts for bulk purchases for sales promotion, premiums, fund-raising, educational or institutional use. Special book excerpts or customized printings can also be created to fit specific needs. For details, write or phone the office of the Kensington special sales manager: Kensington Publishing Corp., 850 Third Avenue, New York, NY 10022, attn. Special Sales Department, Phone: 1-800-221-2647.

Pinnacle and the P logo Reg. U.S. Pat. & TM Off.

First Printing: September 2004

10 9 8 7 6 5 4 3 2 1

Printed in the United States of America

1

The two men stood on the sidewalk in front of the small white church on the narrow street in the town of Mormontown, population 2,190, in the northwest corner of Utah. A sign on the small ragged lawn that fronted the church stated JESUS MERCY in large black capital letters, and beneath it were detailed the times when the services were going to be conducted. One of the men was the minister of the church, the First Mormon. His name was Frederick Baker, mid-fifties, dressed in a dark, dusty, rumpled suit. He had a fringe of mussed gray hair, plain, pale, even features, light blue eyes, and a little paunch. He looked tired—and very sad, with an air of hopelessness about him. The man facing him—and looking down on him—was in stark physical contrast. He was only thirty, very tall and lean, dressed in a denim shirt and pants, short black hair, deeply tanned. He was, at first glance, movie-star handsome, but on second glance one would know that he was hardly the Hollywood type. He had a rough-hewn quality, a certain crinkling here and there, particularly when he smiled, that clearly showed that he had spent a lot more time in the great outdoors—climbing, hunting, fishing—than on a soundstage.

His most striking features, though, were his eyes.

Indeed, when some people looked into them they became a little disconcerted, even afraid. The eyes were emerald-green and behind them was an almost feral intensity, the clear message: mess with me and you do so at your own risk. Not aggressive or bullying in any way, but what people saw in his eyes was really there. You didn't want to mess with him.

His name was Jim LaDoux.

Jim had just driven in from the middle of north central Nevada using a camouflage-painted HumVee, the squarish, odd-looking vehicle that was two feet wider and three feet longer than the military jeep, twenty times as useful. Years earlier the HumVee had supplanted the once-great jeep as the official vehicle used by the military. The HumVee—plus the weapons and supplies it contained—was a gift that came about as the result of a chance meeting with General Ben Raines, a legendary soldier who for years, following a devastating nuclear war, "the Great War," had led an army of soldiers called the Rebels against many groups—including the U.S. government—in the fight to create a government that was based on fairness that boiled down to following the simple but profound precepts formulated by a bunch of very smart and very heroic men who had lived in the 1770s in a country they created called the United States of America.

Jim had never driven a HumVee, but during the long trip he had found it a fine vehicle. It was very roomy and comfortable and had a sixteen-inch clearance from the ground as opposed to the seven to eight inches of a jeep. This allowed him to traverse rocky terrain that would have rolled over the jeep. Indeed, some of the land the HumVee went over would have given a mountain goat pause. In addition, Jim had learned that the vehicle could drive through deep creeks, rivers, whatever, as long as the water wasn't so high that it engulfed certain parts of the engine. He could also get better traction because he could partially deflate the tires with a control in the cab, then reinflate them when on dry land. And despite the vehicle's bulkiness and heaviness it was fast. Jim had traveled most of the way, because he was not in any hurry, at thirty-five to forty miles an hour. It had a V-8 engine and a couple of times he had roared along at over seventy miles an hour. Small wonder that the military used it for everything—a gun truck (machine and other guns could be mounted on top), an ambulance, a signal truck, a supply truck (you could load well over ten thousand pounds on it), and more.

Jim had started his trip from his mountain home in northwest Idaho, where he had been raised outside a small town called Jaynesville. He meant the trip to be cathartic, to help deal with the loneliness and sadness that had besieged him for the last six months, when his grandfather, the last of his immediate family, had died and he had been living alone in the mountain cabin that his great-grandfather had built over a hundred years earlier.

There had been no other human beings to talk to, no living thing that was close. Even the family dog, Brandy, had died, perhaps of a broken heart when his master, Jim's grandpa, died. As the months had gone by, Jim, isolated except for an intermittently working radio, had become more and more depressed, curtailing and then stopping the hunting, trapping, and fishing that were his livelihood. And he was sleeping a lot even when he wasn't really tired. He knew that there was only one thing to do.

Get on the road, head somewhere. Start living—or finish dying.

He did not have any specific destination in mind, though at first he had an idea that he would head east. He had read about New Hampshire, Maine, and Vermont and they sounded like places he would like to at least visit. They weren't the Rocky Mountains but they had mountains, wildlife, extremes of temperature—all the stuff he had grown up with. Plus, he had never seen an ocean and would like to, and he knew that parts of New Hampshire and Maine touched the Atlantic. Still, for some reason when he left Jaynesville and came to a junction in the road that would take him south or east, he headed south.

He didn't attribute anything particularly significant to that direction. But he knew his grandpa would. "There's no such thing as coincidence," Grandpa used to say. "Everything happens for a reason, large and small."

What it could mean to him, Jim had no idea. He was just a mountain man trying to get his heart working again. Certainly, he thought, no large destiny awaited him.

He knew the trip south was going to be rough in one way. The tubercular-sounding intermittent transmission from the radio had filled him in on something horrific happening in America as well as the rest of the world, something not designed to make you happy, unless you were a hyena or a vulture.

But the radio reports hardly painted pictures as vivid as the reality of what the plague had wrought. It seemed to have struck in pockets, and he started seeing the result of it when he crossed over the southern border of Idaho into Nevada. What he had understood in the abstract he now grasped in a visceral, in-your-face way. In fact his first experience with plague had made him vomit so hard that he saw blood mixed with the excretions. He had actually smelled a town in Nevada before he saw it. As a hunter and outdoorsman he was very attuned to the wind and what was riding on it, in this case a thick, pervasive stench that was a cross between methane gas and fetid Limburger cheese.

As he drove into the town, which was called Nevada City, the sight was horrific, the streets lined and littered with stinking corpses, bloated bodies, covered with raised, black masses of flesh that commentators had named *bubas*.

He had been able to make it halfway through the town before he was outside the HumVee, bent at the waist, vomiting violently.

He found, as he rolled slowly along that the plague played no favorites. Men, women, and children, babies, teenagers had all been felled by it. And from what Jim had heard on the radio, all had died quickly. The average life span of persons contracting the disease was three to five days.

Jim was a hard man who came out of a hard life. Hardly a day went by when he didn't see death. But nothing had prepared him for this.

Nevada City and the other towns also deepened Jim's depression. He was traveling to get away from it all but heading right into it.

The radio had been right about survivors. One broadcast had said that the plague usually killed nine of ten people that were in contact with it, and Jim found this to be true. But sometimes the body count was nil. Entire towns had survived. He would pull into a town expecting to see bodies strewn all over or piled up like cordwood, if the town had the man-power to do it, but everyone was alive. People would be walking the streets, working, playing, doing whatever people do. Living. This had occurred in three different towns, and when he saw it it gave him a jolt of joy.

Something else made his spirits soar as well. The plague was having zero effect on the animal kingdom. The survival rate was 100 percent. Why? He had no idea. But he knew that anyone who would hope to come up with a treatment could start by learning what made the animals resistant.

We were all animals, Jim reasoned, and if grizzlies survived, so could people.

Still, as he experienced all this he found a certain anger building. An anger toward God. No one knew for sure where the plague had come from. Some said from an alien universe, others from a mistake in a government lab, others from nature itself. But that was all speculation. All anyone knew for sure was that it was an aggressive and new form of bubonic plague, the so-called "Black Death" that had wiped out twenty-five million of the sixty million people on earth in the fourteenth century. But the bottom line, Jim thought, was that the entity who was ultimately responsible for it was God. And try as he might, he could not begin to explain why God allowed it to be. And that pissed him off.

Now, standing opposite Reverend Blake, Jim had the chance to utter a question that had been generated by the anger, and had popped into his head when he stopped to ask Blake if he was still heading east. Blake had confirmed that and then Jim asked the question.

"Was this God's doing?" he asked, and he didn't

have to identify what he was asking about. Mormontown had not been one of the towns that had escaped the plague, as indicated by the neat stacks of coffins—at least three hundred—that lined the streets. In Mormontown people didn't put out their papers for collection. They put out their corpses.

Reverend Blake was silent. Surely, he had heard the edge in Jim's voice and seen the intensity in his eyes. But Jim was not going away. He waited for a reply.

"No," Blake finally said. "It was not."

"How can you be sure of that?"

"Because in my heart I know it was not."

"That's not much of an answer."

"It's the best one I can give." Blake turned to walk away.

"Wait," Jim said softly.

The minister paused, turned, and looked at Jim.

"Where are you going?" Jim asked.

"I'm going inside God's house to pray. God be with you, young man."

You should be out here, Jim thought, praying for the people whom God had seen fit to turn into breakfast for vultures. Jim blinked. He felt guilty to think that way. He should not think like that. God had been there many times for him and his family. Why rip at Him when things went wrong? And who was Jim to question what happened? Who was Jim to try to decipher why God did what He did?

He looked down the street again and then had a flashing image, like a slide show at high speed, of towns where death and destruction had descended, and all he could do was sigh. "Whole world's screwed up," Jim muttered, shaking his head, as he walked back to the HumVee. He climbed in behind the wheel and looked at "Reb"—a stray dog who, at least, proved something was still a little right with the world. He had encountered Reb just as he crossed into Nevada. In fact he had almost turned him into roadkill, and Jim took to him immediately. Jim had always been partial to mutts, and Reb—whom he named after Ben Raines—had a Heinz-57 lineage. He was a big dog who looked more like a police dog than any other kind, but Jim, who was somewhat of an expert on dog behavior because he had owned them all his life, knew that no matter the kind or kinds, it was it was a good dog, a well-trained one who had belonged to someone. Jim had tried various commands, everything from "Sit" to "Fetch," even "Quiet," and Reb had passed the tests with flying colors. Jim would not have been surprised if Reb had been owned by a dog trainer.

At first, Jim had debated with himself whether to take Reb with him or not. Jim knew that on the way east he would be camping out in bear country, and bears and dogs didn't mix too well. Dogs would run after a bear, and if they caught up it could lead to the dog's demise, or the bear's if the dog's owner was on the scene with a rifle. Recognizing this natural hostility, park service rangers banned traveling with dogs through national parks.

Of course it occurred to Jim that national parks were not going to be overrun with park rangers, but that really didn't matter. He liked to think he set his own rules for ethics and morality. It was sometimes the hardest way to do things this way, he had discovered, but ultimately it made you the happiest.

On the other hand, this was a special circumstance, and in a pragmatic sense Jim had done it before. He had taken his golden retriever–shepherd "King" with him and there had been no problem at all, because the dog remained quiet and suppressed his exploratory nature.

Immediately after Jim had decided to take Reb with him he started to feel, in general, a little better. Reb had acknowledged Jim as the alpha or leader of the pack, as all dogs will to the most dominant member of their packs, and they were getting along very well. Moreover, Jim enjoyed just occasionally looking at Reb, lying on a blanket on the floor on the passenger side. And every time—every time—he did it, Reb would look up and get his tail going. And the times they stopped in the park had proved no problem at all. Jim said, "Stay," and Reb stayed.

Now, Jim climbed into the HumVee, which was parked on the street heading east, and Reb took his customary spot.

"Ready, Reb?" Jim said. "Let's roll."

Jim fired up the HumVee and they pulled out. As he went, he thought that he hoped it would be the last time he would see the plague in action. Maybe he would get lucky. And maybe he would be lucky enough to avoid marauders, which was what he had encountered shortly after meeting General Ben Raines. Some marauders had attacked him and a badly weakened General Raines, and Jim and the general had killed them quickly.

Marauders were the reason Jim had tried to stick to the back roads: the possibility of more of them showing up. Finding back roads was made very much easier with military maps he found in the glove compartment, though he had gotten lost once. The maps were highly detailed. He had read somewhere a quote of General Raines that he couldn't help but recall when he had discovered the maps: *Wars are won with men and material,* Raines had said, *but maybe the greatest asset is information.*

These maps, Jim thought, did nothing to deny that statement.

The only bad thing about back roads was a lack of service stations. Jim had found around twenty so far. All had been abandoned. The problem with the HumVee was that it was an oat burner. Jim figured he was averaging only about six miles a gallon, and the tank held twenty-five gallons. To ensure that he didn't get stuck on some back road, he filled up the five-gallon containers that Raines had set up side by side in the bed of the vehicle.

Occasionally, he would have to travel a main road or highway until he found one. These were all abandoned as well, but they had gas. The plague had drastically cut down on the number of customers.

When he did stop, he brought the weapons he had out from under the front seat and laid them on the passenger seat, fully loaded. Ready to go.

Jim was great with a rifle and a pistol. He had been shooting since he was ten years old and he had never missed hitting his target, whether it be stationary or moving. But he had never used automatic weapons, nor had the experience—until he was with General Raines—of firing them with someone firing back. Jim was thankful now for what his older brother, Ray, had taught him about guns. Thanks to Ray he had a good idea what automatic weapons were all about. Ray was surely a good teacher with a lot of experience. He had fought in two wars.

Included in Jim's inventory were a variety of handguns and two AK-47s, which Ray told him had been produced in larger numbers than any other rifle. Ray said that though precise figures weren't available, it was estimated that over twelve million were made, and more were being made. The AK-47, popularly known as the Kalisnikov, actually had come out of research first developed by the Germans, finding that most combat situations involved fights at four hundred meters or less, so a new cartridge, a Soviet 7.62-by-39mm cartridge had been developed. A so-called assault rifle, it could fire its relatively low-powered ammunition—low-powered compared to conventional rifle ammunition—either on single shot or fully automatic to a maximum effective combat range of around four hundred meters. "It's a great weapon in an assault situation," Ray had said, "because you can use it single shot or automatic. It uses thirty-bullet clips, and it's the kind of gun that's easy to field-strip and can take a lot of kicking and keep on ticking."

Apparently so. It was the weapon of choice of guerilla armies all over the world.

Yes, Jim, thought, but he never wanted to have to use it except to protect himself. Jim hated war. Ray had carried automatic weapons, and had gone to those wars, and now his thirty-five-year-old body lay in a plot in David Rook Rural Cemetery near Jaynesville. Jim's father had been in another war, and he knew about guns too. And he had also lost his life in combat. He had died of shrapnel wounds at the ripe old age of thirty-three, and Jim's mother shortly thereafter of cancer, so Jim had been raised by his grandfather and Ray, until he died too.

There had to be a better way, Jim thought, to work things out with other people than to try to kill each other. He had read about war, and many times the reasons for the war were unclear. You needed a real clear reason to die. He was not about to die for some fuzzy political principle, or to grab some land that didn't amount to a hill of crap. He remembered he had read once about McNamara, who had been secretary of defense during the Vietnam War, crying years after the fact because he later knew he was wrong for sending all those innocent boys to their deaths.

That was a bunch of woodpecker crap. No way would he fight for that.

Ben Rainses sounded like he had the right idea, but Jim would not have been willing to fight any wars for him either. You lost your father and your brother in war and it tended to turn you off on it. Way off. Talk it out. Talk it through. People had done that. There had been many wars, true. But many wars had been avoided because people gave in to each other.

In addition to the AK-47, Jim also had an old-fashioned Thompson submachine, or tommy gun, which Ray had explained was the "weapon of choice of gangsters," but eventually it became great and popular when modified for use in World War II, a formidable weapon that was not that easy to handle but could fire six hundred rounds a minute. Jim knew this was a favorite of General Raines and Jim had used it to dispatch two of four marauders he met while he was with Raines.

Above all, Jim liked the Glock handgun, which was light, 9mm, and held sixteen shots. He had heard the story of why the New York City Police Department carried these pistols—because of a death. One NYPD officer had been in a shootout with a perp and the cop was using a six-shot .38 while the bad guy was using a 9mm. When the bad guy knew that the cop had used up all his ammunition—he'd counted six shots—he just walked up and put two bullets in the twenty-three-year-old cop's head—and had five left in the clip.

Jim withdrew a cigarette paper from his jacket pocket, folded it like a little trough with his fingers, then used the other hand to sprinkle on and tamp down some Prince Albert tobacco. He rolled the cigarette closed, licked it, popped it in his mouth, and lit it with a Zippo lighter.

He took a deep drag and focused inward. He smiled. For a moment he got an image that was straight out of a movie. A wonderful movie. He could see himself, knee deep in rapidly running water that was so clear that he could see the pebble-covered creek bed almost as clearly as if the water wasn't there, and then flicking his wrist to make a fly sail out on the end of his fishing line, there to make a little splash and wait for one of the fat trout that, hopefully, would get a hankering for the fly bobbing above him on the silvery water.

He knew he could he could live indefinitely in the wild, and in harmony with everything from bears to marmots. His grandfather had once said, "Jimmy boy, you know the wild so well I sometimes think you were born part wolf."

The relatively narrow road was flanked by evergreens, and Jim knew that this was an ideal situation. The trees provided great cover though he knew that many parts of Wyoming, which he had traveled through extensively while still living in Idaho, were not forested. Besides its spectacular mountain ranges, much of it was desert, and most of it was covered with various kinds of sagebrush, which provided zero cover when you were traveling by vehicle, particularly a camouflage-painted HumVee.

His route was typical backcountry road, mile after

mile of forest; occasionally he could see a house through the veil of trees. So far, he thought, so good. His mood, he sensed, had gotten just a little better. It wasn't a square dance on Saturday night in Jaynesville but it was better than it had been.

Most of the road was straight, but of course some was curved, and as he came around one curve he got a surprise that put him on full alert.

The road was blocked by a barricade. It looked like a steel I-beam had been placed across the road, the ends of the beams housed in some sort of sawhorse arrangement about four feet above the ground. But that wasn't the only thing barring passing. There were six men all wearing khaki uniforms, all wearing the same short beards, albeit different colors, and red berets. And armed to the teeth. Four of the men looked like they had shotguns, and two Kalisnikovs. They also had holstered handguns and belts of grenades.

Jim slowed the HumVee and then stopped but kept the engine idling. Just like he had done when he was hunting game, he started to calculate what he would do if they would, in effect, charge—started to fire on him. There wasn't much he could do. The firepower they were toting would make Swiss cheese of the HumVee, and him, in short order and maybe turn it into a fireball, this thanks to the gas cans he had stored in back.

And if he wanted to make his butt scarce, he couldn't do that either. There was no room to turn. If he wanted to move out, all he could do was throw it in reverse and put the pedal to the metal.

Then two of the men, both muscular, maybe in their thirties, one tall, the other short, starting walking toward him, each carrying his gun at port arms. They did not seem threatening, but one never knew. Jim pulled the Glock, which was on the passenger seat in a holster, flicked the holster out of sight near Reb, and pushed the gun under his right thigh. Then a plan hit him. He was very conscious that he had a loaded, thirty-cartridge AK-47 under his seat. If the men were hostile and drew down on him he would shoot first one and then the other in the head, and bolt out of the Hummer, using it for cover, hopefully before the other four men made mincemeat of him with their weapons.

Then something glittering on their chests caught Jim's eye. He saw something he hadn't noticed because of the grenades. Each had silver medallions held by silver chains hanging from their necks. The medallions were maybe three inches in diameter, and inside the circular edge was a cross, the ages-old symbol of Jesus Christ, a modern depiction of the crucifixion.

The tall man looked at Jim with narrow blue eyes.

"What do you want here?" the man demanded.

"Just passing through," Jim replied. "Heading east."

The man's eyes narrowed to the point where they were just about slits. Jim tried to read what was in them, but couldn't. The other man's hazel eyes were blank.

"Everything east of here," Slit Eyes said, "is known as the Zone, stranger. It's no-man's land."

"Why is this so special?"

The shorter man stepped forward.

"Are you a Christian?"

That was, Jim thought, none of their business. But if he didn't answer he didn't know if it would lead to violence. He decided to answer, but he also wondered if he should tell the man that he was born Catholic though, in truth, he hadn't been to Mass or confession in more years than he could recall. Churches were few and far between in Idaho's wilderness. Still, he felt that he and his family had lived a Christian life. But something inside would not let him go into all this. His attitude was accommodating—to a point.

"I believe in God, yes. Why do you ask?"

"Them folks in the Zone—that's what we call it—don't," the man replied.

Jim stared at the man for a moment, then shrugged, and said quietly, "Well, so what?"

The man nodded slowly, his eyebrows arched a little.

"You'll find out, fella," he said. "You go in there and you'll sure find out. We're suggesting you don't."

"I'll be okay," Jim said.

The man backed away, apparently a signal that Jim would be allowed to pass.

"Go on," the man said. "Just don't say we didn't warn you."

The man waved and the two of the other four men went over and swung the big I-beam out of the way.

Jim put the HumVee in gear and drove forward slowly, very conscious of the Glock under his haunch. As he passed the other men, he noticed their expressions. They were looking at him as if he were a steer going into a slaughterhouse. And then, twenty or so yards beyond them, he glanced in the rearview mirror still wary that this might be some sort of trick, that they were going to open up on him. But he saw only one action: one of the men was making the sign of the cross.

2

The so-called Zone did not seem dangerous to Jim. It was very ordinary. Just mile after mile of evergreen forest, an occasional home spotted through the trees, and a few times some animals. Once he had seen an elk, another time a buck deer, and another—the treat of the ride so far—a black bear sow and two teddy-bear-size cubs trailing after her. And once he had a close call—or the skunk did—when Jim narrowly missed turning it into roadkill which he did not need, with what he had put his nose through already.

Despite the lack of an open threat, Jim stayed alert. He was sure that the medallion men on the barricade were not telling him that the Zone was dangerous as a joke. Jim knew that there was always the possibility—and it could be a strong possibility—of being attacked. He knew this was the time of the predator, because when people were down was when predators emerged. They preyed on the sick, the young, the old, the helpless. So, too, men. They would much rather attack someone who was defenseless than someone who was not. Such people always struck Jim as not only evil, but shortsighted, just plain stupid. He had always been raised to believe that far and away the most important person in anyone's life was the one looking back at you from a mirror, and when you prey on the helpless, what did that make you? Of course people like that had a very simple solution to self-image. They never looked in the mirror.

But Jim also knew something else. That it was in bad times that always produced the best people, like Mother Teresa, who would work the streets of Calcutta where the dead lay out in the open even before the plague came, ministering to the dead and dying, the forlorn and forgotten. Or the doctor who would stand in some godforsaken place in Africa and use himself as a guinea pig for an experimental serum, or a guy like his brother Ray who had his whole life ahead of him but would die jumping on a grenade so others could live.

Jim swallowed hard. God, he missed Ray. He loved him and idolized him and he didn't need a psychiatrist to tell him that Ray was his surrogate father. He remembered that one of Ray's favorite TV shows was a very old one called *Superman,* where the father, as the planet dies around him, saves his son, and before he goes he tell him: "And all that I have is in you."

Jim swallowed again. So it was with him and Ray. Jim had modeled his life after him—except for the war part—and knew that he would always be with him no matter what he did or where he went. Ray had been a model for the way you should live your life. That was his gift to his young brother, Jim, and it was as good as gifts get. And Jim hoped, someday, that he could pass on what was in him to his own son.

Despite his awareness of potential danger, Jim relaxed more and more as the miles piled up. Still, part of him remained alert, a quiet but observant eye inside him always scanning for potentially hazardous situations. Maybe, he thought, smiling, he was part wolf or some other animal. That's how they survived: by staying alert always.

While there was no one to keep him company on his journey, he would occasionally have a "conversation" with Reb, who would invariably respond to his name by raising his head and wagging his tail.

"So how you doing, Reb? You're lucky. Lucky that I found you." Jim smiled. "A lucky dog."

But Jim knew that he was lucky too. Dogs were wonderful creatures. As a trapper he once knew in Idaho had put it, "God was having a real good day when He made the dog." Indeed, Jim had often thought that the world would be a much better place if people acted more like dogs and horses, another animal favorite of Jim's. (Though, in truth, horses were not that bright. In fact when asked if they were smart, his grandfather had a standard answer: "If you were that big and that beautiful, would you spend your entire day eating grass?") If you treated a dog or a horse a certain way, you could be sure that was the way it would treat you back. Not people. You could treat people as if they were the queen of Sheba and they would stab you in the back.

At one point, Jim pulled off the road onto the shoulder to stretch, take a leak, top off the gas tank by emptying two of the five-gallon gas cans into it. As he did, he thought again that he did not like carrying this much gas in the vehicle. It made him, in effect, a mobile bomb, but it was either that, at this point, or start walking. And the HumVee had too much going for it to make him want to look for another vehicle, which, he was sure, he could get. Many had been abandoned. Indeed, half of Nevada was now a used car lot. Jim smiled: with nothing down required, now or later!

Once back in the cab, the kinks gone, he rolled a cigarette, lit up, took a couple of drags, and was on his way again.

Besides the occasional animal, Jim also had the flora and fauna itself to view.

It was early June and the forest was in full flower, so he did not see as much as he would if it were another season. But the animals he had seen reminded him—if he needed that—that no animal, as far as anyone could tell, had come down with the plague. That gave him hope. More than that, if he were a medical investigator he would start looking into what kept animals well to try to determine what made people sick.

Occasionally, too, the forest would clear a little and he could see mountains and the big sky. As many times as he had seen the mountains, they still moved him. In fact, his favorite song was "America the Beautiful." He loved the words. "Oh, beautiful, for spacious skies, for amber waves of grain, for purple mountain majesties."

"There's only one thing more beautiful than the mountains," Ray had said, "and that's a beautiful woman."

That, Jim thought, was hard to argue with. And someday he hoped to be able to see if Ray was right!

Every now and then, Jim would also see narrow dirt roads leading off the road he was on to somewhere, either a house or nowhere, and he would be tempted just to follow it to God knew where. But he resisted the urge. The width of the HumVee said no. The roads were narrow and the HumVee was twelve feet wide. There might not be a turnaround and he did not relish having to back out.

What he did not see, aside from marauders or whatever this danger was, was more dead people. He was grateful. Christ, he thought. It must be a bitch to be a coroner. That's all these guys and gals ever saw all the time: dead people. After awhile it had to get to you. Indeed, he had heard on the radio once that reporters who were involved in death scenes suffered posttraumatic stress syndrome, the problem first discovered in soldiers who fought in Vietnam.

And, thinking of death, what about the plague? What hope, ultimately, could humanity have if the plague wasn't brought under control? Or, maybe, it would go away by itself. That's what happened to the one in the fourteenth century. This one would too, though Jim knew that a far better answer would be to cure it through scientific means. Who wanted to be sitting on what, in effect, was a plague bomb that might go off again at any moment?

One thing Jim knew, he was immune. In some of the towns he had passed through, the bodies were everywhere. There was ample opportunity for him to come down with the disease. If he hadn't by now, he wasn't going to.

At another point along his journey, Jim stopped again, but this time for Reb to do his business. And as he watched, Jim thought again how well trained Reb was. Training was so important . . . so important . . .

Abruptly, Jim remembered a friend of his named Luke McGovern and his German shepherd, who was named Cap. People used to laugh at how hard Luke worked to train Cap, but one day it paid off handsomely—by saving the dog's life. Luke had gone camping. He had let Cap run free—it was an unrestricted area—and at one point Cap wandered across a fairly well traveled road while Luke stayed at the other side at the camp.

It all happened in an instant. Luke was looking at

some fishing gear and he glanced up to see Cap starting to run back toward his camp, maybe three yards from the edge of the road; and speeding down the road, not ten yards away, was a pickup truck. They were sure to collide, but in that instant Luke yelled the command that he had taught over and over and over again to Cap: "Down!" The dog dropped like a stone and the pickup went whizzing by, missing him by a foot.

Like the rest of the road he had traveled, most of it was straight, but there were some curves and he was coming around one when he got another surprise. Directly to his right was a two-story white building, on the side of which someone had painted—in huge red letters two stories high—GOD IS DEAD.

The sign was stark. Not only were the words big, but the paint had run down from the letters, making it look as if they were bleeding

And the sign writer or writers made sure that people would see the sign. All the evergreens that were in front of the side of the building and would have at least partially blocked the view had been sawn down, and lay in a jumble on the ground.

The building, Jim saw, looked like it had housed a business. In the front was a plate-glass window at street level—though it was knocked in—and a framework jutting out over a door that had held a sign.

There was also a road that ran past the building on the side where the sign was. This, he thought, was probably the road that customers used to get whatever the building sold; there was a packed-dirt parking area in front of the building. And across the road, to his left, there was a modest home.

Jim, Glock in his pocket, got out of the HumVee,

still keeping it running, and took a few steps toward the building. The people who ran whatever was in the building, he thought, probably lived in the house.

Jim reflected on the words again: *God is dead?* he thought. *I don't think so.*

Jim thought of what the medallion people back at the barricade had said to him, implying that there were people in "the Zone" who would not take kindly to someone who believed in God—like Jim.

Jim took out paper and the tobacco and rolled a cigarette, licked it closed, and lit up. He took a few more steps toward the sign and stopped and looked up, thinking as he smoked.

The thing about the sign, he thought, was that it was filled with hatred. People who would take that long to clear the area and deface a building with what was really a sacrilegious sign like that had a lot of hatred in their heart. And what could he infer from it if they truly believed it? True, he had not been that religious, but a world without God in it and at the end of it all was a world that was guaranteed to be in chaos, simply because there were no laws. It was Moses, Jim thought, who brought the Ten Commandments down from the mountain, but it was God who had handed them to him.

"Thou shalt not kill, thou shalt not commit adultery, thou shalt not covet thy neighbor's wife, thou shalt honor thy father and thy mother. . . ." These laws, Jim thought, were created because God recognized the weakness of man. He knew that people must be given laws to adhere to. But if "God is Dead," the clear implication was that so were His laws.

Jim took a deep drag, let the smoke trail out his nose. It was, he thought, disturbing.

After a while, he went back to the HumVee. If nothing else, the sign had reinforced what the medallion wearers said, and his experience here confirmed that he was in an area where there were some very dangerous people prowling around.

He looked down at Reb.

"Hey, buddy," he said, "we got some nuts around here. And not the kind squirrels gather."

Reb wagged his tail rapidly in affirmation.

Jim put the HumVee in gear and moved forward. For a moment, he thought about turning around and heading back, but just as quickly realized that it was too late for that. The medallion wearers had told him if he went through the barricade he was on a one-way trip.

Jim hoped again that he didn't meet anyone. The last thing he wanted was some firefight with nutcases. *Just leave me alone,* he thought, *and I'll leave you alone.*

But another thing Jim knew was that life doesn't care what an individual wants, it just plays out the way it wishes. A miles down the road as he rounded yet another curve he got another surprise, this one even worse than the barricade and the sign. Hanging from the lowest branch of an oak tree was a dead person.

He drove close to it. It looked like a woman—the body had long blond hair—and she had large breasts. Her thick tongue was protruding from her lips, her eyes were bulging, weird looking like people with the plague because the pupils were fixed and dilated, and her body was obviously bloated around the belly and feces and urine had collected in a pool beneath her bloody bare feet, two feet off the ground. Her legs and arms were cut and bruised. And she stunk. Around her neck was hung a crudely lettered sign: BELIEVER.

Jim got out of the vehicle, first shoving the Glock in his pocket, and walked around the body. He looked at its shape . . . and then something hit him in a profoundly sad way. The body was not bloated by death alone. The woman had been pregnant.

"God Almighty," Jim said out loud. "God Almighty."

No way, he thought, was he going to leave her like this. It was going to be a messy, stomach-churning job but he was going to bury her, albeit in a shallow grave. All he had to do was get up high enough so he could cut her free. Standing on the HumVee would allow him to do that easily. And he also had to cover himself or dress in some sort of protective gear, or wrap her, so that the oozings from her body would not get on him. Yes, it was not, he thought, going to be a pleasant task.

He was about to pull the HumVee next to the woman, calculating at the same time where he might bury here, when he heard a sound in the distance, like thunder. He realized it was approaching from the road to his right.

He had been so preoccupied with the woman that he had not really examined the area. Now he did, because instinct had told him to get away from that sound as quickly as he could. Directly across from the end of the road and set back somewhat was an ordinary-looking residence with beige vinyl siding, a brown asphalt shingle roof, a patch of grass in front, bushes lined up all around it, and all set on a crawl-space type of foundation. And—all important—a backyard.

Quickly, he drove the HumVee up a driveway that flanked the left side of the house and then pulled it around to the back. Fortunately, there was no deck, just grass.

Room for the HumVee. He turned it off, then

rubbed Reb on the side of the head and said, "Be quiet, boy."

Reb looked at him, Jim swore, as if he understood. He didn't even shake his head in response. This would be an acid test.

He grabbed the Glock, the AK-47, and the Thompson submachine gun, which were under the driver's-side seat, and moving in a half crouch, went up along the right side of the building, then set himself up at the corner behind a couple of thick holly bushes. He had a clear view of the entire scene. He placed the Thompson on the ground and checked the AK-47. The clip was firmly in place, safety off. The Glock was shoved down into his back pocket.

A fleeting thought. He was a hell of a shot. In fact—and he was legend in his hometown for this—once he squeezed off a round at an animal he sighted, he never missed.

A thought. Now he was about to find out again just how good he was with automatic weapons. Well, he had done pretty well with the Thompson when with Raines.

Abruptly, the scene was filled with smoke, dust, and noise as vehicles emerged from the woods. One by one they stopped, and before the engines were turned off, people—or more specifically, uniformed people—were starting to pour out of them.

There were five vehicles in all, three jeeps, and two SUVs. All were painted dull flat black and had an insignia painted on the doors, the letter R with a red lightning bolt through it.

All of the people were dressed in gray uniforms, the kind that convicts wore, and all wore soft gray caps and were armed to the teeth. He counted twenty people—

or soldiers. Most brandished AK-47s. By everything human it should have been a nerve-racking sight for one man. But, as was usual in hazardous situations, Jim found himself getting calmer, able to think as clearly as if he were standing in the middle of a river trying to hook a nice big walleye.

"Hey," one of the people said, "look who's still hanging around!"

Jim blinked. He felt something cold and hard, and had a momentary urge to shoot the wise guy right in the mouth. No, he told himself, not yet.

Some of the other people laughed, but a tall man with a very deep voice was all business. He acted as if he had not heard the joke at all.

"Let's find that other bitch," he said to no one in particular. "You sure you seen her around here?"

"I'm sure," one of the people, a man, replied. "She was right here not more than half an hour ago."

"Anyone else with her?" Deep Voice said.

"I didn't see nobody else."

"We'll search that house for her," Deep Voice said, pointing with an AK-47 in Jim's direction. "When we find her, don't shoot her. Take her alive. I want to crucify the bitch as an example to all of them that followed her and her pa."

Crucify! Jim thought. *Where am I! Caught up in some time warp going back two thousand years? What in the hell is going on here?*

That silent question was answered in the next heartbeat when one of the women, the bustier of the two, said: "Killing Beverly will go a long way toward dropping this God crap that's springing up around here unless they want to die for their beliefs."

God crap? Jim thought. *God crap!*

Jim waited, calm and clear. He knew a lot of people

were close to dying, and maybe him as well. But it didn't bother him. Death was an abstract thought. If he died, he died. So be it. Certain things you had to do in life, and if you didn't you were dead anyway.

He raised the Kalisnikov. If someone had taken his pulse at that moment it would be about fifty-five.

Then Deep Voice motioned forward with his arm and the entire group started to saunter slowly toward the house.

It occurred to Jim that he might pop up and tell them to freeze. But then what? An instinct told him that they then would spend their time looking for him to drop his guard for a millisecond so they could blow him away.

Then a question occurred to him: how would Ben Raines handle it? Jim knew, and in the same mental breath, as it were, he knew the die was cast. These were killers and if he didn't kill them they would kill him. It was just a matter of them getting close enough. He would unload on them from the bushes. He would start firing from the left, then sweep back to the right. Hopefully the last man would discover where the firing was coming from just as he died.

If he needed more firepower, he would use the Thompson.

He was ready. They marched slowly toward him.

Then, abruptly, he heard a noise to his left that raised the hair on his neck. He looked. There, on her hands and knees under the crawl space, was a young woman. She looked thoroughly spooked.

"Please," she whispered.

"Be quiet," Jim barely whispered back, putting his finger on his mouth.

"If they catch me they'll kill me and you."

Jim nodded and thought: *Tell me something I don't know.*

"I mean it," the young woman persisted.

"Shut up! If you don't, we're going to have problems for sure."

Without the element of surprise, he thought, he would have very big problems.

The woman, Jim guessed, keeping his eye on the group advancing toward him, was the Beverly the group was looking to nail to a cross. She slipped back under the house and out of sight. Jim made a motion with his hand that said *stay there.* He got a sense that Beverly didn't need to be told again.

Jim drew a bead on the person to the far left, which was a woman.

He took a deep breath and then held his sights on her as still as a stone and slowly started to squeeze the trigger. He was less than a millisecond from all hell breaking loose when the crackle of a walkie-talkie made him release the pressure. Deep Voice stopped as if frozen and so did everyone else. Deep Voice picked a walkie-talkie off his belt and put it on his ear and said, "Unit Five."

Deep Voice listened for ten seconds. Then: "They want us back at the compound. Let's go."

Jim had not lowered his rifle. *Whatever,* he thought.

"What about the bitch?" one of the men asked. "What if she's in the house?"

"No one would go into the house and hide fifty yards from where her best friend was hung," Deep Voice said. "I was just checking it out routinely. And by the way, what the fuck do you have in your head, brains or sawdust?"

The rest of group laughed and Jim was close

enough to see the face of the man who was chewed out get red.

"Okay! She can wait," Deep Voice said. "Hell, she's running scared. She'll screw up and we'll get her eventually."

Jim, trigger finger still at the ready, watched as the group turned en masse and walked back across the road. He lowered the rifle as they got into their vehicles, started them up in a cacophony of dust, exhaust, and noise, then pulled out and formed a caravan that headed back up the dirt road they had arrived on, raising yet another cloud of dust. Jim waited until he could no longer hear the rev of the engines before he turned his attention to the woman. He looked into the crawl space. The woman looked back at him, her face filled with anticipation—and fear . . . and maybe a little relief.

"C'mon out," Jim said. "They're gone."

The young woman crawled out and stood up. For the first time, Jim got a good look at her. She was about five feet five inches tall, he guessed. She had light brown hair cut almost as short as a boy's, large dark brown eyes, and full, pouty lips. And very shapely in her jeans. Quite pretty, Jim thought, except she was covered with assorted dirt and smelled like a dead polecat.

"I guess you're Beverly," Jim said. "You want to tell me what is going on around here?"

"Who are you?"

"Jim LaDoux. No affiliations, no nothing. Just traveling. So?"

"They're Rejects. My friend Ida and I were trying to start a church around here, and they found out and starting about a week ago hunted us down. They raped her repeatedly and then hung her."

She paused, and tears came to her eyes.

"I narrowly missed the same thing. And they might come back at any time looking for me. They're unpredictable. I've got to get out of here. But . . . I have to bury her first."

"What exactly is a Reject?"

"Where have you been?" She paused. "They're a group of fanatics who, based on what has happened in the world now and in the recent past, deny the existence of God, any concept of God. They're a group of different people, good and bad, including ex-cons, ordinary people, ex-religious, soldiers, you name it, but the thing that binds them all together is the common belief that any God who could put humanity through what has happened to it in the last few decades isn't worth believing in. So God is, for them, in effect, dead. And they're determined to establish a society that God is a not a part of—which includes terminating those who believe in Him."

"I was stopped earlier by a group of people who wore medallions around their necks. How do they figure in? They told me that this was 'the Zone.'"

"The Zone is wherever the Rejects control the land. It shifts. The people with the medallions are the other side of the coin. They've organized into a Christian army called the Believers to protect themselves. They're the archenemies of the Rejects. They believe in God totally. But if you have different beliefs than theirs you're ostracized by them, ostracized to the point where they'll expel you from the country. They're bad, misguided, not really true Christians in my book, whatever you want to say, but they're not murderers like the Rejects are. And they're the only group that we have right now that's big enough and strong enough to stop the Rejects. In fact, that's exactly what has been happening. The two groups are constantly battling, and the control of territory is constantly shifting. The Believers are trying to save people—add them to their army."

"Neither," Jim said, "sounds like they're worth more than a bucket of warm spit."

Beverly paused. Her eyes glittered with anger.

"I hope the Rejects are stopped—cold. They executed my father."

"I'm sorry. Why? Spreading the word like you and Ida?"

"He was a minister of a nondenominational faith. They demanded that he renounce Christ and he refused. They hung him after a five-minute mock trial conducted by Alex Szabo."

"Who's he?"

"A muscle-bound geek who runs the Rejects. He is the so-called premier."

"Why are you in this particular area?"

"We were trying to start the church in Nevada. I ran to here."

"Is that where your father wanted to start the church?"

"Yes."

"What are you going to do?"

"If things work out, start another church."

"Are you a minister?"

"No, I'm not holy enough to be that."

"You grow up around here?"

"No. I grew up mostly in Japan in various places where he was a missionary. After my mother died we moved to the States and ended up in a little town outside of Salt Lake City. But the Rejects invaded that and Salt Lake and killed a lot of the survivors of the plague. My dad and I escaped and ended up Nevada.

He was trying to start a new church when the Rejects came here."

"Sounds like a good man."

"He was a great man There was only one thing I disagreed with."

"What was that?"

"He was too much of a pacifist. He never would take up arms."

Jim nodded.

"You want some coffee, Beverly?"

"Coffee? You want to take time to make coffee? Man . . . you're crazy! I haven't time. I have to bury Ida."

"They're not coming back today."

"How do you know that?"

"There's no reason to."

Jim paused.

"You don't have a gun, I see," he said.

"No," she said, smiling. "I have an M-16 on my back and two six-guns belted around my waist."

"It's kind of crazy being on your own, particularly a woman, and unarmed."

"I have weapons," Beverly said. "I know empty-hand combat and a whole bunch of other stuff."

"How'd you get to know it?"

"I started to train in that when I was a kid. But I have never used it in a violent way. Just to help myself spiritually."

"Just what is empty-hand combat?"

"Like karate."

Jim nodded.

"Well," he said, "empty-hand combat isn't going to help if you have bullets coming at you. I have some guns. I'm going to give you something. And maybe we can find something even better if we search some of these wrecked houses."

"Maybe not," Beverly said. "The Rejects collect them all."

`"Well, let's get to burying Ida."

"You're going to help?"

"Yeah. Follow me."

Jim walked to the HumVee and took something off the back.

"Here's an entrenching tool," he said. "Why don't you find a spot for a grave in the woods and start digging? I'll take down Ida."

"Okay."

Bev went to find a spot, and Jim drove the HumVee back and next to Ida.

Over the next fifteen minutes Jim, his stomach somewhat used to the smell, cut Idea down, wrapping her in four sheets and some plastic he had in the HumVee. Then he carried her back to where Beverly was digging in a place just inside the woods but well out of sight. Jim came over and placed her on the ground. No part of her was visible to Beverly.

"Good spot," he said. "Let me try for a while."

Ten minutes later, the hole had been dug deep enough and long enough to accommodate her body. Jim placed her in and covered her over with dirt, then covered the grave with leaves and twigs. The grave was invisible. Beverly had placed a small stone at the head.

"Okay," he said. "Do you want to say a prayer?"

"Yes, I do."

With tears in her eyes, Beverly said a silent prayer and Jim stood by respectfully. Then Beverly wiped her eyes.

"Where are you headed?" she asked.

"I was going to go east. But I think I'm going to go north now. Maybe I can get out of the Zone."

"Do you mind if I come with you?"

"Not at all," Jim said.

"It could be dangerous. The Rejects are not going to stop looking for me."

"It wouldn't matter if you're with me or not. These guys are into killing."

"I think you're right. By the way, my full name is Beverly Harper. Everybody calls me Bev."

"Okay, Bev," Jim said. "But before we leave we have to do one important thing."

"What's that?" she said.

"Have coffee," Jim said with a straight face.

For a moment she didn't read him. Then she did and smiled.

"I'm kidding," he said. "By the way, I hope you like dogs. I have a puppy with me."

"I love dogs. What kind of puppy is it?"

"I don't know. Heinz 57. He sort of adopted me a couple of weeks ago. I'll show you."

Beverly and Jim went out of the woods and around the house to the HumVee and opened the driver's-side door. Reb was looking up at them, his eyes glistening.

"Good dog," Jim said, mussing the hair on the top of his head. "Good dog."

Jim turned to Bev.

"One bark today could have meant disaster. I wonder what he's got in him."

"Malumute, German shepherd, and some wolf." She smiled. "I used to work in a vet's office part-time. I was studying to be vet at Cornell Veterinary College but I had to drop out. Whatever, he's a cutie pie."

"The war?"

"No. Money. But I was saving to go back to school."

"Okay, let's go."

"No coffee?"

"Later," Jim said.

Bev got in and sat on the passenger side and Jim climbed up onto the driver's side. Before settling in behind the wheel he put the Thompson back under the seat, but kept the Glock and AK-47 out. Then he fired up the HumVee. They pulled out onto the road and soon were in a nonpopulated area, miles of flanking forest.

"Thank you," she said.

"Not a problem," Jim said.

He could feel Bev's look linger on him.

3

Ten miles from the spot where Jim almost had the confrontation with the Rejects, he and Bev stopped for coffee, turning off on a road that the HumVee, again, was barely able, because of its width, to fit through. Jim had the coffee already made. Last time he had stopped when alone he made two thermoses full.

They stepped outside. Jim took the thermoses from the bed of the vehicle.

"I hope you like it black," he said. "No latte available."

"I do. Black and strong. I don't even use sugar."

Jim poured the coffee, which was hot enough so it steamed, into two foam cups.

They both sipped it.

"Delicious," Bev said.

"You made fun of me wanting coffee," Jim said, "but maybe you don't know the power of it."

"What do you mean?"

"I remember about ten years ago when meat prices really started to go up, and women were up in arms. So they stopped buying meat and brought the vendors to their knees. The prices went back down."

Bev nodded.

"And then the stores did the same thing with coffee."

"And what happened?"

"Nothing! They paid the price. Coffee is as addictive as heroin."

"Well, I love coffee too. It just seemed you weren't worried enough at the moment."

"I'm worried," Jim said. "But I try not to let it get the better of me."

"I think you succeed," Bev said. "While you waited for them it seemed to me that you were so calm that I expected to see flies swirling around your head."

"I was calm," Jim said. "It's later that I shake." And he stuck out his free hand and shook it in mock fear.

Beverly smiled.

"So, which way are we going?"

"Like I said, I was heading east, but I was thinking of going north. I want to stay off main roads. I figure when I get far enough north in Wyoming I'll head east. Maybe. These Rejects can't be everywhere."

She paused, and coughed.

"Do you have any water?"

"Help yourself. There's a whole case of bottled water behind the passenger seat."

Beverly took a bottle, opened it, and drained it empty.

"You were thirsty."

"Yeah, that's something even coffee can't solve."

They finished their coffee, then got back in the vehicle, as did Reb.

Back in his seat, Jim knew her eyes were on him again. He smiled.

"Thinking you might have made a mistake coming with me?"

"No. You have a good face, nice eyes, and you like dogs. You can't be all bad. Plus, I'd like to live."

They laughed.

"Don't forget I'm a fellow coffee lover too."

Jim paused.

"So, what do you think about continuing north?"

"Good. I think you'll have a better chance of going without meeting more Rejects than if you continue east. I don't know how far up the Rejects are. But I haven't seen any Believers in this area."

"I guess for the time being they own it."

Bev shook her head in wonderment.

"They've had many, many battles with the Rejects. And towns and positions are regularly fought for and won and lost. The Believers can retake a town and hold it for several days, then the Rejects will counterattack and drive them out—or vice versa."

"Who's winning overall?"

"I don't know. No one."

Jim shook his head in disbelief. "I guess I'm not really surprised about the Rejects and Believers."

"My dad told me this has been building for a long time," Bev said. "He said he remembered back before the Great War certain factions in America were trying to remove religion from all aspects of American life. And when the plague came and knocked everything askew, that was the signal for bad people to do their thing."

"I remember my grandpa saying something about that too."

"Did you come from a religious family, Jim?"

"Well . . . when I was a little boy we said grace before our meals and sometimes on Sundays we would go to Mass. That's about it."

"Catholic, huh? Do you go to Mass now?"

"Not in years."

"But you believe in God?"

"Oh, sure. What's not to believe?"

"That's a relief. I thought there for a moment you might be a Reject in disguise."

Jim smiled. Then: "Bev, how much do you know about what is happening outside this area?"

"May I ask you a question before I answer that?"

"Of course."

"You don't seem to know much about what is going on, so where have you been?"

"I lived in a very remote area of Idaho, way up in the northwest. All the network newscasts had gone off the air before this stuff started, and the only news I could get was on radio, which was intermittent. And that wasn't much."

"And your family?"

"All passed on. What I know about this plague thing and what it's done to the world I learned from speaking to Ben Raines."

Bev's eyes widened. "General Ben Raines?"

"Yes. I was with him for the last few days of his life—when he died. I buried him."

Abruptly, a darkness swept across Bev's face. Jim picked up on it.

"That's it then," Bev said.

"What do you mean?"

"Ben Raines was the one man who might have been able to build something out of this godawful mess. With him gone, it's . . ." She paused, shrugged her shoulders. "Over."

"You're giving up, just like that?"

Bev paused before she spoke. Then she held up her hand and waved it, as if waving away what she had just said.

"No," she said, "I don't think so. I was just feeling sort of melancholy for a moment."

"I've felt that way several times myself recently. That, and angry at God."

"I've experienced that too."

"Things have a way of righting themselves though. At least I hope so. But you do need people like Ben Raines. I also know that history's quirky, and individuals matter."

"What do you mean?"

"Just a little change here or there can shape the course of humanity. I remember reading a book that spoke about how important individuals were in history. Just a little change in an event might have eliminated one person and made all the difference."

"Like who?"

"Well, for example," Jim said, "there was this British diplomat who was in New York City in 1931 and was crossing a street and got hit by a car. He survived. Good thing."

"Why?"

"His name was Winston Churchill."

"Interesting."

"And during World II a guy seated next to Franklin Delano Roosevelt was almost but not quite assassinated, but Roosevelt survived. Lenin got typhoid but didn't die, and Hitler was in a war in 1923 in Germany and unfortunately for humanity he didn't get killed. Just think about where the world night have been without Hitler having come on the scene. No one was that nuts or zealous."

"I agree."

"Yeah, that's one of the pleasures of life in northwest Idaho."

"What's that?"

"No TV. You're forced to read—and think. Nothing like a cup of coffee and a book."

Bev laughed.

"Tell you what let's do, Bev. Let's find us a house that has heat and take a shower or bath. I could sure use one."

Her face brightened. "Yeah! That sounds great to me. But I don't have any clean clothes."

"So when we stop at houses we'll look for some. We're sure to find something that will fit you. First, we have to find some houses."

They got back in the HumVee and on the road. Over the next twenty miles or so, they found three houses, none directly on the road—which of course Jim liked—and all reachable by roads that were just wide enough to accommodate the HumVee.

All of the homes had been ransacked and pillaged. Only one of them was powered by propane, and there was no chance of taking a bath there: all the propane had been depleted. But Bev found some clean clothes around her size and took them. They also found some blankets and loaded these into the HumVee, as well as a winter coat for Bev, which they took, since they would be traveling into the mountains, and Jim knew that it could be eighty-five degrees during the day, as it was now, and drop down to thirty-five or forty at night.

At another of the homes they found a new pair of lace-up boots that fit her and a half dozen pairs of socks.

"You should put those boots on," Jim said.

"Why?"

"If we stay off the main roads and camp out you never know what's in the ground cover."

"What do you mean?"

"Wyoming has its share of rattlesnakes. Sometimes they give a warning by rattling, but sometimes they're just in the bushes or under a rock. You got to be careful."

Jim had gotten Bev's attention.

"What will we do if one of us gets bitten?"

"Die," Jim said with a straight face, then smiled. Bev laughed. "Actually," Jim said, "the prairie rattlers aren't that dangerous. You won't die from their bites but you can get sick. The one that's really dangerous is the smaller midget rattlesnake. They're found just about where we are within the lower Green River valley. They're ten to thirty times more poisonous than the prairie variety. Fortunately, they're very timid and pose little or no threat to us."

"Okay," Bev said, smiling, "no problem wearing the boots."

In one of the houses Jim also found a pistol that the Rejects had overlooked, a Soviet TT-33 automatic pistol, which Ray had once shown to Jim in a book and said it was very widely used by guerillas. He also found several hundred rounds of 7.62-by-39mm cartridges for it. It was a simple, well-made gun and seemed ideal for Bev.

"My brother Ray told me that this gun was one of the most commonly made guns of all time. It used to be used by the Soviet army front-line forces, but no more. But reserves and militia still use it."

Jim paused.

"I think it's a good weapon for you. You shouldn't be without a weapon, even though you know empty-hand combat."

"You're right," Bev said.

Jim showed her how to use the gun, then loaded it and put the safety on and handed it to her. It looked large in her small hand.

"Lord," she said, "I'm a long way from Sunday services and listening to my father give a homily."

"You ever shoot a gun?"

"No."

"All you have to do is point it at the person like you're pointing your finger and squeeze the trigger."

"How come you know so much about guns?"

"I'm from Idaho, remember?"

"Yes, but this looks like a military weapon."

"I learned about guns from my brother Ray, who was in the Great War."

"Where is he?"

"He got killed."

"I'm so sorry."

"Thank you. We were very proud of him," Jim said, lost for a moment in the memory. "Just an ordinary mountain man, like me, like so many other guys who were very ordinary, but when war came he changed."

"What do you mean?"

"He just . . . became great. A warrior. I remember how the Blackfeet Indians in the area used to admire him. To us, that was great praise."

"Were you ever in any war?"

"No. I was too young. And I'm glad."

Bev was going to ask him why. But the appearance of two homes in the wood distracted her. They investigated. Both were devoid of people, but in one of them they found the skeletal remains of a couple and a small child, all huddled together on the master bed upstairs. It was a very, very sad sight. They left that home immediately after the discovery.

They continued on, and within a couple of miles they came to a tiny town with a few stores that looked like a holdover from the 1800s, the Wild West days. Jim stopped and parked the HumVee behind the buildings, as they did when they investigated homes. Then, Jim toting the AK-47 and Bev the TT-33, safety off, they entered the stores, all of which were open. There was no one inside. No one alive. Just skeletal remains.

They had some luck. At a ladies' FINE APPAREL store she found some panties in their original packages on a shelf, and at a drugstore both she and Jim were able to load up with toiletry articles.

The other store they entered was a tiny gift shop. Bev picked up a small Bible and put it in her knapsack. She was conscious of Jim watching her and smiled.

"I noticed you didn't have a Bible in your gear."

He returned the smile.

"We do now. Good thinking. Get another one for me, will you?"

She looked surprised.

"You read the Bible, Jim?"

"Occasionally. I read anything that contains wisdom. You ready to go?"

"I'm ready."

They pulled out from behind the stores and were soon on the main road. There was no sign of life.

"It's hard to believe there's no one in the town," Bev said.

"They either all died, or fled, or were off to look for others who had escaped," Jim said.

"Left?" Bev said. "To go where?"

"I don't know."

"Or maybe," Bev said, "they were rounded up by the Rejects and shot."

Jim nodded. Mass executions wouldn't surprise him at all.

"We should find a junction heading north about twenty miles from here," he said.

"Good."

They would both be glad to get away from the Zone.

4

"Look at that home over there," Bev said, pointing to a house set back maybe thirty yards from the road. Jim had stopped the HumVee because the house was, in fact, beautiful—and unusual. They had traveled a long way down the road, and the houses, when they appeared, were either small ranches or Colonials or trailers, very much unlike this one.

The house looked as if it had come out of the pages of an architectural magazine whose intent was to show beautiful homes, as if it had sort of arisen out of the earth. It was set on a little hill, and the walls were made with individual stones that had obviously been created by nature rather than man. The roof was a dull orange concrete tile and the windows and door were made of dark wood that looked like it had been coated with some sort of dark, clear material. The house was fringed with all kinds of greenery and flowers at one end of a large pond that reflected it all perfectly. There was no fence, but the entire property was surrounded by evergreen bushes. It was quite obvious that the people who lived in the house loved nature.

"A beauty," Jim said.

"You want to check it out?" Bev asked.

Jim did not answer immediately. He had noticed something else odd about the house. Almost all of the other places they had seen or entered showed some exterior sign that they had been pillaged, such as a broken window or stuff strewn in the yard. And in one case, the siding and roofing had been ripped off. From the outside, at least, this one looked like it was in perfect condition, as if it were oblivious of the chaos in the world swirling around it.

It occurred to him that, as beautiful as it was, perhaps someone was living in it. Perhaps some Rejects, and that would mean trouble with a capital T.

He finally nodded, then reached down and picked up the AK-47. Bev noticed him, but seemed oblivious of its implication.

"Good," Bev said. "Maybe they have propane and everything is still working. Then I can take a shower and wash my hair. I'm getting a little gamy."

"I won't argue with that," Jim said with a smile, but keeping his eyes trained on the house. "Got your gun off safety?" he asked.

"You think this is dangerous?"

"I doubt it, but like my grandmother used to say, 'A stitch in time saves nine.'"

"What does that mean?"

"I have no idea."

Jim scanned to his left. There was a natural opening in the forest, as if vehicles had parked there regularly. Jim liked it. He could go deep enough into the woods so that the HumVee would be concealed.

"We'll park over here," he said.

He moved the HumVee into the gap, then stopped it but did not get out. Bev looked at him.

"Aren't we going in?" she said after fifteen or twenty seconds of sitting there.

"I just want to listen to things a bit," he said.

"Where I come from, what you hear is as important as what you see. Sometimes more important.

"Okay," he said, after another ten seconds or so, "let's go."

As he got out, he looked at Bev. He liked what he saw. She did not seem that afraid, just alert, as he was. He didn't need someone with a loaded gun who was nervous going in with him. They left Reb in the truck. Again, he was silent.

They walked across the road, glanced up and down it—nothing—then crossed it and continued until they were at the front gate. It was held by a regular latch. Jim disengaged it and they entered. Bev followed him partway up the brick path, and then was surprised when he didn't continue to the front door. Rather, he veered off toward one side, the business end of the AK-47 raised.

He walked slowly around the house, Bev following, and as he went she was surprised. He stepped so lightly that she could hardly hear his footfalls, and she got the sense that she was following an animal rather than a man. If she hadn't earlier gotten a sense that this man had lived in the mountains, she had now.

He stopped at every window and tried to look in, but he couldn't. In every instance, the blinds or drapes or other window coverings had been pulled. Somebody, it occurred to Bev, did not want anyone looking in—or maybe out.

A couple of times he stopped and held up his hand for her to do the same, and once put an ear against one of the windows.

In the back of the house there was a beautiful multilevel redwood deck. It had some handsome wooden chairs on it. The woods had been cleared around it to a distance of about fifty feet and the grass was dotted with flower beds.

Jim went down the other side of the house, glanced in a window—blinds pulled as on the others—and as he approached the front of the house he raised his weapon. Bev followed suit.

They had noticed when they first came to the front of the house that the blinds had been pulled in the windows on both sides of the front door. "I don't see any fresh vehicle or man tracks," Jim said quietly, "so the house is probably empty. But one never knows."

He smiled. God, Bev thought, this guy was cool. She felt nervous, but in control of herself.

He proceeded toward the front door, motioning to Bev to stop as he got within a few yards of the door, but he did not walk out in front of it. He was well aware that someone standing behind it could fire through the door. Though oak, it would not withstand a fusillade of shots, which would kill whoever was standing there.

Instead, he kneeled down and sort of scuttled up to the door. Anyone shooting would fire over his head, expecting that the kill zone would be at least five feet off the ground.

He tried the doorknob with his left hand. It turned. He pushed the door open an inch with the muzzle of his weapon. No one fired. He pushed the door back, stepping out of the potential line of fire.

He waited a moment, listening, then walked in, AK-47 leveled, quickly scanning as he entered the living room. He knew Bev was behind him. She also had her TT-33 up, both of her hands on it as she had seen in movies.

The house was not trashed outside, but it certainly had been inside. Against the far wall was a built-in unit with cubicles, like boxes, for holding a wide variety of stuff, everything from a television to knickknacks and vases with flowers in them. But the cubicles were empty. The contents had been pulled out onto the polished wood floor in an obvious attempt to find valuables.

Everything else was a mess as well. A couch and two chairs had been ripped up and virtually disassembled. The base molding had been pried off and the electrical outlets pulled out.

Jim lowered his AK-47 and Bev followed suit. Jim turned and made a silence gesture with his finger over his mouth and just stood there. She knew that he was listening for any sign that someone might be in the house.

He moved and continued his scanning of the living room. One of the walls was covered with built-in bookcases but there was not a single book in them. All had been pulled out, torn apart, apparently in an attempt to see if any money had been slipped between the pages.

In essence, the room had been reduced to a pile of junk.

Jim thought it was unlikely that anyone was still in the house, which he guessed had at least a dozen rooms, but one never knew. As he left the living room he kept his guard up, his ears peeled for sounds, just as he did when he was hunting grizzlies in the woods of northern Idaho.

They went down a long hall, off of which were a number of rooms. Everything they saw had been torn apart, reduced to junk.

At the back of the house was the kitchen and pantry, and there was a back door. Pots and pans and utensils were all over the floor, dishes and the like pulled out of cabinets and smashed.

The laundry room held a very unpleasant surprise. Someone had defecated on the floor and stuck a crucifix in it. Without comment, Jim went over and pulled the cross out and went over to the sink and turned on the water. The water sputtered, but then flowed—hot. Jim washed the crucifix, dried it off with one of the T-shirts he found on the floor, and placed the statue on a shelf above a washer, leaning it against the wall so it could stand up straight. Then he used two pieces of soft cardboard to pick the crap up and went into a nearby bathroom and flushed it away.

Bev, who had witnessed what he did, said when he returned, "Thanks for doing that."

"It's the least I could do," Jim said.

"I bet it was the Rejects."

"I wouldn't bet against you," Jim said.

When you're on the road as Jim had been for weeks—the places where you can actually buy food no less find it are few and far between, so you're reduced to your own looting of sorts. During the last few days, however, Jim had not found much of anything, so he felt doubly good when he saw, strewn all over the floor among the debris, unopened and intact, a treasure trove of canned goods, everything, at a quick glance, from tuna fish to Spam to spinach.

"Look at these canned goods," Jim said. "We're going to travel in style."

"You mean we're not going to starve?" Bev added.

"Yeah, that's what I meant," Jim said, his face lighting up with a smile, his teeth appearing very white against his tanned skin.

Bev's look at him lingered. The sight of him was, she thought, doing strange things to her stomach.

They continued their search.

In a closet in a hall that she almost passed by, Bev hit pay dirt as well. It was a narrow closet, its contents intact. The looters had obviously neglected to go through it. In it Bev found a dozen clean, thick fluffy towels. She knew there was hot water, and she had found some soap. A winning trio!

"Do you mind if I bathe while you go through the rest of the house?"

"Hey, no problem," Jim said. "No problem at all. Have a good time."

"See you in a few minutes," she said, and for a flashing millisecond wondered what Jim would look like without any clothes on and in the shower with her. He looked like he had a very wiry body with a washboard for a stomach. These were decidedly unpreacher-like thoughts. But there you were.

"By the way," Jim said, "lock the door and take a weapon in with you."

"How can a gun help me clean myself?" Bev asked with a straight face.

"If you see any cooties you can shoot them," Jim said with an equally straight face.

"I have to get some clean clothes from the HumVee," she said.

"Go ahead, I'll watch you from the window."

Bev did, and two minutes later, Jim watching, stepped into the bathroom, locking the door behind her. She righted a hamper that had been knocked down and put the Glock and clean clothing on top of it. Then she peeled the clothing from her body, feeling as if she were peeling off some sort of alligator skin.

Nude, filthy, stinking, she turned on the shower and manipulated the hot water handle. It didn't take long before the hot water was flowing, so hot it steamed, and Bev turned it down and turned on the cold water. When the mix was perfect she stepped under it.

"Hallelujah," she said softly. "Praise the Lord and pass the soap." And then she was lost in the luxuriant feeling of applying soap to her slick skin.

Jim waited until he heard the click of the bathroom door lock, then headed toward what he thought was the only other downstairs room left to check, the garage. There was a door to it off the kitchen. He opened it and was immediately accosted by the smell of oil and chemicals.

The condition of the garage told the story. Tools, lumber, and other materials were strewn all over the floor of the empty room. Here, too, a search had been made but apparently not as thoroughly as the other rooms, because there were a few paint cans on a shelf that had not been touched.

He scanned the rest of the room—there was no car. The last of the walls, the one that was behind him when he had stepped in through the door, had a surprise, and confirmed that this was the work of the Rejects. Someone had used green spray paint to paint the words GOD IS DEAD all over one masonry wall.

Jim found himself pissed and he went over to the shelf where the spray cans were and selected one with orange paint. Then he walked back across the room, shaking the can as he went to distribute the paint, and then used it to obliterate the obscenity.

Then he went back inside the house and as he passed the bathroom he heard Bev singing something. He stopped to listen. She was singing "Rock of Ages." Jim had heard it before and liked it and he just lingered there, the sound enveloping his body as the warm water was enveloping Bev—even though she was butchering the song. He smiled, recalling a favorite expression of his grandfather: "Don't give up your day job, honey!"

He debated whether to leave Bev alone in the shower while he went upstairs. But she had brought the Glock in with her and the search should only take him a few minutes. She would be all right. He knew that if anyone approached the house he would know it. For a moment, he thought that maybe he should have brought Reb in with them but then decided against it.

He climbed polished, elegant oak stairs to the second-floor landing and once up there he was accosted again, though very faintly, by the smell of death.

There was a full bath directly across from the stairway and five rooms leading off the hall, which extended to both his left and right. The lavatory and three of the rooms had their doors open and one had it closed. It wasn't hard to figure where the foul smell was coming from. Someone had stuffed a towel along the space under the closed door on the third room down.

He went into each of the rooms where the doors were open, and predictably they had been trashed. The first one he looked at was a master bedroom, and here again he found evidence of sacrilege. There was a painting of Jesus Christ on the wall, and someone had sprayed brown paint all over it.

One was the room of a teenage girl, which he could tell from the young feminine touches and the canopy over the bed, one was the room of a teenage boy, one of a young boy, and one was a guest room, Jim thought, and another was empty.

Sadness surged in Jim—and anger. It was so sad that people who had once enjoyed so many privileges and rights in the greatest country that ever existed should now not even have the right to live in their own homes, the right that a lot of people had risked their lives for, and died for. Goddamn bastards.

Jim took out a handkerchief and put it over his nose. If the smell was coming through the door, it would be much more potent, of course, inside the room. He turned the knob and pushed the door open.

The smell was not as bad as he thought, and whoever or whatever or wherever the smell was coming from was not immediately apparent. The room was a study, every single inch of the walls covered with bookshelves, but as was the situation downstairs, all of the books had been pulled out of the bookcases and onto the floor, which was so covered with books it was barely visible. A number of the books had their pages pulled out of them, perhaps, Jim thought, because the looters found nothing and were enraged.

There was a large oak desk in front of a bay window, but nothing on it except what looked like a leather-bound journal, or diary. It was open, and something was written on one of the pages.

Jim picked his way through the piles of books and glanced behind the desk. The source of the smell was there. It was the body of a man, lying on his back, his eyes open, pupils fixed and dilated, who had only recently died. He was past rigor mortis, Jim guessed, but there was extensive lividity and he was just starting to smell.

The man was bald except for a fringe of dark hair

and a short goatee. There was a small red hole in the middle of his forehead. He had been shot, Jim thought, judging from the size of the hole, with a small-caliber weapon, probably a .22. He was fully dressed, complete with vest. Jim also guessed that, granted all the books, he was some sort of professor.

Jim covered the remains with a blanket from a nearby couch and leaned over the desk so he could read the journal.

The page began: *I strongly suspect, despite the rather ludicrous claims from our government that the bug came from outer space, the virus that is rapidly killing off the world's population was homegrown, right here on earth. I believe it was an experiment gone awry, released into the air quite by accident from some top-secret lab, perhaps even one financed by our own government. I . . .*

That was all that was written.

Lying, Jim thought. The U.S. government was lying? So what the hell else was new?

Jim wondered who the dead man was. He flipped the journal back to the first page, and there was a sticker on it with the name Harold Charles, Ph.D.

Definitely a teacher.

Jim put the book down, and as he did he saw, on the floor among the books, what looked like a diploma—at least the paper was parchmentlike—and he reached down and picked it up and turned it over. It was something else that he decided to read when he was downstairs. He disliked leaving Bev alone longer.

He left the room, closing the door behind him and replacing the towel.

He went downstairs and stood in the hall. The water in the bathroom was off and Bev had stopped singing.

SUSA Manifesto

Freedom, like respect, is earned and must be constantly nurtured and protected from those who would take it away.

It is the right of every law-abiding citizen to protect his or her life, liberty, and personal property by any means at hand without fear of arrest, criminal prosecution, or lawsuit. The right to bear arms is central to maintaining true personal freedom.

That liberal politicians, theorists, and socialists are the greatest threat to freedom-loving Americans. Their misguided efforts have caused grave injustices in the fields of criminal law, education, and public welfare.

Therefore in respect to criminal law:

An effective criminal justice system should be guided by these basic tenets:

- Our courts must stop pampering criminals.
- The punishment must fit the crime.
- Justice must be fair but also be swift and, if necessary, harsh.
- There is no perfect society, only a fair one.

Therefore in respect to education:

Education is the key to solving problems in society and the lack of it is the root cause of America's decline.

An effective system of education:

- Must stress hard discipline along with the arts, sciences, fine music, and basic skills in reading, writing, and mathematics.
- Must teach fairness and respect.
- Must teach morals, the dignity of labor, and the value of family.

Therefore in respect to welfare:

Welfare (we prefer workfare) is reserved only for the elderly, the infirm, and those who need a temporary helping hand. And the welfare system must also:

- Instill the concept that everyone must work if able and be forced to work if necessary.
- Instill the concept that there is no free lunch and that being productive in a free society is the only honorable path to take.

That racial prejudice and bigotry are intolerable in a free and vital society.

No one is worthy of respect simply because of the color of their skin.

Respect is earned by actions and by deeds, not by birthright.

There are only two types of people on earth, decent and indecent. Those who are decent will flourish, those who are indecent will perish.

No laws laid down by a body of government can make one person like another.

A free and just society must be protected at all costs even if it means shedding the blood of its citizens. The willingness of citizens to lay down their lives for the belief in freedom is a cornerstone of true democracy; without that willingness the structure of society will surely crumble and fall into the ashes of history.

Therefore:

Along with the inalienable right to bear arms, and the inalienable right to personal protection, a strong, skilled, and well-equipped military is essential to maintaining a free society.

A strong military eliminates the need for "allies," allowing the society to focus on the needs of its citizens.

The business of citizens is not the business of the world unless the rights of citizens are infringed upon by outside forces.

The duty of those who live in a free society is clear. Personal freedom is not negotiable.

In conclusion:

We who support the tri-state philosophy and live by its code and its laws pledge to defend it by any means necessary. We pledge to work fairly and justly to build and maintain a society without fear and without intervention.

General Ben Raines

Jim nodded. Yes, he was lucky to have met Ben Raines. A great man had written these things. Ben Raines was a great man.

Not thirty seconds after he finished reading the manifesto, Bev came out of the bathroom.

"I feel a hundred percent better," she said. "Now it's your turn."

Jim looked at her for a moment. She was really a beautiful woman, with her large dark eyes even more striking against the newly washed paleness of her skin, and for a moment Jim thought that she had put on lipstick. But she hadn't. Her lips were naturally that red. She had on her new clothing, and now she smelled good. Real good.

Jim told her about finding the dead man and what he had written in the journal.

"That's what my father suspected, too," Bev said.

"Could be," Jim replied, "but we'll probably never

know for sure. It certainly makes more sense than things from outer space. . . ." His voice trailed off.

"Here's something else I found."

Bev glanced at it.

"I'm familiar with it," she said.

"Pretty powerful stuff in it."

"General Raines was one of a kind. A warrior and a thinker, a philosopher. My father said that when Raines died people were going to be asking the same thing a character in Shakespeare asked when Caesar died: 'When comes such another?'"

"There'll be others," Jim said. "That's the way life is. My grandfather once said that it's heat and pressure that produce diamonds. That happens to people too."

"I hope you're right," Bev said.

Jim nodded.

"I'm going to shower and shave. Then we'll have supper."

"Anything I can do to help?" Bev said, her face reddening a little when she realized the double entendre. "I mean with supper."

Jim did not react to the mistake. But he surely understood it. Bev did too.

"All we have to do is open some cans and heat them up," he said.

She smiled at him. "I was hoping you found some T-bone steaks."

"I wish. Be back in a few minutes."

Jim was not gamy. He had washed regularly in creeks, lakes, and rivers on the way down. But he figured that hot showers might not be too plentiful in his future and a cold river was not the same thing to bathe in as a tub with a shower.

He took a couple of the towels that Bev had found

and went into the bathroom. He also took the AK-47. He didn't want to, as it were, be caught with his pants down.

The hot shower felt good, and after he dried himself thoroughly and donned clean clothes, then he went into the kitchen. He saw that Bev had already heated up their supper and made a pot of coffee. She had also brought Reb in from the HumVee and fed him. He was polishing off the final bit of something in a bowl. Jim rolled a cigarette and smoked slowly. It had been a long time since anyone waited on him, and he liked the feeling.

They slowly consumed the supper, cleaned up, and then just sat there, relaxing, with Reb lying quietly near the stove, a classic scene of domestic tranquility, ironic given the world outside.

"We going to check out Jackson?" Bev said, referring to a large town in Wyoming that was directly north.

"Why not?" Jim said. " It's directly on our way. I was there when I was a kid. But of course we'll take back roads to stay out of harm's way. There's a limit to how big this Zone can be."

Bev looked at Jim. He was growing on her by leaps and bounds.

"Aren't you a little afraid to be with me?" she said.

"Oh no," he said with a straight face, which she was learning was the way he was when he was being funny. "I'm not that afraid of you."

Bev laughed so hard that Reb raised his head from sleep.

"You know what I mean."

"Listen, Bev," Jim said, "you don't have to be a psychiatrist to figure these guys out. They're bad. They want to kill. That's their religion and like I said before, whether I'm with you or alone doesn't matter."

Bev nodded.

"What," she asked, "exactly are you looking for?"

He smiled at her.

"I don't really know, Bev. Just a place where I can live in harmony with nature. Peace. Be happy."

"But you may have to fight to get it. That's what Ben Raines said."

"Not me. I'm tired of war—or at least the effects of it. I lost my brother and my father in wars. I'm just turned off by the whole experience."

Bev nodded. She knew that Jim was a little shortsighted on this picture. But right now maybe he needed to think that he wouldn't have to fight for peace. She changed subjects.

"You married?"

"No."

"Girl?"

"No. Not much opportunity to meet someone where I'm from."

Bev nodded, hiding her feeling, which was that she was very, very happy that Jim was not connected to someone else.

"How about you?" Jim asked.

"I had a boyfriend in Japan. But the commute was hellish."

They laughed heartily. Then they went into the living room.

"There are two couches," Jim pointed out. "All you have to do is turn the cushions over, torn-up side down. I don't think that either of us feels like making up a bed."

"You got that right," Bev said. "I'm going to sleep. See you in the morning."

They looked on each other for one lingering moment before they went to their separate couches. Jim sensed that it could have been a one-couch deal, but something inside told him not to. Bev had been through hell, losing her father, being pursued by the Rejects, had seen her friend Ida raped and murdered, had a pack of beasts after her. Jim knew that, beneath the laughter, she was in a very vulnerable state emotionally, and that making love to her wouldn't be difficult. But he couldn't do it, just like he wouldn't hunt an animal with one wing, or an elk with a game leg, or fight a man with one arm. It was unfair, and he knew that being fair was a super-important thing in life. If you weren't fair, somebody somewhere would have a bone to pick with you, and one day they might. Oh yeah, what goes around definitely does come around.

5

Jim had a backup security system with him when he went to sleep: Reb the dog had come in to lie next to the couch that Jim was on. Jim was also a very light sleeper, and he was ninety-nine percent sure that nothing would surprise him as long as Reb was around. Dogs were hundreds of times more proficient than people when it came to hearing and smelling. Like his grandpa once said about his dog Brandy, "That old dog can hear a flea pass wind at a hundred yards. And smell it."

Jim kept his firepower close, the AK-47, the tommy gun, and the Glock. He also made sure that Bev had her TT-33 nearby when she settled in on the couch across from him.

Jim had, additionally, formulated various scenarios before going to bed. He had reconnoitered the back of the house as well as the woods on the fringe of the open area, and had both front and back doors locked. If someone tried to come in the back way he would just stand his ground in the living room, to exit via the front door to the HumVee in the woods across the road.

Finally, he had found some Christmas decorations with bells that actually tinkled, and he had nailed these just above the doors so the bells lay against their tops. If someone succeeded in compromising the locks and opened the doors they would go tinkle-tinkle—and he would go boom-boom.

It was nice going to sleep on a couch. When he was traveling down from his home he would sleep in a tent, and once, when he was very tired, he had slept in the cab of the HumVee, but just to be in a house, on a couch, and with another person around was good.

Jim woke up three times during the night because of noises. But they turned out to be nothing. Once it was just the sound of the wind coming through the trees, once it was the occasional plink of the shower faucet in the downstairs bathroom, once it was because Bev was snoring, and she stopped when he awakened. Two of the times he was back to sleep within a minute. The third time he didn't go back to sleep for at least five minutes.

He spent the five minutes looking at Bev, who was clearly visible thanks to the moonlight coming through the window. She was sleeping on her stomach, and he couldn't help but notice her butt. In fact, he found himself focusing on it, but after a while he stopped looking at it because the sight was increasing his heart rate and it was taking him down a path that he didn't want to go.

All told, except for the three times he awoke, he slept very soundly, and when he awakened at dawn he felt deeply refreshed.

He checked out Bev, which was a mistake Now she was lying on her back, her sheet and blanket had slipped down past her waist, and her shirt had hiked up a bit, exposing a flat bare belly including her belly button.

Jim felt himself about to sneeze, something weird

given that it was what he always did when he felt sexual desire for the opposite sex. He shook the feeling off and got up, shoved the Glock in his waistband, and went—Reb following him—to the bathroom, then to the front door, Reb still behind him. He opened it a crack and looked out.

The pond was as flat and still as dark green glass. Even the relatively few leaves floating on it were not moving.

He stepped out of the house and closed the door quietly behind him, first letting Reb out, who promptly went into the woods and returned within seconds.

Jim really loved the house and wanted to take a better look at it, take another stroll around it and look at it in a more leisurely mood than he was in yesterday. He started out. He had only his Glock with him, but that was okay. His other weapons were his eyes and ears and Reb, who now seemed to have grown into his constant companion, which was fine with Jim.

As he had grown up in Idaho he and his family had lived in the plainest of circumstances, and it was fine. But occasionally he would dream about living in another kind of house, very much like this one, just he and his wife and kids. People would sometimes ask him: "Don't you want more out of life than that?"

Jim's answer was what he profoundly believed: "I don't think there's much more."

Of course the house would probably be located in Idaho. Maybe he would do some farming or maybe something else, raise horses or cattle or sheep, but always something close to the land. He knew that he was not to return to Idaho for a long time, but he also knew that it would always be in his heart, and thinking about it every now and then sent a surge of joy, almost like a zap with electricity, through him. And, of course, a little sadness.

He stopped halfway along the back wall and examined the fine masonry work. The craftsman who did this was no beginner. All the rocks, smooth and about half the size of a bowling ball, had probably been gathered from the surrounding countryside, a job in itself. They had been laid up in an orderly manner, but they were still very natural looking. That was art, it seemed. He was no professional architecture or art critic, but it seemed to him that all the best art cut out the middleman—the artist—and just presented itself, simply and beautifully.

Jim continued on, basking in the beauty of it all, and then walked across the road, first looking each way—no one seemed to be in sight.

He walked toward the HumVee, and he was in the woods about halfway to it when he sensed—he couldn't hear or see it—that he had company. Reb was busy doing something on the other side of the house, so he was no help in this instance.

Jim scanned the woods, just like he did when he was ten years old and hunting squirrels or some other small game. Animals were not stupid. To protect themselves they would stand stock-still and, given their coloration, would be almost impossible to see. But after a while Jim had been able to detect them.

He did not know if the visitor was animal or human. He drew the Glock, keeping it down, and walked forward. Then he saw it. It wasn't human. It was a pronghorn antelope, partially obscured because it was standing behind a cluster of tree trunks.

It was standing as still as a statue, and Jim just reveled in watching it.

If Wyoming had a state animal, the pronghorn antelope was it. The greatest mass of them in the world lived within Wyoming's borders and they were amazing animals. Though small as a deer they were super powerful with oversize lungs and the ability to turn oxygen into energy that was so efficient that they could run an astonishing sixty miles an hour for an hour. More than once he had watched a herd of them in full gallop along a flat plain in sagebrush country, and it was an amazing sight. It didn't seem that they were expending much effort, even moving quickly, because they ran so fluidly, except when you heard the thundering of their hooves and saw the massive cloud of dust that was raised behind them, and watched the ground they covered disappear in great chunks.

But a pronghorn couldn't outrun a bullet, and on the occasions when Jim had encountered them and had a chance to take one or more of them down he found he could not do it. They were too glorious a creature to have their head end up mounted on a wall someplace.

He used his open palm to slap a smooth tree trunk and that's all the pronghorn needed to take off like a sprinter starting at the sound of a gun; within seconds the animal was gone. Talk about zero to sixty in ten seconds!

Jim proceeded on to the HumVee. It was still locked, and there was nothing amiss. The camouflage paint did a good job of concealing it in the particular stand of lodgepole pine where it stood.

Jim knew pretty much how much gas he had left. He was perhaps ten gallons shy of a full tank, so he opened the hatch in the back, got out his trusty funnel, and poured two full five-gallon cans in. As he did, he knew that he was lessening his risk just a little, because a full tank is less likely to blow than one half-full of fumes. It wasn't a big deal, but you did what you could. At one point when he had earlier thought he might switch to a smaller, more gas-efficient vehicle, he immediately thought of Ben Raines. Raines had given him the HumVee. Somehow, to not use the vehicle anymore was to cut off any remaining contact. He had no obligation whatsoever to Raines, and yet Raines had, in his way, been as glorious an example of the human species as there could be. Jim was coming to realize that he wanted to honor that memory in any way he could.

On the way back to the house, he stopped on the road and looked east, toward the sun, which was not fully over a distant line of mountains. A wave of sadness swept across him. His eyes slowly closed and he remembered the days, endless, joyful days he had spent with his grandfather, waiting quietly in the forest for a bird or bear or maybe in a blind by a lake, him and Grandpa with shotguns, and then a gaggle of mallards floating on the lake would abruptly lift off, squawking and carrying on, and Grandpa and he would get a good shot, at least two and sometimes three. And it was then that he discovered that he never missed, and Grandpa would say that he never had seen anyone who could shoot as well as Jim. Those were good days. No, not good. Wonderful.

Back in the house, he rolled himself a cigarette from a diminishing supply of Prince Albert tobacco, and then made some powdered milk for cereal and a pot of coffee. He found some cat food for Reb, who ate it greedily.

Bev awakened about eight o'clock and wandered into the kitchen, yawning.

Her hair was a little mussed and her eyes looked

sleepy, details that seemed to accentuate rather than diminish her beauty. In total, the sight of her made Jim's stomach tighten.

"That coffee smells wonderful."

"Tastes wonderful too. Pull up a chair and have a couple of cups. We got plenty.

"Also," he said expressionlessly, "how about some ham and eggs and biscuits?"

"Dream on, big boy," she replied. "I'll just settle for a bowl of cornflakes."

"Gee, that's what I'm having too." Pouring two mugs of coffee, Jim asked, "Did you sleep well?"

"Like that much-talked-about log."

"Me too. But I did wake up several times to give a listen, just in case anybody might be prowling around outside. Then it dawned on me that Reb would sound an alarm if that were the case. I'm pretty good about hearing noises that don't belong, but I'm not better than a dog."

It occurred to him that he might tell her the analogy of hearing a flea pass wind, but he held himself in check. His instincts told him she would laugh, but he might embarrass her—and himself also. She was not only a sexy and attractive woman, she was a lady.

Bev mixed some milk in her mug and then carefully sipped it.

"Delicious," she said.

"Have you listened to the CB this morning?" Jim asked.

"No," she said.

"I was out and nothing was moving—except an antelope I saw—and I didn't hear the sounds of any shooting," he said.

"That's a good sign. Maybe," she said.

"What do you mean by maybe?"

"I know the Rejects are up to something. People like that are always planning something," she said.

Jim nodded. "Down through history they've been plenty of groups like the Rejects, and they always seem to show up when the world is in chaos."

"Like a mob after a riot," she said.

"How about the Believers?" he asked.

"I don't know what they're planning now. Perhaps getting ready to invade the Zone. It's just back and forth, back and forth between them and the Rejects," she said.

"It really galls me that they say they're Christians. No blacks allowed, no Hispanics, and no brand of the Christian religion except theirs. Christians! What they forget is that the word *Christian* comes from Christ, and He didn't die on the cross just for white people. His greatness is that He died for us all," she said.

Jim looked at her.

"Are you crying?"

"Just a little misty. I guess part of it is my father. He always said that God is love, and that love is blind—color blind, sex blind, and blind in every way imaginable. Jeez, I miss him."

"In reading the SUSA manifesto, it's clear that that was the way Ben Raines felt too."

"Absolutely."

"Do you think that the Believers will be able to stop the Rejects?"

"I don't know. As bad as it would be, at least, like I said before, they're not murderers."

"Not yet," Jim said. "But it has always struck me that narrow-minded thinking can lead to violence."

"Hey, that's pretty good."

"Yeah." Jim smiled. "Jim LaDoux, philosopher."

He paused.

"Well, I guess," he said, "we should be moving on."

Bev nodded.

"I guess we should."

Fifteen minutes later, they were back on the road.

At a few points during the journey north, to stay off the main roads they had to take some very narrow, out-of-the-way roads, one of which was not even on Ben Raines's maps.

And once, for a while, the lodgepole pine forest they were traveling through gave out to high desert and sagebrush, and continued as they traveled past the town of Green River and through the Flaming Gorge—named for its spectacular red color—and they were relatively exposed to danger. But they saw no one or more importantly, no one saw them.

Once they stopped for a bathroom break, and then they were on their way again.

So far, they had not seen anyone, hostile or friendly. It would be easy to think that they were the only two people left on earth.

At one point, Jim, smoking a cigarette, looked over at Bev.

"We have a decision to make," he said.

"What's that?"

"Should we go around Jackson, or through it?"

"I'd rather go through it," Bev said.

"Why?"

"Maybe we could hook up with someone. There'd be more safety in numbers."

"Maybe," Jim said.

"What about trying to find the Believers? Maybe we could hook up with them."

"I don't think so. I don't want to be associated with them."

"For the reasons mentioned?"

"Absolutely."

Bev thought before answering.

"You're right," she said.

"How about taking 191 into Jackson?" Jim said.

"That's the main highway."

"I know. I figure we'd get on and off it fairly fast."

"Okay," Bev said. "I have a feeling you have good instincts."

"I do when it comes to mountain trails. I hope it spills over onto asphalt ones!"

Bev laughed, and Reb, sitting on the floor beneath her, wagged his tail as if he got it too.

Jim nodded.

About five miles up they turned west, and soon they were on 191, heading into Jackson. It was weird. Jim knew 191 was a well-traveled road. But now, there was no one on it.

He wondered what would be going on in Jackson.

"How you doing?" he said to Bev.

"Okay," she said.

"I find it curious that there's no one on the road. But I'm also glad."

As they got to within a few miles of Jackson they saw their first sign of human life. They had spotted three passenger cars going south at a high speed on 191. They knew that the people in the cars saw them but did not attempt to make any contact.

"I'm hoping those cars we saw are a sign that Jackson is free of hostiles," Jim said. "They didn't try to stop us, so they're not Rejects, and if Rejects had taken over Jackson I doubt very much if they would have been traveling so freely."

"You said you had visited Jackson."

"I visited there when I was ten. I went with my father.

I think it's mostly a tourist town, everything designed to separate the tourist from his dollar."

"There's nothing wrong with that."

"I know. I'm just telling you what it is."

"Okay."

"I think the population is less than ten thousand, but on the day we went there it had to be three times that many, and I remember seeing license plates on cars from every state in the union. Don't expect to see an old western town. From what I've heard about it over the years, there're all kinds of gift shops, art galleries, fine restaurants, western-style saloons, and fancy boutiques."

"Oh."

"My father told me that other people in Wyoming don't like Jackson, maybe because they're jealous, but also because they consider it a false town, all just geared to sell things to tourists. But the country around it is pure. You got Grand Teton National Park or Bridger Teton National Forest."

"That's good."

"The thing I remember most about it, though, is the antler arches."

"What's that?"

"Jackson has a town square, and they build arches of elk antlers."

"Where do they get them from?"

"Bull elk. They fall off every year and people pick them up."

"Oh."

Almost abruptly, Jim and Bev stopped talking because they could see the town. They would soon be in it, and whatever it held. Both were alone with their own thoughts as they approached, but they shared one idea: it could be dangerous.

6

The HumVee rolled slowly into Jackson.

Jackson held no sign of life, but plenty of signs of death. It was horrific. The streets were virtually lined with dead bodies in various states of decomposition from skeletal to black and bloated. The stink seemed worse in certain sections as they drove along—and it was a cool day—thick enough to be visible. Jim rolled up his windows.

The entire town had been trashed. Buildings, exclusively stores, were intact, but it seemed that every one of them had their windows broken. Some of the buildings had the doors pulled off, while two had the roofing ripped off, and one small building was totally collapsed.

"It looked like a tornado touched down here," Jim said.

"How horrible," Bev said. "Let's keep going."

"Okay, but first I want to check something out."

He stopped the HumVee and took a handkerchief from his breast pocket, then reached back and grabbed a bottle of water, opened it, and poured some on the handkerchief so it was damp.

He handed it to Bev.

"Here," he said, "just breathe in it and concentrate on not breathing through your nose."

"Okay."

"I'll be right back."

Jim had brought the HumVee to a stop in the middle of the town square where, indeed, U-shape arches made of elk horns were intact. One of them had a pair of bodies under it, a man and a woman, lying side by side. They were lying faceup and looked as though they were taking in the sun. Jim grabbed the AK-47 and headed over to them.

Bev watched as he looked at the male body, then knelt down. He lingered a moment, then got up and went to the female body.

What, Bev thought, could he be doing?

At the point when she was about to join him—as ugly as she found the whole thing—he headed back to the vehicle. He got back in the HumVee and did not say anything until he had closed the door.

"Okay, let's go."

"What's up?" she said as Jim put the HumVee in gear.

"It looks like half of these people died of plague," he said. "But the rest were shot."

"The Rejects?"

"I wouldn't bet against that. The woman I looked at was a Believer."

"How do you know?"

"She was wearing a Believer medallion, and she wasn't alone."

"This is like a holy war," Bev said.

"I think it's more like a fight for survival. A fight to the death. What I don't understand," Jim said, "is what Believers were doing in Jackson. These people have been dead about a week, I'd say, and it doesn't look like it was an all-out battle. More like plague mixed with executions."

Jim was silent for a moment.

"It's quite a shock," he said. "This was once, like I said, a tourist town, full of life and kids and . . . just a shock. Hard to believe it could happen."

Bev took the handkerchief off her face.

"I know," she said. "I was shocked when I first encountered the Rejects near Salt Lake . . . and all the rest. I mean, you go through your life thinking that God will protect you from stuff like this. No, not even that. You can't imagine it happening to you. And then it does."

Jim nodded.

"Are you game to cruise some of the residential areas?"

"Where are they?"

"Outside the town."

"Why?"

"In case someone asks about this place, I want to be able to give them a complete report on what's going on."

"Who, someone like General Raines?"

"Maybe someone like him. I hope there's someone around like him."

"You sound like a GI out on patrol."

"Maybe in this instance I am."

"Okay," Bev said. "It can't get worse than this."

Jim glanced at the CB. Nothing. He put the HumVee in gear.

For the next fifteen minutes they drove up and down the residential streets that were close to the center of town, and then to one or two of the condos. When Jackson had started to grow exponentially because of the hordes of tourists that visited the place each year, so did the homes of people involved in the town's activities, creating a host of expensive private homes and condos.

Jim did not check out all the homes, but he saw enough to realize that quite a force had been through. Windows were broken and dead bodies, some shot, some having died of the plague, abounded, ordinary people as well as Believers.

And a number of the buildings had signs on them in red paint that said GOD IS DEAD as well as ones that were a lot worse, including FUCK GOD.

"It's just as bad as town," Bev said.

Jim nodded, and after a while he didn't have to be asked again by Bev to drive out of Jackson. It was depressing, and there wasn't much to do, wasn't much to say, and he felt that he had grasped, for the first time, just how sick the Rejects were.

"The Rejects have their own religion," he said.

"What's that?"

"Murder. They believe in it totally."

"I couldn't agree more."

Jim drove back to 191 and got on it, heading north. Both he and Bev couldn't wait to get back into the country, God's country, and cleanse themselves as much as possible of what they had just seen, smelled, and felt.

They had gone only a few miles when Bev said: "I think that the hardest part of religion is forgiving."

"You're probably right," Jim said, "but you can't forgive people like the Rejects."

"I think you ultimately can. That's the way of Christ."

"Yeah, maybe ultimately. But the best way to handle them right now is to kill them."

"Unfortunately," Bev said, "I think you're right."

She paused.

"And what do you think, Reb?" she said.

Reb looked up at her.

"Look at the expression on his face. I swear that he seems depressed too."

"I wouldn't doubt it," Jim said. "He's probably picking up on our moods. They say that while we can tell what dogs are feeling, they can do the same by us."

"I wouldn't doubt it," Bev said.

They had driven about five miles when they spotted a fair-sized white church set back a good hundred yards off the road with access to it by a narrow asphalt road.

"Could we stop?" Bev asked. "I'd like to say a few prayers for those poor souls back there."

"Sure," Jim said. "I wouldn't mind going into God's house myself."

"I hope they haven't wrecked it," she said.

A minute later, Jim slowed the HumVee and made a right turn and went up the road toward the church.

From afar, they had seen that the church was lined with stained-glass windows, but when they got close enough they saw that it, too, had been visited by the Rejects. Every single one of the windows had been broken. Part of one looked like it been caved in, as if someone had driven into it.

"I guess," Bev said, "that it was too much to hope for."

The asphalt road widened into a lined parking area on the right. There were no cars in it. Jim drove through it, then followed the "road" around to the back of the church. There was a single vehicle there, an SUV, but it didn't look like anyone was in it. Jim stopped abreast of the vehicle and confirmed that it was empty—of people. The back was filled with all kinds of boxes piled high to the ceiling. He had no way to tell what was in them. The presence of the vehicle meant that either someone was inside or had departed in haste or . . . Jim just wasn't sure.

He continued driving down the other side of the church. There was a line of stained-glass windows there, too. All had been broken. Neither he nor Bev said anything, but their silence spoke volumes.

He stopped the HumVee in front of the church.

"What do you think we should do?" Bev asked.

"I'm going to check it out. It's still a church. You can say a prayer if you want."

"Maybe there's somebody in there."

"They're not necessarily Rejects. When I first encountered the Rejects, all the vehicles they had were painted black. I would assume that they're not. Or at least it's not an official vehicle."

"That doesn't mean that some of them couldn't be in there."

"You can stay out here if you want."

"No way," Bev said. "I'm okay. I want to help you if you need help."

She paused.

"It's sad, though," she said, "that we couldn't find an intact church now. We're afraid to go into a church—because something bad might be waiting. How bizarre."

"I can imagine how the inside looks. This is not just any house but God's house. I'm surprised, in a way, that they didn't burn it to the ground."

"So am I."

Jim turned off the vehicle.

"We should go in loaded for bear," he said.

"I got my TT-33."

"Make sure the safety's off."

"It is."

"Let's go," Jim said, grabbing his AK-47.

They got out of the HumVee and went up to the front door, a massive carved oak entry that had been left, for some strange reason, unmarred.

Jim, holding the AK-47 level with one hand, went first. Bev, also holding her gun up, followed him.

Jim turned the knob, it clicked, and then he pushed the door open with his foot, his body out of the line of possible fire, Bev behind him.

There was no sound, no gunfire. Nothing. Jim listened for ten seconds, then poked his head in.

The door let them into a kind of foyer that looked okay, except for a glass-encased announcement board on the wall to the left of the double doors that led into the church proper. The glass was intact, but someone had carefully spray-painted on it, again in red, a single sentence. GOD IS LOVE . . . MAKING. But someone had crossed out LOVE . . . MAKING and had written above it in smaller letters FUCKING.

Jim was startled when Bev made a quick movement and smashed the glass with the heel of the gun, obliterating the words.

"Bastards!" she said.

Jim looked at her.

"I wish you hadn't done that."

"I'm sorry. A rage came over me."

"Well, if there's a reception committee in there, they know someone has arrived."

"Wouldn't they know that already," Bev said, "us driving around the church?"

"Maybe so," Jim said, and thought: *This girl has grit.*

He turned his attention back to the doors, first leveling the AK-47, and Bev the TT-33. He tried the doorknob, just as he did the outside one. It turned. He pushed one of the doors open with his foot and he and Bev looked in.

It was a disaster. The pews were smashed, in a jumble, obscenities were spray-painted in red on the walls and on the altar, and the things on the top, such as the tabernacle, and around it, such as candles, were smashed. Above the altar was a large crucifix. Someone had looped a rope around the neck of the statue of Jesus Christ and pulled it down to the point where it stayed on the cross but looked like it was in bowing position. The only thing that seemed to be intact were two side-by-side confessional booths on the right wall of the church, and the ceiling. Why they had missed them was anyone's guess.

One thing particularly bothered Jim. In the corner of a church was a statue of the Virgin Mary carrying the Christ child. Both had been beheaded.

"Good Lord!" Jim said quietly

"Yes," Bev said flatly, almost rhetorically, "the Rejects were definitely here."

"I'm going to check the sacristy," he said, referring to the room in the rear of the church where the priests and altar boys changed clothes.

"Okay. I'll check in here under the benches to see if I can find anyone—dead or maybe alive."

"Good."

Bev started to look carefully under the jumble of benches and debris, but had half an eye on Jim as he approached the sacristy door. He used the same caution as he had in entering the church foyer and the church itself. He pushed the door open, keeping his body out of the firing line, peeked in, then stepped inside.

Bev started to make a search of the church, looking as best she could in the dark spaces under the jumble of benches. And what if they found someone injured? Jim probably had some basic medical supplies, but they were not set up to help anyone seriously wounded.

But her mind was not totally focused. At any moment, she knew, she could hear the sound of gunfire.

Inside the sacristy, there did not appear to Jim to be anyone there. At least there was no one in the room. There were a couple of closets, and he knew he should check these out also.

He tapped on one with the muzzle of the AK-47, again keeping his body out of the line of fire. When there was no response he opened the door, stepping aside as much as he could.

The closet was empty, except for vestments and other priestly accouterments as well as shorter garments, red ones with white collars. Altar boy stuff, he thought.

Jim closed the door, then repeated the procedure for the remaining door, which was wider than the first one and, he guessed, a walk-in type.

It was a walk-in—but it wasn't empty. On the floor were three bodies, a young man and woman and, next to them, a child, maybe five years old. There was a massive amount of fresh blood on the floor, so fresh it was still liquid, and Jim could see why. All three throats been cut ear to ear. A little blood, Jim knew, could always look like a lot of blood. But this scene looked like a lot of blood because there was a lot.

"Jesus," he said softly, feeling a lump in his throat. Instinctively, he made the sign of the cross. There was just one shock after another. If it wasn't plague it was murder. If it wasn't murder it was nutcases running around the countryside.

He pondered what to do, and also wondered if he should tell Bev. She was obviously tough. So, he thought, was he. But why visit crap on people unless you had to? He would tell her what he had found, but in due time.

There was nothing more to do. He walked across the sacristy and opened the door, which he had closed on his way in, and stepped into the church.

An unpleasant surprise awaited him.

Bev was in an open space in the aisle and someone was behind her and had his arm around her neck, holding a pistol to her head. And the parts of his clothing Jim could see were gray. This was a Reject, up close and personal.

"Drop the hardware, big boy," he said in a gravelly voice, "or I'll put this sexy lady's brains on the ceiling of this church, which would be a shame."

Jim hesitated, but then he felt something behind him: a muzzle on his neck.

"Do what he says, or your brains will join hers," a man with a high-pitched voice said.

Jim laid down his AK-47, and he felt his Glock being torn out of his belt. Bev's gun was nowhere in sight. She looked very scared, and Jim was surprised. It was a very bad situation, but he wouldn't have bet she'd act like this when in this type of situation. He had thought she was tougher than that.

He himself was very calm. Jim knew this attitude was invaluable in bad situations, though all it was was the ability to see and think clearly despite being in imminent danger of losing your life. It could lead to solutions to problems where nothing seemed possible.

"Tie him up," Gravelly Voice said, "then we'll get to the first order of business."

"What's that?" Jim said.

"Having sex in church for the first time," Gravelly Voice said, "with both of you." For a moment, Jim heard guttural laughter, and then he saw stars. He had been hit in the head from behind, and he fell to the floor. But adrenaline was surging and he knew that if he did not stay conscious he and Bev were dead. Bev had been released by the man. They knew that managing a woman was easy.

"You should have gone to confession," the man behind him said. And both men laughed heartily. The other was also dressed in gray—another Reject. "That's where we were."

"Did you find that little family in the closet?" Gravelly Voice said.

"Yes," Jim said.

"They believed in God," Gravelly Voice continued.

"Do you believe in God?" High Voice asked Jim.

"Yes," Jim said. Maybe, Jim thought, if he answered in the negative he could begin to talk his way out of the situation, but probably not. But he knew he had to tell the truth.

"I don't believe in God!" Bev screeched. "I don't believe. Look at what God has done to the world."

"Our feelings exactly," Gravelly Voice said. "But I want to see something."

With that, Gravelly Voice reached down Bev's shirt, grasped something and pulled it out, and held it up. It was a thin gold chain and, dangling, light reflecting off it, a cross.

"And this," Gravelly Voice said, "is evidence of how much you hate God, right?"

Both Rejects laughed heartily.

"Well, don't worry," High Voice said, "me and my partner are going to give you plenty of opportunity to get down on your knees and adore Him."

For a moment, Gravelly Voice didn't get it, but then he did and laughed heartily as well.

"Just take me with you," Bev pleaded, "then you can have me all the time."

"I don't know," Gravelly Voice said.

On the floor on his belly, listening to this, Jim was appalled, but some part of him wondered. Could he have been that wrong about Bev? Was she that cowardly? *I guess,* he thought, *you never know people until it comes down to their survival. Still . . .*

Jim looked up at her as the Reject behind him started to tie him up. He caught Bev's eye. Her face was terrified and pleading, but there was a faraway look in her eyes, as if she was thinking about something else.

Jim calculated what he might do. But there weren't many options.

Then he was aware that Bev was falling forward, as if fainting, and he shouted, but her fall seemed controlled and then her hands contacted the floor and faster than his eye could follow, she whirled on her head like a break-dancer and her foot smashed first in the head of the gravelly-voiced Reject, and before the other could react he, too, had been smashed in the head by a high-powered kick. Jim was amazed. The central fact was that within milliseconds both men were on the floor and he saw that one was unconscious, the other semiconscious, and both of their weapons had gone clattering away harmlessly.

Jim was on his feet in seconds with renewed vigor, and he ran over and picked up one of the AK-47s and whirled. Speed, he saw, was not necessary. The Rejects were still sprawled on the floor, one still unconscious, the other semiconscious, neither with any ability to get up.

Jim looked at Bev. Her demeanor, which had been of a young woman about to be raped and pleading for mercy, was now calm and hard. It occurred to Jim that the safest place for these jerk-weeds was the floor.

"What the hell was that?" Jim asked. "Some kind of karate?"

"No," she said softly, "it's a defensive move within the art of ninjutsu, which is not karate. Karate emphasizes the physical. Ninjutsu is a marriage of mind and body."

"So your pleading with them was an act."

"I was scared. But ninjutsu teaches you to understand that fear, takes it into account and teaches you to use it, to direct the power within yourself and the universe into your hand or foot or arm or head—whatever you intend to use."

Jim shook his head.

"What's next?" Bev asked.

"Why don't you check around outside? I'll be out in a minute."

"What are you going to do with them?"

"I don't know."

"Okay, I'll see you outside."

Jim watched Bev as she walked to and disappeared into the foyer, then he turned his attention back to the gray-uniformed duo sprawled on the floor. He did, in fact, know what he was going to do with them. It had occurred to him when he opened the walk-in closet and seen the butchered family there, and it was also an outgrowth of something that Ben Raines had said in the SUSA. And he knew he wasn't going to hesitate.

Jim pulled a knife from a scabbard on his belt. It was a wicked-looking knife, one that U.S. SEALs used. It had a six-inch blade with the serrated part on the cutting edge one and a half inches from the tip. Jim kept it so sharp he could give himself a close shave without soap and water.

He leaned over the gravelly-voiced man who was semiconscious and then Jim swung his arm in a vicious arc and ran the blade across his neck, almost taking his head off with the depth of the cut, cutting halfway through the spinal column, then leaped out of the way to escape the gushing blood. He did the same to the other man, and he did it with the same efficiency and proficiency that he might use in butchering a deer, except he had never felt the same rage he felt now. He looked dispassionately at them. Now, he thought, they would never rape and kill again.

He wiped the knife clean on one of the men's shirt, avoiding the spurting bright red blood as he did, then replaced the knife in its sheaf and walked outside. Bev was just completing her reconnoiter.

"That was fast," she said.

"Yep."

"What'd you do?"

"I'll tell you on the way," he said.

7

Jim and Bev continued to head north, going deeper into Wyoming. As before, Jim took one of the safer county roads. They did not speak for ten miles, even though both knew that there were things to discuss. Finally, Jim said: "I guess you want to know what happened at the church?"

"Yes," Bev said, "I do."

"I killed them both. Let me tell you why."

He then detailed the horror show he had found in the sacristy, and how he wanted "to make sure that the duo did not kill again."

"I figured you did," she said.

"I didn't give it much thought. It was the only thing to do."

Jim paused.

"By the way," he said, "I want to thank you for saving my life."

Bev laughed.

"All in a day's work."

Jim laughed. Then: "I was wondering," he said. "How come your father allowed you to learn this empty-hand combat? You're the daughter of a preacher. Didn't he preach against violence?"

"This is the first time I ever used it to harm anybody, and I hope it's the last."

"How did you ever get into it?"

"Like I said, I was raised in Japan. There I met a relative of Dr. Masaki Hatsumi, of Noda, Japan, a thirty-fourth-generation ninja of the Togakure Ryu, a ninjutsu style founded in approximately 1550 in the Iga Province near Kyoto, which was the capital of Japan then."

"Ninja. I thought they were all criminals, or just existed in comic books."

"That's a misconception. There are some criminal types, but most are good people. And they certainly do exist."

"Why were you interested in it?"

"I don't know. I didn't like dolls. Empty-hand combat was just part of it."

Jim laughed.

"Actually," Bev said, "I liked the spirituality of it all."

"What was that shout you made?"

"That's what is known at the 'ki' or 'kiai' or 'spirit shout.' It's used by ninja as well as other martial artists in empty-hand fighting. It's a natural release of breath and noise that accompanies the expending of physical and mental energy. The Togakure masters compare the sounds ninja make to the sounds dogs make when growling and barking while fighting, or the yell used at the moment of lifting something heavy, such as weightlifters use."

"Amazing."

"There are other yells too, attacking shouts, victory shouts, discovery shouts . . . and the highest form of kiai is the internal shout of what is known as 'silent kiai'—a low, rumbling growl . . . of vibrations so low in pitch that they're inaudible."

"What else do you know?"

"Weapons. Everything a ninja knows."

"Like what?"

"Oh, I can throw a shuriken—"

"That's the star, right?"

"Yes."

"I can handle a bo and jo—sticks—as well as the kurisgama, which is a weighted chain, and much more."

"I really am amazed."

"But I think the most interesting thing I was taught was the art of invisibility."

"How does that work?"

"Well, I didn't practice all of them, but some I did."

"Like what?"

"Well, first of all there's the night. The ninja were taught how to stay invisible in it, but all the ground and plants—"

"Like?"

"It's called do-ton jutsu, or earth techniques, where you learn how to hide yourself and your gear among rocks or uneven ground. For example, we were taught how to shape our bodies like natural or man-made objects, such as boulders or statues, which are undetectable in darkness. There's also moku-ton jutsu, wood and plant techniques, involving hiding in trees and foliage or tall grass. I was also taught how to hide underground."

"Underground?"

"Yes, you bury yourself completely except for bamboo snorkels. You can imagine," Bev said laughing, "how disconcerting it would be for a guard to be walking along and then see someone come up out of the ground at him."

"I can imagine."

"There're also techniques for hiding in a house. The one I liked best was the one where a ninja could climb up near a ceiling and brace him- or herself . . . People never look up when they come into a room."

"By the way, do you have a black belt in ninjutsu?"

"I'm way past that. There are only a few other people in America who rose to my level. I'm one of the few people in America to be allowed to establish and promote the Togakure style in this country."

"Wow. I better steer clear of you."

Bev smiled.

"That's right," she said.

Jim looked at her. He knew that their relationship had gotten a couple of notches deeper, something that tends to happen when someone saves your life, or may depend on you for his or her life. He had heard once that when male and female cops rode in a radio car together the chance of them having sex was almost one hundred percent. Now he understood that totally.

They were quiet for a while.

"I was wondering," Jim said. "How, ultimately, are the Rejects going to be controlled?"

"I don't know," Bev said. "Since the wars and the plague and all the chaos that's been released, the American Constitution means nothing because it cannot be backed up with force."

"So what is going to happen?"

"I think until some sort of stable government is created the chaos is going to continue."

"What do you mean by stable?"

"Fair. That's what's wrong with the Believer philosophy. It's unfair, therefore it ultimately won't work."

"I agree with that," Jim said. "And what you said is

exactly what Ben Raines would say." Jim paused. Then: "The calamities didn't shake my family's faith."

"Nor mine. So that's two out of three or four billion. Add it up, Jim."

Jim came to a crossroads and slowed the HumVee, then stopped. The land was flat sagebrush country, the powder-blue sky cloudless and immense. Wyoming was either mountains or desert—and the big sky. The only sky that was bigger than Wyoming's as well as the other states was Montana, which was due north.

"You want to continue north," he questioned, "or go east, west?"

"You're driving," Bev said.

Jim reached over and took one of the maps that Ben Raines had given him and examined it carefully.

"North, of course, will take us into Yellowstone. We have a couple of roads we can take there that will keep us off 191."

"Suits me," Bev said. "I've always wanted to see Old Faithful. Hope it's still gushing."

"I don't think fanatics are going to stop it," Jim said.

"In fact," Bev said, "Yellowstone Geyser is a miracle that some people look on as proof of God's existence."

"Isn't there a name for that? I mean people who believe that the wonders of the universe are proof of the existence of God."

"Pantheism," Bev said.

"We got a lot of stuff around here that would make you believe that. As long as I've lived in this country, there are still sights that take my breath away."

"Japan is also beautiful," Bev said, "and when we

settled in Salt Lake City, of course, the beauty was incredible. All those weird colored rock formations, like in Arches National Park. You ever been there?"

"Yep. I went down to see the mountains once, and the salt lake."

"Yeah. People think that Utah is all desert, but they have a bunch of mountains that are thirteen thousand feet high."

Jim nodded.

"I just rode through some of it."

"The city itself is beautiful," Bev said. "I used to love to drive up into the mountains. From certain points on the road you could see the entire city, complete with all its lights, laid out. It reminded me of diamonds laid on black velvet."

"That's pretty poetic."

"I call 'em as I see 'em."

"Listen," Jim said, "after seeing what you could do in that church and what you've been telling me, I'm not going to disagree with you in any way!"

Bev laughed.

They continued to drive north. Meanwhile, Bev worked the radio dial, which was on the AM band. She stayed at it a while and got nothing, finally turning off the radio in frustration.

"What happened to all the network people?" Jim asked. "What happened to the major networks in New York and Los Angeles? The satellites are still up there." He automatically pointed upward. "And will be for years. Major cities were not destroyed in the Great War, nor did everyone die of the plague. The networks stayed on the air until a few weeks ago. Then they just stopped broadcasting. What happened?"

"I heard the newspeople got sick and died, they

got scared and ran off, the cities exploded in religious violence and they couldn't get to work, or a combination of these things—take your pick. The Rejects killed them or scared everyone off," Bev said. "Or . . . " She paused.

"Or what?"

"Or they joined the Rejects."

Jim nodded. He believed her. Some people would do anything to survive, from selling their children into prostitution to turning their mothers in to the authorities. It had happened over and over again in history.

"Yes," Bev said, "survival is everything to most people."

"No question," Jim said. "The urge, the absolute need to survive is so strong . . . You know what the most dangerous person you can face is?"

"No," Bev said, "what?"

"Someone who doesn't care if they live or die. That person is very dangerous."

"No question," Bev said.

When they were about fifteen miles from the church, and out of the desert and tooling through the forest, Jim got another surprise—this one pleasant. There was a Mobil gas station virtually in the middle of nowhere, and the pumps worked, and here were no cadavers around, or live people for that matter. In a way it was bizarre, as if he and Bev had started out some Sunday afternoon, taken a back road, and then decided to stop at this off-the-beaten-track gas station.

Jim filled up the tank, as well as the empty five-gallon gas cans in the bed of the HumVee, and topped off the oil, storing a couple of extra cases in the bed of the vehicle.

"I'd love to discard these gas cans," Jim said, "but it's not likely that I will. There will be fewer and fewer gas stations as we travel farther north."

Bev nodded.

"The one thing that I don't need," Jim said, "is what gas stations commonly have, a mechanic. With all the farming and other motorized equipment we had around us I've been working on internal-combustion engines since I was knee-high to a spark plug. Because anyone who lives in the wilderness with the nearest mechanic a hundred miles away must learn. And as it happened I tuned up this little baby a couple of days before I met you, so we should be in good shape. Since it gets such low gas mileage you have to keep it well tuned."

"Interesting," Bev said.

"You have to be part doctor. Know how to perform a tracheotomy."

"What for?"

"In case someone chokes."

"Oh."

"We also learn CPR and a lot of other stuff, including delivering a baby."

"Wow."

"Dr. LaDoux at your service."

They stopped in midafternoon for lunch. Jim drove the HumVee deep into one of the rest areas to hide it. Bev cooked up some Spam and sliced potatoes, sprinkled liberally with onion salt, and it was quite delicious. The fire with which they cooked the Spam burned smokeless enough so it wouldn't give them away should there be Rejects in the area.

After lunch—or more particularly as Jim and Bev were sipping on cups of fresh coffee and Jim was smoking a cigarette—she brought up a subject that had been on her mind.

"Let me ask you," Bev said, "how did you like living in Idaho?"

"I loved it."

"Like what?"

"The country, the mountains and water, the food . . . everything."

"Somehow I got the idea that it was the breeding ground for a lot of crazy people."

"That's a myth. I mean, people say that Idaho harbors a large number of hate groups and white supremacists, but there are only small groups concentrated up in northern Idaho where I was from. For example, a few years ago when the Aryan Nations had their national gathering, only a few people attended. One thing I do know. Idaho really cares about liberty and freedom, that its laws don't infringe on individual or property rights. That really came out during the Ruby Ridge assault years ago by the FBI."

"I vaguely remember that. . . ."

"It happened in 1992," Jim said. "U.S. Marshals and FBI and BATF agents assaulted the home of Randy and Vicki Weaver, killing Vicki, son Sammy, and the family dog. So in 1993 Randy Weaver was found innocent of weapon and murder charges and got $3.1 million in civil damages. But that didn't bring his family back."

"How terrible."

"Let me ask you a question," Jim said, topping off their coffee cups. "Do you expect to get married one day?"

"Not if the world stays like this. I've always thought I wanted kids, and I certainly wouldn't want to bring them into the world the way it is now. It's so unstable."

"I agree."

Jim mashed his cigarette out on a rock. Preventing fires in the wilderness was as natural to him as breathing.

"Do you think the world will change?" Bev asked.

"If it doesn't it won't survive."

"Why do you say that?"

"Again, and I don't want to harp on it, but I've always thought that life was about fair play. If you don't treat people right, one day your behavior will bite you in the butt. That's why wars start. People don't treat other people fairly. I know you're too young to have experienced it, and so am I, but I'm sure you know about Communism?"

"Sure."

"I remember my grandfather telling me that the reason the Berlin Wall came down was that the general populace wasn't being treated fairly. The bigwigs lived in relative luxury while the rest of the people had to scrape to get by. And meanwhile the bigwigs were telling everybody to believe in Communism, with everybody sharing equally. The general public knew that was baloney—or knockwurst—and they took it for a long time, but one fine day they said we've had enough and revolted."

"Absolutely.

"Changing the subject," Bev continued, "it's hard to believe you weren't married, or don't have a girl."

"No," Jim said. "Like I said before, not many eligible girls where I live. And I always seemed to be busy with other stuff."

"I would imagine that women would flock to you."

"The only thing I had flocking to me was sheep."

Bev laughed.

"You don't like girls?"

"You mean do I prefer boys?"

Bev laughed.

"No," she said.

"I would imagine boys would flock to you," Jim said.

"My father discouraged them. I had a boyfriend when I was about fifteen," Bev said. "We went out about six weeks."

"What ended it?"

"Daddy. He heard that the boy was interested in only one thing."

Jim laughed.

"At that age the world is—how did one writer say it?—all legs and breasts," Jim said.

He paused, then continued. "That's what all boys are interested in. That's just the way nature is."

"Not to a Bible thumper like my father."

"Well, he must have been interested in something other than religion at one point in his life."

"What do you mean?"

"You didn't crawl out from under a rock, did you? You had a mother, right?"

"Yes," Bev said. "Are you . . . uh, liberal about that stuff?"

"I'm not liberal about anything. I would totally agree with Ben Raines when it comes to liberalism. You treat people like they're crippled and guess what, they turn out to be."

"Crippled?"

"That's it. I guess I'm sort of old-fashioned," he said.

"What do you mean?"

"I don't believe that men should live like caribou,

mating with everything in sight. I guess I always told myself that I had to really feel something for a woman before I would have sex."

"I think that's the way it should be too," Bev said.

Jim nodded. He was right on the verge of telling Bev that he was starting to feel something for her but he held it back. Maybe, he thought, she didn't feel anything for him. And if she had to say that, it would be disappointing and possibly add to the tenseness of their relationship.

They drove on for many more miles, still in forest, and at one point Jim knew that more desert was coming up.

"Do you want to stop for the night now?" he said.

"Why?"

"I'd just like to camp out in the forest. We'll be totally safe, and every now and then I just like to stay in the forest. It sort of renews me. And I sure need renewal now."

"What do you mean?"

"I don't know about you, but all this—plus the last of my family dying—has taken its toll. It gets to you."

"Absolutely," Bev said. "Absolutely. But you can't go to the corner drugstore for an antidepressant."

"There are plants you can use if you want," Jim said, "to pump yourself up."

"No, I'm okay. I just say a couple of prayers. And talking to you really helps."

"I'm glad," Jim said.

Bev looked at him. A little color had come into her cheeks.

"You know, you're a very sensitive man. I mean you look like this very strong, tough guy—and you are. But you have a very sensitive, concerned side. Sort of unusual for a man."

Jim nodded.

"I don't take any credit for that," he said, "it's the way I was raised."

He paused. Then: "We have about an hour of daylight left," he said, "and that will give us up time to set up before we hit the hay."

"What do you mean 'set up'?" Bev said.

"I want to show you my mountain man side," he said.

"Okay."

A couple of miles later Jim drove through an opening in the trees to an area deep in the woods.

"We can camp here," he said. "Of course we're breaking the law."

"What do you mean?"

"It's against the law to bring dogs into national parks like this. They don't mix well with the bears."

"Oh."

"But old Reb here—or should I say young Reb here?—is very well behaved. I'll let him stay in the HumVee cab overnight. I don't want him arrested!"

Bev laughed.

"Now," he said, "our first chore is to find a place to store our food."

"What do you mean?"

"This is brown and black bear country and occasionally you get a grizzly coming down from Yellowstone. They usually don't bother people but they are attracted to food. And they can be dangerous."

Bev nodded.

"You know the difference," Jim said with a deadpan expression, "between a black bear and a grizzly?"

"No."

"If you climb up a tree a black bear will climb up after you. A grizzly will snap the tree off at the base."

For a moment, Bev thought Jim was serious, then started laughing. Jim joined her.

"We have to cook and hang our food about a hundred feet from where our tents are. That puts enough space between us and the bears."

"Okay," Bev said, "lead the way."

They carried the food about a hundred yards away from where they intended to camp, and Jim climbed a small ladder he had brought with him to hang the food from a branch that was fifteen feet off the ground and five feet from the trunk of the tree. The branch was high enough off the ground so no bear could reach the food, and strong enough to support the food, but not a hungry bear whose natural smarts about not climbing out onto a branch would keep him from attempting to get the food.

"Want to eat now?"

"Sure. I'm hungry."

"Let's do it."

Together, they got a fire going, first clearing away all brush and leaves. They made coffee and eggs seasoned with herbs Jim found and they were delicious. Reb also got some dried cat food—suitably seasoned. Then they lingered over a final cup of coffee, Jim had a smoke, and then Bev helped him hang all their food up high and make sure that the fire was out. He got the feeling, without being able to nail it down, that she wanted him to notice the way she positioned her body during all this, and a couple of times she caught him looking at her. He was embarrassed, but he couldn't help it. She was gorgeous.

Then they walked back to where the HumVee was parked, and Jim unloaded the tents and other gear.

Jim set up one of the tents, and then he said: "Where would you like yours?"

Bev looked at him in a way that he had not seen before. Almost as if she had never seen him before, but what she saw she liked very much.

"I think one tent will be okay," she said. "What do you think?"

"I think one tent will be fine," Jim said, his voice a little husky.

Fifteen minutes later, night came to the forest. Reb was placed in the HumVee and then Jim and Bev—and the AK-47 and her TT-33—went into the tent and closed the flap behind them.

"I got three blankets," Jim said. "It gets chilly here."

But Bev did not seem to be listening, and the next thing Jim knew she had his face in her hands and kissed him with first a closed and then an open mouth. He felt a certain electricity go through him, and then he kissed her neck, and soon their clothes were coming off and they were at each other with a controlled, highly efficient, but soft intensity, and then they were making love, two human beings who, no matter how strong they were, had seen and felt far too much in the days and weeks and months and years that had gone before, and now needed each other not only as lovers, but as human beings, ministering to the wounds and hurts that both felt, melding, blending, not knowing where each other's body began and left off, emptying the pain and heartache and love into each other over and over again.

8

As the man walked as quickly as he could through the forest he recalled something he had read once: in a racc between a hare and a fox, the hare usually won, because he had stronger motivation than the fox. The fox was running for its dinner. The hare was running for its life.

The analogy for him, he thought, was inaccurate. He had nothing concrete to base it on. He could not be sure that someone was pursuing him, but based on what he had seen back in "Compound W," he didn't want to take any chances.

His name was Morty Rosen. Normally, his hair was as long as a woman's but part of his undercover persona before he hooked up with the Rejects was to get his head shaved. He had also joined a local atheistic society so that if someone questioned him he would know the lingo and the ideas of people who didn't believe in God. In fact, he wasn't sure he believed in God anyway, but it seemed more logical to believe there was one than that there wasn't. Ironically, when he was in college he took a philosophy course and went along with the proof for the existence of God furnished by Thomas Acquinas, a great Catholic thinker. To wit, there had to be an "uncaused cause," and that was God. It was hard to argue with. You could trace man all the way back to some one-celled animal. But someone had to cause the one-celled animal to begin with.

Perhaps the best part of his God-is-dead cover, however, was the tattoo he had done on his right forearm. He had asked and the tatooist had blurred the edges a little and made the image faint, so it looked like Morty had had it for a long time, the implication, of course, being that Morty had been a nonbeliever for a long time. He understood that before they did anything to you the Rejects would determine where your—ho, ho—faith lay.

He was also thirty years old, thin and wiry, and before this night was over he knew he was going to be thinner. He hoped he didn't make a meal for a damn grizzly. Once he had read a story about two campers who were attacked by a grizzly without all his marbles and when they found the duo all that was left was twelve pounds of meat and bone. The rest of the duo was inside the grizzly.

Morty was a city-bred guy, having been raised in the Bronx and having worked in a number of cities including Chicago, Baltimore, and New York, so before he had come to Wyoming, where Compound W was, he had also done research on how to survive in the wild if he had to, and now he was putting what he knew to the test. Of course before he had decided to head west he had taken a test in a magazine on his suitability to survive in the wild and he fell into a category that said: *Stay in Gotham.*

He knew he should have been exhausted. He had gone at least forty miles, most of it at a fast clip but some of it trotting and, occasionally, running flat out, just to bleed off the anxiety that would boil up inside him. But you don't get tired when you're running scared. Good thing he wasn't swimming where sharks were. Along the way he had collided with a number of brushes and branches, and once had fallen and his head had missed a big, jagged rock by a half inch. Those scratches would have been an invite to dinner for every shark with a nose.

He had been able to keep in the woods all the way—though he was tempted to run out in the open where he didn't have to worry about wild animals and where he could really put some distance between himself and them. But he wondered just how visible he would be if they got close. The moon was almost full, and the sky was blanketed with stars to an unbelievable degree. Christ, he might be visible in the woods. He knew the Rejects didn't have any planes or choppers—at least not yet—but he did not doubt their determination if they found out who he was. But they did have tracking dogs, and a special "escape unit" for just this kind of thing. If they found out who he was, they would come after him fast, and if they caught up with him, he didn't want to think of what they would do. The easiest way, which they sometimes did, was to shoot you. But they were great on making examples of people, and to make sure you suffered, so they might hang you, garrote you, boil you alive, draw and quarter you, crucify you. Or a recent favorite, mount you on a sharpened stake that would slowly drive up into your intestines. He had seen one guy who had been caught with a prayer missal pulled apart by wild horses, his arms being torn from their sockets, the horses running away with the man's arms bouncing along the ground like two legs of lamb. Watching this—and it was compulsory for everyone in the compound to watch it—had almost made him puke. In fact, a number of people did puke, and a couple cried. But they all had gotten the message.

Loyalty was high on the Rejects's bill of particulars, and he was hardly that. If they found out about him, and went after him and caught him, he would not see the sun come up. That he knew absolutely and surely as he knew his name. His real name, not Mort Adams, which he had ID'd himself as.

Still, when he was in the woods he was not thinking so much of the Rejects as he was of animals. Bears were nocturnal creatures. One fantasy had him coming around a bend and face-to-face with a black bear or grizzly, though he had heard that if they heard you coming they would run the other way.

Whatever, when he was moving through the woods he carried the .45 the Rejects had issued to him, safety off. If something appeared he would shoot first and ask questions later. He had also had the foresight to take a box of cartridges with him. He had this stored in his backpack. He would probably be so nervous if he encountered *Ursus horribilis* he would empty all sixteen shots into him—or whatever found its mark.

Right now, Morty was not feeling so good, not only because he knew he was facing great danger, but because he wasn't facing it too well, something he had been able to do quite handily before. And he had been in some badass places, like Bosnia, during various wars in Africa, as well as going undercover in a motorcycle club in the States. All had required great chutzpah, and his balls had come through with flying colors. But he had never seen such savagery as with the Rejects, and after a while watching people die in such horrible ways every single day of the week started to get to him.

Abruptly now, he heard something. He stopped and listened. It was in the distance, the direction he was coming from. It was the yip-yip-yip of a coyote, and the sound of something light and fast running across the forest floor.

He looked around. There didn't seem to be anything dangerous around. A couple of times when he had stopped he saw pairs of red eyes—fortunately very low to the ground—looking at him, but then the eyes had dissolved and the creatures had run away.

He was not, of course, defenseless in case a wild animal came at him. He had wanted to steal a shotgun or any number of other weapons that the Rejects had stockpiled, but if he was caught with one he would have been questioned exhaustively, and if they suspected anything they would invite him to sit on a stake. The Rejects didn't trouble themselves with the finer points, like proof and corroboration. They just killed you and moved on.

The yip-yipping sound stopped, and Rosen listened a little more, then clapped his hands, this to alert any bear in the area that he was coming through. You didn't want to surprise a bear, he had heard, particularly a sow with cubs. And if you came across a cub you'd better move out of the area quickly. Mama was sure to be nearby.

Of course, the Rejects might not have found out who he was. That was in his head. But chances were, that they would, and if he didn't act on that he knew that he would have no way to talk his way out. They would take him and before he knew it he would be killed in a very special way.

There was no question that if they found out who he was they would come after him. No question at all. And not just anyone. Part of the compound was earmarked as a prison, and despite the severe penalties for trying to escape, a number of people had tried it and then were pursued by the escape unit. So far as Rosen knew, no one had escaped yet.

He had to get out and tell the world what was going on. He wouldn't win a Pulitzer, he'd win a Nobel. He actually did think he would win a Pulitzer. This story was huge.

Ahead, he heard a sound and slowed, then stopped. It was a creek, a brook, or maybe a river. He thought it was a creek, the water running but not too intensely. *Hey,* he thought, *I'm turning into a fucking naturalist.*

He started to trot toward it and then he saw that it was a creek, a thin ribbon of silver, illuminated by moonlight, running through the forest. He knew how he would get across. He sped up and leaped. The creek or whatever they called it was about six feet wide. He made it across with three feet to spare. Fear had made him a world-class broad jumper.

He was glad he had kept moving. No matter how hot the day, Wyoming nights were cool or cold. He was sweating. He had not had time to get the best gear to travel in—he would have preferred shorts—but he had to get out of there fast. The work pants and shirt were not the ideal things to be wearing when you wanted to move fast through the forest. And the pack on his back didn't help either.

Occasionally, he would come across a path and follow it and if he saw that it curved he would be particularly careful to clap his hands. At one point, about five minutes after he had jumped the stream, Rosen saw something in the distance, maybe a hundred yards away, that stopped him dead. It looked like there was a large, even huge animal standing in the woods.

But how big could it be? he thought. There weren't any elephants in the woods of Wyoming, and this animal was big enough to be an elephant. He took a few steps closer, where he got a better angle and saw that it was a HumVee, the kind of vehicle that was popularized in the Iraq wars.

Rosen stopped, not knowing what to do next. Maybe, he thought, the Rejects had gotten wise to him and found a road and circled around to head him off. No way. Also, he never saw any of them with a HumVee. Only those black jeeps and SUVs.

He gripped the .45 hard. He might as well face it now. He could start to run, but they would catch him. He'd better try to shoot his way out now. Maybe he would win. Maybe he would be able to commandeer the vehicle. He knew one thing. If they were going to get him, he'd be sure to keep one bullet—for himself. No way would be go through whatever it was they would put him through.

Then, another idea. Maybe he should just take off back the way he came, cut across the desert section. He had his trusty compass, he could keep going east, at least.

No, he'd keep going. Maybe it wasn't them, maybe it was, but they didn't have a clue it was him. . . . Maybe he could slip by.

As stealthily as he could, he threaded his way through the forest, each step bringing him closer to the vehicle. Then he saw a tent. A tent. It couldn't be the Rejects'. Why would they set up a tent? They wouldn't. It was someone else. Of course there was no telling if they were hostile or not. The Rejects weren't the only bad guys in the forest.

One good thing about the Rejects. They were required to wear the gray uniforms and stupid little caps to ID themselves. And it was bright enough for him to see what color whoever it was was wearing—or wasn't.

But he couldn't see anyone.

He crept closer, going from tree to tree, and finally he was only fifteen yards away. He looked at the vehicle and the tent. Where were the people? he thought. Probably inside the tent.

And why was he so curious who they were and what they were? He should just slip by and get away. He was curious because that's just the way he was. He was a reporter, and that was the nature of the beast, at least the good ones.

And then he heard a tiny crunching sound behind him and everything went black.

9

Rosen became aware that he was awake, lying on his back, and that it was dark—or night. His stomach squeezed. The silhouettes of two people loomed above him and appeared to be looking down at him. He was also aware that the .45 was no longer in his hand. He realized he was on the run, that these were Rejects. That before too long he would be dead. All he could hope for was that it would happen quickly.

He could make out shapes—and color. No gray. They weren't Rejects. It was a man and a woman. There was no gun in sight, but he still got the feeling that these were not people to be trifled with.

"Who are you?" the man asked. It was impossible to see his face. All Rosen knew was that he was tall.

"Morton Adams."

"What are you doing here?"

"I was just walking through the woods," Rosen said, immediately realizing how lame, even stupid, his explanation was.

"Why?" the man said.

"I don't know. I'm just a traveler walking through the woods."

"With a loaded .45?"

"Well, there's wildlife in the woods."

"A .45 isn't the kind of gun one often uses for that."

"Who are you?" Rosen asked. "Are you Rejects?"

"No. We're just people traveling north."

Maybe he would not die. He had to take a chance. He debated with himself. Maybe they were Rejects in disguise. Maybe they weren't. If he guessed wrong about these people he could be watching the world go by from his perch on a stake that was anchored in his butt and going deeper at the rate of about an inch an hour.

"Actually, I'm running away from the Rejects."

There was a pause, and the man and woman looked at each other, then down at him.

"Why?"

Again, Rosen had a choice to make. He could tell them everything, or just a bit. He was always against full disclosure. When you did that you had no cards left to play.

"Because I'm a reporter for *Rolling Stone* magazine. My real name is Morton Rosen. And I was sent out here to do a story on them. I was undercover among them. If they ever found out, I'd be dead."

"Are they after you now?"

"I don't think so," Rosen said, "but I got the feeling that my days with them were numbered. That's why I took off from their camp."

"What camp?" the man asked.

"They call it Compound W."

"Where is it?"

"About forty miles from here. Near Little Piney, Wyoming."

There was a pause. Rosen got the feeling that the couple had relaxed. Maybe he had made the right move.

"My name is Jim LaDoux. This is Beverly Harper. You want something to eat?"

"You better believe it. I lit out of there so fast I forgot to take food."

"Sorry I whacked you," Jim said, "but I didn't know who you were and you were approaching our campsite carrying a weapon."

"No problem," Rosen said. "I understand."

Jim grabbed Rosen by the hand and pulled him to his feet. Rosen got the sense that this was one strong dude.

"Why don't you wait here with Bev?" LaDoux said. "I got the food in a tree about a hundred yards from here."

Rosen nodded. He had learned that when he had researched going UC. He just nodded, but he thought: *Morty Rosen, woodsman.*

He and the woman, "Bev," waited, watching as the man disappeared into the woods. He had glanced at her when he was pulled to his feet, and now he glanced again. Food, he thought, wasn't the only thing he hadn't had much of. He had had sex with one of the Reject soldiers, but she was a hard bitch with all the warmth of an entrenching tool and screwed with about the same effect on his body. He could have had sex with any of the young female prisoners any time he wanted, but he wondered how he would write that up. Also, he wondered what it would do to his high-flying morality.

He smiled inwardly. Wouldn't the guy be surprised to return and see Rosen on top of his girlfriend going at it the forest floor? He thought not. Rosen had a good sense about people. This was a dude you didn't want to mess with.

LaDoux returned within a few minutes carrying a sack with him.

"I don't want to risk making a fire," Jim said, "so how about some peanut butter and jelly sandwiches?"

"Excellent."

"How many sandwiches could you eat?" Bev asked, taking the sack from Jim.

"I could eat the sack," Rosen said, "but two should do it."

Bev made the sandwiches and gave them to him, along with some chocolate cookies, and a bottle of water. Rosen tried not to eat the sandwiches like a wild animal. Plus, he didn't want to choke to death.

"Where are you headed?" Rosen asked as they sat down on some big logs near the tent.

"We don't know," Jim said, "just north. Trying to avoid any further contact with Rejects."

"Going north is a good idea," Rosen said. "There are fewer of them up that way, I think."

In fact, Rosen knew exactly where concentrations of Rejects were, but he was not about to reveal what he knew.

"So *Rolling Stone* is still publishing?" Bev asked.

"On a limited basis. But our publisher feels it's important to get the truth out there about the Rejects. His idea is that the truth is the only basis for America to be able to come back."

"I agree with that," Bev said.

"So do I," Jim said. Then: "I'd like to hear some more about the Rejects, but you look really beat. Why don't we wait until the sun comes up?"

Rosen did not nod or say okay.

"What's the matter?" Jim asked.

"I just don't want these whacks showing up."

"Well, if they don't know you're a reporter," Jim said, "there's no reason for them to come after you, is there? I mean you could have just disappeared for no apparent reason, right?"

"Yes."

"Of course if they did," Bev said, "then I could see it."

"I can't think of any way how they could," he said. "I just sensed it." And he thought: *Unless they found my ID, which is highly likely.*

Rosen knew he was lying, but he had perfected this skill as a reporter. He was quite accomplished. Good reporters were. And they would lie—convincingly—to their mothers if it meant getting a good story.

Jim listened, and though Rosen made his statement forcefully there was an undertow of indecision beneath the surface. But he let it go.

"Why don't you sleep in the cab of the HumVee?" Jim said. "That should be fine and it's plenty big for you. As long as you don't mind the company of Reb."

"Who's Reb?"

"My dog."

"No, not a problem. As long as he's friendly."

"Very," Jim said. "Good night."

"Okay, Good night," Morty said. "And thanks for the sandwiches. They tasted like filet mignon."

Later, in the tent, Jim and Bev lay down side by side. Bev said: "I get the feeling that's there's more here than meets the eye."

"You mean he's not who he said he is?"

"No. Just like he's leaving out something."

"I got the same feeling," Jim said. "Well, maybe we can find out tomorrow."

Jim gave Bev a long kiss, and it wasn't long before both of them had fallen back to sleep.

* * *

In the HumVee, Rosen thought about what he should do. Maybe he should wait an hour or so, then take off. There was nothing to prevent him from going.

Wouldn't it be nice to take off in the HumVee?

Yeah, but that wouldn't be kosher. Rosen had done some questionable things in his life, but that was crossing the line. Just like humping a prisoner would have been.

He was still pondering what he would do when exhaustion overtook him and he fell into a deep sleep.

10

Jim, Bev, and Rosen awakened at dawn. Bev volunteered to make breakfast, and after they had finished it— waffles that were no longer frozen and a couple of cups of strong coffee—they sat around for a while on some logs and then Jim looked at Rosen and asked: "So what did you find about the Rejects?"

"First of all, they have about twenty compounds spread over the Northwest—Utah, Wyoming, Nevada, Colorado. They're mostly in northern Utah and Wyoming and Colorado. But there are also cells of them in major cities, and they have all intentions of covering America."

"What is their goal?" Bev asked.

"To turn America into a secular country."

"Godless?" Jim asked.

"That's the idea," Rosen said. "And anyone caught practicing religion will be summarily executed."

"Sounds like the way the English treated the Irish in the 1800s," Jim said.

"What do you mean?" Bev asked.

"Well, stories came down to me from my grandparents—I'm Irish on my mother's side—of how if you were caught, by the British, in the mid 1800s going to Mass or attending school you would be executed."

"Why?" Rosen asked.

"I think the English felt that going to church would somehow bind the people together into a dangerous group, and certainly an educated person was more dangerous to the English than one who wasn't so educated. Ideas can move mountains, right?"

"Hey," Rosen said, "I like that. Ideas can move mountains."

"I can see that," Bev said. "Absolutely."

"Who's their leader?" Jim asked. "Must be a fanatic."

"And then some. Fruitcake, wacko, and nutcase all rolled into one. But a brilliant nutcase. His name is Alex Szabo. He's in the same league with Saddam Hussein, Hitler, Stalin, people of those ilk. He's what they call, as the doctor who did a report on him for the *Stone* said, a 'psychopath, a personality disorder, especially one manifested in aggressively antisocial behavior.'"

"You said a doctor did a report?" Bev asked.

"Yeah," Rosen said, "my editor—and I—wanted to get a sense of who the players were before we played the game. Intel like that can save your life."

"What else did you find out?"

"You want to read the report? I have it with me."

"How did you get away with that?" Jim asked.

"I kept ninety-nine percent of the stuff I needed in a plastic container outside the base camp."

"No, how did you obtain the report?"

"One night I was able to get into Szabo's private office and into his personal crap. The report was there."

"I'd definitely like to see it," Jim said.

"Me too," Bev said.

Rosen went away, and a short while later returned

with a bunch of papers, which he unfolded and handed to Jim.

"The name of the doctor has been removed. He never wanted Szabo to know that he wrote a report like this. I remember him telling me with a smile that was not such a smile that he didn't want to be one of the people on which Szabo manifested his aggressively antisocial behavior."

"But obviously he found out."

"He surely did," Rosen said.

Jim read, Bev looking over his shoulder.

To: Jon Wagner
Publisher
The Rolling Stone magazine

Subject: the personality of Alex Szabo

Dear Mr.Wagner:

I have examined all of the available court, prison, and other papers connected with Alex Szabo, as well as having conducted a few interviews with him while I was staff psychiatrist at Marion Maximum-Security Prison in Marion, Indiana, and this is my conclusions about the man.

Mr. Szabo, who is now head of a paramilitary group that is getting larger and larger in the United States, is an extraordinarily hostile and dangerous person, and when dealing with him there is always the danger that he will abruptly explode in violence. Indeed, while he was in prison he lifted weights constantly, apparently building himself up to a strength that would allow him to better manifest his violence on those who would conceivably cross his path.

As in the vast majority of cases like this, Mr. Szabo's personality was formed when he was a little boy. When he was one year old, his father deserted his mother, leaving her in appalling fiscal straits, and apparently she was unable to make ends meet and rather quickly married Raymond Harel, a man who worked in the steel mills of Gary, Indiana, and who quickly got into the habit of being cruel to young Alex in a variety of ways. While there was no evidence of sexual abuse, there was extreme mental and physical abuse; I think the mental abuse was even more potent on the young boy's personality than the physical aspect, which usually consisted of Alex being beaten with a strap or broom handle.

To give you one example of the mental anguish, there was a brutal incident involving a chicken. Instead of a dog, Alex had a pet chicken that he loved, and one day when he came to dinner his father announced that they were having his pet chicken for dinner, that he had killed it and his mother was cooking it, and his father demanded that he eat it as well, something he did, crying through the entire experience. His father's rationale was that Alex must be strong to survive, able to withstand anything.

After ten years, his mother was no longer able to tolerate her husband's cruelty to Alex, and she left him. She remarried shortly thereafter, but it was too late, emotionally speaking, for Alex. He had a lot of trouble in school. He had a reputation as a class bully, and would take great pleasure in beating other children to the point of unconsciousness. Once, for example, a fight he had with another boy, thirteen, resulted in the boy having to get sixty-two stitches in his face.

He may have murdered someone as well. Apparently one of the boys who fought got his older brother after Alex and the boy threatened to "beat Alex up." Two days later the brother was found beaten to death, apparently with some blunt instrument like a baseball bat or piece of metal and so badly that they had to use his teeth to identify him.

In high school, the pattern of violence continued, until he was discharged from school, but it was here, a school psychologist said, that he developed a desire to be a king, a ruler of some sort, and it was the psychologists' interpretation, with which I concur, that these delusions of grandeur were brought about by a deep-seated feeling of insecurity and worthlessness, the latter the message that his stepfather constantly reinforced as Alex was growing up.

He also developed a pattern of sociopathic behavior—meaning he does not appreciate the consequences of his actions on others, nor does he care. He also uses lying, deviousness, and cleverness to serve his own ends in a way that is quite remarkable. Those who know him well say that the time to fear him the most is when he's smiling, because when he's smiling he always has some other agenda to follow.

He got married fifteen years ago, but he discovered that his wife was cheating on him, and that there was a strong possibility that his two children—a little boy and girl—were not his.

To teach her a lesson that she would never forget, he bound her very securely and also bound the children—and understand that one was three and the other four—and while his wife watched threw first one and then the other into a wood chipper while they were still very much alive. He then fed her, very slowly, into the same chipper and threw the shredded and chopped-up remains into a river.

He received life without the possibility of parole, but one day he and three other inmates pulled a daring escape, killing four guards in the process.

Gradually, he formed the Rejects, composed strictly of people who did not believe in God.

It is a wonder that he can get anyone to work for him, because his violence is closely connected to his quickness to be insulted, or to his belief that someone is being disloyal to him. He holds regular conferences, and these are terrifying ordeals for the people who attend them. His brother-in-law, for example, who was his minister of health, once told him that he thought he should take a break, a week or so off, because he looked peaked. Szabo then invited his brother-in-law into the hall and shot him dead. He actually returned to the conference blowing the smoke away from the end of his pistol. Szabo's interpretation was that his brother-in-law was plotting something against him, but there was nothing concrete to support this.

To sum up, I would say anyone dealing with

him must be extremely conscious of his paranoia and how he gets offended so easily, how prone he is to violence, and the delusions of grandeur that he has about himself. It has been said that those in the know compliment him all the time in hopes of not only currying his favor—he gives out money and property awards all the time—but to stay alive.

Very Truly Yours,

The name of the doctor had been blacked out.

"Wow," Bev said.

Jim smiled.

"You have a lot of chutzpah getting this," he said, pronouncing the C as hard.

"The C is silent," Rosen said. "It's pronounced *hutzpah,* like you're trying to clear your throat."

"Well," Jim said, "whatever way, it spells courage."

"I'd be interested to know what you're thinking about when you go into these situations," Bev said.

"You mean UC?"

"What's that?"

"Undercover."

"Yes."

"I don't think anything," Rosen said, "I just become the person they think I am and that's it. Doing it any other way would be very dangerous. Because if someone had a nagging suspicion about you, the whole operation could start to unravel."

"And you with it," Jim said.

"Absolutely."

Rosen paused, then continued.

"You know Szabo found out about this memo and who wrote it, of course."

"What happened?" Bev asked.

"He murdered the entire family, including grandparents. The method was gruesome. He tied up the doctor, his wife, and three young children, and then strangled each of them with the others watching."

"My God," Bev said.

"And as the years have gone by," Rosen said, "he's gotten worse."

"What do you mean 'worse'?" Jim said.

"He kills more and more people every day, and sometimes for no reason. He always seems to be looking for a reason to kill. And he's got a quick, savage temper. I saw him shoot a guy in the head while they were standing at a urinal because he laughed where he wasn't supposed to at something Szabo said."

Rosen paused.

"They say his eyes have gotten colder the longer he's killed. Christ, I had trouble looking into his eyes. It was like looking into the eyes of a goat, you know, flat and without any depth of human compassion."

Rosen took a deep breath. He was reliving some of the experiences he had as he described them.

"But like I say, he seems to enjoy killing with his bare hands the most," Rosen said. "He mostly lives like an animal, too."

"In what sense?" Jim asked.

"He lives in a cave."

"In a cave?" Bev asked.

"Absolutely Whenever he can, he tries to use natural landscapes to billet his army. It's reminiscent of what the Vietcong used to do in North Vietnam. The ones the U.S. tunnel rats used to go after."

"Yeah, my brother told me about that," Jim said.

"What are they?" Bev asked.

"The caves that the Vietcong lived in were accessible only by narrow tunnels. And the tunnel rats, who usually were little guys armed only with a .45 and a flashlight, would crawl through them to find them."

"Sounds really scary," Bev said.

Jim continued, "My brother told me that no one had more grit than tunnel rats. Because not only would they possibly shine their flashlight into the face of an armed Vietcong soldier, but most of the tunnels had poisonous snakes and spiders in them, as well as rats."

"Wow!" Bev said.

Rosen said, "There are differences between those tunnels and caves and these. Here, you have horizontal tunnels, which are accessible by shafts that have been dug, as well as natural caves with mouths large enough to allow trucks to enter. And everything interconnects, sometimes for miles."

"Who dug the shafts?"

"Slaves," Rosen said, "people the Rejects have captured in war, such as Believers or just ordinary people from towns they conquer. And once they run out of gas they kill them."

"Sounds familiar," Bev said.

"Yeah," Rosen said, "sounds a lot like Nazis."

"He sounds like a man who would want to conquer more than America," Bev said.

"I wouldn't doubt it," Rosen said, "not for a moment."

"You have to have an army to do all this," Jim said.

"He's got about 25,000 Reject soldiers and he's building every day."

"He must have trouble getting recruits based on the way the plague—" Bev said.

"What plague?" Rosen said. "The information I have is that the plague is gone."

"Gone? How?"

"I heard that it's run its course."

"Really?"

"Yeah, the strain died out just as quickly as it came."

"Do you have any details?" Jim asked.

"Yes," Rosen said, "but you have to understand I got this all secondhand from a Reject, so I don't know how accurate it is. But I think it's true. It sounds true."

"Where did the plague come from?" Bev asked. "Someone said that alien space capsules were a possibility."

"No, the way it was explained to me," Rosen said, "was that someone was working on what was first a medieval form of bubonic plague, which, in case you don't know, has never really been banished from the earth, and in the course of their research, which was geared to finding a total cure for it, developed a form of it that was not receptive to antibiotics that normally were used to treat it. The scientists were all set to shut own the entire experiment—"

"Where did this occur?" Jim asked.

"Palo Alto, California."

"Okay."

"Anyway, before they had a chance to do it a bunch of kids broke into the lab, compromised what was a relatively unsophisticated security system, and trashed the place, something that resulted in the plague becoming unencapsulated. And it started killing people, just like the old-fashioned plague."

"That's great news," Bev said.

"You got that right."

"So I take it that all the Rejects are plague survivors, or immune to it?" Jim said.

"Same with the Believers," Rosen said. "Every single one of them was exposed to but survived the plague."

"Well, maybe the country is on the road back."

"Unless it returns."

"Twenty-five thousand soldiers," Jim said. "That seems like an awful lot of Rejects. How does this Szabo attract them?"

"Well, one place he goes to is prisons. A lot of people there don't believe in God. First he would take over the prison by force, then take each and every prisoner into a room and ask them a single question."

"What was it?" Jim asked.

"Do you believe in God?"

"And . . ." Jim said.

"If they said yes they would shoot a single bullet into their foreheads. He killed hundreds of inmates himself, and so did his underlings." Rosen laughed. "It's said that the percentage of people who didn't believe in God got to be almost a hundred by the time they got to the last of them.

"Sometimes he doesn't kill people, though."

"When?" Bev asked.

"When they're useful."

"Where does he keep them?" Bev asked.

"In a compound within a compound. But there's no fence."

"Why not?" Jim asked.

"It's too dangerous to try to escape and fail. Because if he catches you—and his escape units are always successful if they go after you—the penalty is always death. But a special death."

"What do you mean?" Bev asked.

"Whatever Szabo and his henchman can dream up. Most popular now is death by being impaled. They sit you on a sharp stake and you die real slow."

"He hung my girlfriend Ida," Bev said.

"Oh, really?" Rosen asked. "Why?"

"She and I were doing missionary work."

"Who are his slaves?" Jim asked.

"Different people. Anyone who is useful to his army. People who are specialists such as mechanics, gun experts, cooks, and the like. And women—all pretty, particularly teenagers. This guy and his inner circle are rapists of the first stripe." Rosen paused. "Just imagine a philosophy where the concept of sin doesn't exist and neither, in a sense, does evil. You can do what you want when you want with no payback at all."

"How well armed are they?" Jim asked.

"Any place they go they steal the guns and whatever else. They're getting better armed as the days go on."

"Do you think the Believers will stop them?" Bev asked.

"Maybe. I was present at a number of battles with them, and in some cases they beat the Rejects. But the reverse holds true as well. The Rejects have routed the Believers."

"Who heads up the Believers?"

"A guy who has some of the same background as Szabo. I understand it's an ex-con who turned born-again Christian. His name is McAulliffe. They call him Father McAulliffe. He spent fifteen years in San Quentin for manslaughter but when he was released he was a changed man. And after things went to hell in the world he started the Believers. His contention is that God is the only way to go."

"I don't disagree," Jim said, "but my sense is that the Believers are fanatics."

"It would seem that way," Rosen said. "But I have no way to confirm it."

Jim poured what was left of the coffee for all of them, then said to Rosen, "How did you get the idea that the Rejects might find out who you are?"

Rosen's face colored slightly, something that Jim noticed.

"I don't know. It was just a sense of it. Call it a reporter's instincts."

Jim sipped his coffee and glanced gently at Rosen.

"Why did the question upset you?"

"What question?"

"That the Rejects might find out who you are."

"I'm not upset."

Jim nodded.

"I think we should get on the road," he said.

"Can I go with you?" Rosen asked.

"Yeah," Jim said, "sure."

"Good," Rosen said, smiling.

They loaded the gear, with Rosen helping Jim and Bev. At one point Jim and Bev were alone.

"I don't believe him," Jim said, "about not being upset. But I can't figure out why."

"I agree," Bev said. "His cheeks became mottled when you asked him that question."

"I know one thing," Jim said, "my brother Ray never liked the press. Didn't trust them. He had a lot of problems with them when he served in Iraq displacing Saddam Hussein."

"What do you mean?"

"At first he admired the press, particularly the guys

who—as he put it—had the 'stones' to become embedded in active combat units."

"You mean ride along with them?"

"Exactly," Jim said. "but he said that the same guys who played buddy with the troops eventually turned against the GIs and wrote stories that were dramatic and upsetting. They used to report that these things were much worse than they were, not report on how things were getting better, and complain about the GIs morale. The morale of the troops in Iraq was fine, Ray said, it was just the usual moaning. And I remember him saying that if a GI isn't moaning 'there's something desperately wrong with his morale. A happy soldier is one who is talking and beefing. An unhappy one is silent.'"

"Their reporting was horrible. They get facts and figures wrong because they never take the time to investigate, to find out the truth of something. My brother told me once that some guy on NBC said something like sixty guys had been killed in combat over a two-month period. What he did not say—because he did not know—was that there were actually only twenty-one killed by Iraqi firepower, while twenty-nine were killed in accidents or other causes, including two guys who died swimming in the Tigris River."

"That's terrible."

"The thing that used to get him, also, was the stupidity of the newspeople. Most of the people really appreciated having America there, but there are certain anti-American groups that would just wait until the TV people showed up and then run out hollering and screaming about how bad things were in Iraq. So this meant that this baloney would show up on the nightly news the next night. It didn't matter that it was untrue. What mattered was that it would play well on TV. Ray used to complain about this all the time."

"I only had one experience with them," Bev said, "when our church was burglarized once. Three different papers had three different sets of 'facts.'"

"Yes," Jim said, "reporters are different from ordinary people. And I read once too, though I don't know if this affects their ability to do their work, is that many of them suffer from posttraumatic stress syndrome, the kind of condition that GIs in the Vietnam War had."

"Why?"

"Because like soldiers they just see too much. It overloads their ability to absorb it all emotionally. I mean think about it. Bad news is always good news for a reporter, so he or she is always covering fires, murders, all kinds of things that people experiencing such things find upsetting close up."

Bev nodded.

A few minutes later the HumVee was tooling north once again. Into what, no one really knew.

11

Alex Szabo was, to put it mildly, an impressive-looking person. He was six feet six inches tall, had a shaved, polished head, flat, broken features, was muscular in the extreme but with an astonishing thirty-two-inch waist. Some of his soldiers called him V. Standing directly in front of you, he did, indeed, look like the letter V.

While his body was impressive, no doubt the scariest thing about him, as Morty Rosen had said, were his eyes, which were light blue but flat, without the depth of human compassion or feeling for others. If what Dante once said, that "the eyes are the windows of the soul," was true, then in Szabo's case the windows looked in on hell.

As Rosen had also told Jim and Bev, the premier enjoyed killing in general but doing it with his bare hands in particular. He had lost count, but he had strangled or beaten to death with his bare hands over four hundred people, including men, women, and children. He usually killed because they believed in God, but he had also done it because of infractions of his rules or refusing a direct order. There was no trial to weigh the circumstances of an event. Decisions were made instantly—and carried out virtually instantly.

And the infraction could be quite minor. Once,

for example, one of his soldiers had neglected to clean up his area as instructed. Without further ado, Szabo, wearing a rubber apron because he had an idea how the man's bowels would react, had come up behind him while he stood in formation, clamped a forearm over the miscreant's windpipe, and strangled him until he lost control of his sphincter muscles, emptying his bowels as he died.

Killing people in front of his underlings was, of course, done by design. It was an object lesson, or lessons, in more ways than one. First, it cultivated the atmosphere of fear that Szabo, like Machiavelli, believed was the best way to motivate people. Second, that people should die so quickly and for such puny reasons was a direct reflection on the absence of God in the world. And the third and final reason was that the premier liked to be in the overall atmosphere. He liked the stink of fear, the smell of death. If he had been alive at the time of World War II he would have been one of the guards at the gas ovens in Auschwitz or someplace similar with his ear against the door trying to hear women, children, and old people screaming as they died in breath-stopping agony.

Premier Szabo had two trusted lieutenants, Jack Dill and R.W. Duyvill. Both were ex-military men, mercenaries who had honed their combat teeth in a variety of wars. But they were not ordinary grunts. Dill had been a two-star general and Duyvill a bird colonel in the American army. Both were excellent military strategists, and the premier depended on their expertise for invading and capturing some fifty towns in the Northwest and giving advice to operatives in the cities. And both men—in fact all of the top people, in the Rejects army—shared one quality that all great soldiers, even professional prizefighters, share: the killer instinct.

In fact, it was people like U.S. Grant and Sherman that Szabo admired the most. In the Civil War Sherman had, of course, conducted the infamous "Sherman's March to the Sea" where, after burning Atlanta to the ground, he had marched with his army all the way to the ocean, burning and killing and destroying everything in sight. On reflection and examination, there was no justifiable reason for doing this, except one big one: to hammer the spirit of the resisters into total, depressed submission.

But Grant was the same way. Indeed, people forgot that it was Sherman who took his orders from Grant, and he would not have done what he did unless Grant ordered it. Grant himself showed this ruthlessness in the assault on the Confederate troops at Vicksburg, Mississippi, and other places and was known as "Unconditional Surrender" Grant.

Szabo and others shared another quality of great soldiers: none of them were afraid to die. In fact, some of them seemed to seek out death. In numerous battles with the Believers, Szabo and other commanders often put themselves in harm's way, oblivious of bullets and sometimes shrapnel whizzing past them, any piece of which could take their lives. They lived within the moment, focusing on what they were doing. They all had that fabulous essential quality of all great soldiers, the ability to suspend the functioning of the imagination that otherwise would conjure up ways to show you how you were going to get killed.

Now Szabo, Duyvill, and Dill were in the "War Room" at the cave headquarters in Compound W, all poring over a large, detailed map showing a variety of things, these indicated by colored push pins and markers. The only viable threat to the Rejects was the Believers, and their number and concentration in various areas were indicated by markers. Towns that the Rejects had taken over were ID'd with green push pins, and areas that the Believers occupied were marked with red ones. The Reject command could tell in a moment where they stood militarily. Overall, of course, they knew that the plague had hobbled the U.S. government and its armies Indeed a number of U.S. servicemen had come over to the Rejects, or the Believers, and the only group—though it was formidable—between the Rejects and total domination of the United States was the Believers. Szabo and the others vowed that someday they would need a forest of lumber and a ton of spikes to create crosses to which they would then spike to the cross all the Believers who were still alive.

The premier was about to speak when the door virtually burst open and his aide de camp, Jerry Upton, came in accompanied by an attractive, dark-haired young woman. Upton had done a dangerous thing. The premier might get a little pissed, and the next thing you knew you could be on your way to the prison compound—or a dirt nap.

Upton and the woman stood a few yards away from the commanders until their presence was acknowledged, this some two minutes after they had arrived.

"Yes?" the premier said.

"Sir, I wanted you to see what Selby here found in the pants of Morton Adams," Jerry said.

"What?"

Selby handed him the card.

The premier looked for a moment and then handed it to Dill and Duyvill, who, taking Szabo's lead, didn't show much visible reaction.

"Tell the troops to fall out," the premier said, "and get me Raymond O'Brien."

It was a simple statement. But a certain hush fell over the room. Everyone knew the real meaning of what the premier had said.

Ten minutes later, the troops, all in uniform, were lined up on either side of the open compound. The premier came out of headquarters flanked by Dill and Duyvill, and stopped when they were roughly in the middle area that the troops flanked.

Thirty seconds later, a tall, wiry man, looking as if he had just been awakened from sleep, his bushy red hair askew, his eyes puffy, approached.

He stopped and saluted. The premier made a half-hearted gesture to salute back.

It wasn't long, however, that O'Brien was fully awake. Everyone was very quiet, a seeming impossibility with so many people in the area, when O'Brien broke the silence with a short but explosive fart. Everyone laughed raucously, including the premier. O'Brien did not laugh.

"I'm sorry, sir," he said when the laughter had died down. "What's this all about?"

The premier said: "Do you know Morton Adams?"

"Yes, I do, sir."

"What did you do for him?"

"I brought him into our ranks."

"Why did you do that?"

"Because," O'Brien said, suppressing more gas, "I thought he would be a good addition."

"And why did you think that?"

"Because I knew he didn't believe in God. He told me his background as a criminal and his membership in the G Group, the atheistic group in New York City."

"And you believed him?" the premier said.

Everyone seemed to get even more quiet, if that were possible. Everyone knew that something bad was going to happen to O'Brien, including the premier. But he enjoyed this, just as he enjoyed watching someone die slowly on the cross, just as he enjoyed the bodies falling off the cross and being devoured by wild animals, just as he enjoyed watching and listening to people scream in agony as their weight drove the sharpened stake they were sitting on deeper into their entrails. The premier was now treating O'Brien like a marshmallow on a stick, turning him this way and that over a low fire, close enough to singe, but not close enough to go up in flames.

"And why did you believe him?"

"Just the way he was in general, but he also showed me a tattoo."

"A tattoo of what?"

"It showed a picture of Jesus Christ and had a cross-out symbol over it. I asked him what it was, and he told me it was Jesus Christ and represented the way he felt. That God was dead—and should be dead."

"And how did you know the tattoo was real?"

"It looked very real. It was faded like he had it a long time."

The premier nodded and smiled. The smile was terrifying. Everyone knew that the premier only smiled as he did when he was contemplating causing someone else pain.

The premier took the card out of his pocket and handed it to O'Brien. "And did you also know that he was a reporter for *Rolling Stone* magazine? Did he have a tattoo for that as well?"

"Where did this come from? It must be a plant," O'Brien said.

The premier disregarded what O'Brien said.

"Why did you vouch for him?"

O'Brien farted again, but only a few people laughed.

"I believed . . . I believe he is okay. I've seen him in action against the Believers. He's shot at them."

"So why does that mean that he isn't a mole?"

"Doesn't it? Would a mole kill?"

"I don't know," the premier said, smiling even more broadly, "but it's a possibility, isn't it? It's the perfect cover. Or maybe he faked it."

"No, his bullets hit people."

"You are aware, are you not, that vouching for an enemy is an extremely serious crime?"

"It's not been proved that he is," O'Brien said, his voice croaky. "It's not been proved!" he yelled.

The premier swiveled his bald dome from side to side.

"I think it has been. Does anyone here disagree with me?"

There was silence. O'Brien farted loudly again. Then abruptly, in total panic, he turned and started to run, but the premier was as quick as a cat and in a few strides he had grabbed him, squealing like a pig, by the shirt and had him down on his back, straddling him, and just as quickly had his massive hands around O'Brien's neck and was squeezing. O'Brien grabbed the premier's forearms in a vain attempt to pry his hands off his neck, but it was useless, like trying to pry away bands of steel. O'Brien kicked and kicked and kicked and gradually his kicks slowed down, then stopped.

The premier stood up, still straddling him. His pants were tight, and careful observers would see that his crotch was slightly engorged, expanded. The killing had been a sexual experience, as all his killings were to one degree or another.

The premier took a few steps away from the body. "Has anyone seen . . . Rosen?"

A trooper in one of the front rows raised his hand. "I saw him last night at chow."

"Anyone seen him today?" the premier asked.

There was silence.

"Are all the vehicles accounted for?"

The director of the motor pool, a portly, balding man in his mid-forties, stepped forward.

"Yes, sir."

"Which means, of course, he's on foot. He no doubt got the idea, somehow, that his true identity was in danger of being compromised."

Heads nodded.

"And I can tell you," the premier said, "that if he writes about what he experienced here it will not be good for us. It could galvanize people against us. He also knows much classified intel. He was here about eight weeks. He knows how we operate, he knows the locations of our compounds, he knows the personnel, he knows everything. And, in the worst-case scenario, he will give the Believers a royal road to attacking and possibly destroying us. We have no greater priority than to find and terminate him and anyone else he has told. Let's go. I want bloodhounds on the scene within fifteen minutes."

The premier glanced down at O'Brien's body. His crotch area was wet and the premier could smell the feces he had expelled when his sphincter muscles shut down.

"Get this farting machine out of my sight," he said.

12

The Rejects were careful where they buried their victims. By executive order, the premier had declared that grave sites be a minimum of two hundred yards from the compound, and that the graves, individual or mass, were to be a minimum of six feet deep so that the animals could not get to them.

Many people used lime on dead bodies to destroy tissue more quickly, but the premier didn't feel that necessary. "The body," he had astutely pointed out, "rots from the inside out, so no lime is required. I used to get a kick," he told one assemblage of troops, "when people would buy these five- or ten-thousand dollar mahogany coffins to keep their dead from rotting. Meanwhile, they were going to rot even if they had them inside kryptonite. Isn't that hilarious?"

The assemblage had laughed appreciatively, though some of them did not think the premier's observations funny at all.

Ten minutes after he was strangled to death by the premier, O'Brien's corpse was dumped into a grave opened up with a backhoe the required distance from the compound, and a few minutes later was filled in. There would be nothing to mark the grave, nothing to remember O'Brien by. The only people who would remember him would be those who watched him die, and some of these people would never forget.

Above all, there was no service to mark his passing, no prayer, no nothing. (A good way to join O'Brien would have been to get caught saying a prayer over his grave.)

Within twenty minutes, a select group of twenty-five Rejects, the "escape unit," gathered in the center of the compound. Also present were two bloodhounds and their handlers, a permanent part of the escape unit.

Otto Krill, the escape unit leader, stood in the front of the men, and reiterated what the premier had told them.

"It is very important that we track down and neutralize Morton Rosen. He has information that is of the utmost sensitivity. I expect everyone to keep pace with the group. If anyone here feels that they cannot do this, drop out now. Anyone?"

No one raised their hands. In fact, all the Rejects were expected to stay in good physical shape, but the elite group that gathered here were special. Each man ran a minimum of five miles before breakfast, did multiple sit-ups and pull-ups with palms facing forward, and innumerable push-ups. There wasn't a person in the group who couldn't do more than a hundred pushups per session, and many of them could do thirty or forty one-arm pushups.

The escape unit was also well schooled in reading the countryside they traveled. Two of them were, in fact, full-blooded Apache Indians who had lived in the Wyoming area their entire lives and were almost otherworldly in their ability to read the slightest disturbances in the natural world, such as the breaking of a twig, the crushing of a leaf. These things spoke volumes to them and they were almost always able to know if the disruption was made by a man or an animal.

But at the heart of the escape unit's success was the special, physically altered bloodhounds: their voice boxes had been surgically removed. While this did not interfere with their olfactory prowess—it was said that the average bloodhound could detect smell hundreds of times better than a human being, even follow a scent underwater—it did allow them to lead the escape unit to an escapee without uttering the usual baying sound that would warn him or her (or them) of the proximity of the unit.

So far, in Compound W, there had been eight attempts at escape, none successful. One of the escapees had had a losing encounter with a grizzly bear, while another had fallen to his death, and another had drowned. The others—except for one—had been captured alive, and the premier personally beat all to death with a three-foot section of lodgepole pine. Just before they took the other man, a forty-five-year-old scientist, into custody, he sprinkled cyanide powder on a pear and ate it, killing himself instantly.

Suicide was preferable for some of these escapees because, as Rosen had told Jim and Bev, the punishment was only limited by the imagination of the premier and his henchmen. One particularly malevolent treatment of women, for example, was what happened to one slightly overweight forty-year-old ex-nurse who escaped and was caught. She attempted her escape in the early fall, and premier Szabo told her, in front of most of the people in the compound, that he was going to give her another chance to escape. But there were going to be a few changes. One was that she would only be allowed to wear a pair of sneakers. All other clothing would be removed from her. She would then be given a half-hour head start, released into the woods, and then three of the escape specialists, armed only with knives, themselves nude, and carrying along a video camera, would pursue her through the woods. If she was found, she would be returned, but first she would be gang-raped by the three pursuers who would tape the entire experience for the pleasure and edification of others in the camp.

As it happened, the woman was caught within two hours, and then raped and sodomized repeatedly over a three-hour period and then, bleeding profusely from her rectum—because someone had also used a part of a tree branch on her—had been returned to the camp. Sometimes during the night, while being sodomized by one long line of soldiers, she died from loss of blood and shock.

The escape unit knew that going after Rosen was not without hazards, the main hazard being the Believers. They would instantly kill every Reject they came across or sometimes emasculate captives, then release them. The Rejects viewed them as every bit as savage as they were. And, at least with them, they were. It was a holy war and anything went.

Exactly forty minutes after O'Brien was killed, the handlers of the bloodhounds pressed a piece of Morton Rosen's soiled clothing in the nose of each of the silent bloodhounds, and within seconds they were pulling on their leashes, his scent found, and fresh, as clear to them as highway signs leading to a particular road, and the escape unit was trotting to keep up with the bloodhounds as they emerged from the compound entrance and started to thread their way through the woods where, less than twenty-four hours earlier, Morty Rosen had slipped out of the compound and started to run for what he knew might be his life. If he had been there, indeed he would have reflected that now his analogy was accurate. He was the hare.

13

For a moment, Bev didn't know where she was, and when she reached over, expecting to feel Jim, he wasn't there. She opened her eyes and sat up. It was windy, the shadows of adjacent tree branches moving on her tent almost ominously.

Where, she wondered, could he be? She felt a quick surge of loss and was surprised very much by her feeling. She cared about him very much. When he had asked her about the loves of her life, she never explained—why, she didn't know—that there had been one boy in high school, Jeff Grimes, whom she loved very much. And one day Jeff and his family had moved away, almost without warning, and she had felt as if her stomach had been hollowed out and she would never get over it. That relationship was on the same level of feeling as this one.

But Jim was all right, she thought, she was making a big deal of this. He probably went to relieve himself.

She looked over at where he slept. Certainly, she thought, it wasn't something he heard that he was investigating. His AK-47 was lying right next to where he had lain. He would have taken that with him.

Then where was he?

She slipped on her denim pants and a long-sleeved

cowboy shirt and put on the lace-up shoes—first checking inside the boots for snakes—without tying them and stood up. She pushed open the flap in the opening of the tent and went outside. It was cool outside, maybe fifty degrees, but not chilly, though there was that wind, most of it blocked by trees. The moon was up, full, so she could see fairly clearly, this helped by the always incredible number of stars.

So where was Jim? she thought, trying to quell a rising sense of panic.

She looked around, and then relief flooded her. She saw his silhouette. He was maybe fifty yards away, standing next to a large evergreen. She saw a brief glow of orange. He was having a smoke.

She took a couple of steps and he turned around—God, his hearing was unbelievable—and waved to her. She waved back. She walked toward him and as she did a simple but profound thought occurred to her. She knew absolutely that their relationship was much more than two people making physical love. She was falling in love with him. He was one of the long-distance runners, the kind of guy that women start looking for when they are little girls, the guy who will walk them down the aisle in a fairy-tale wedding. And then she had a thought that she held until she walked up to him and put her arms around him and kissed him tenderly on the mouth. He made her feel so wanted, so beautiful, so loved, so cared for. It was wonderful.

"I thought of something as I was walking toward you that really sums you up," she said.

"What's that?"

"You're as pure as these mountains that you love so much. And just as strong."

He kissed her again.

"Hey," he said, "that's high praise. I think of you that way too. I mean, not the mountains, but you're one of the good people. People who care. I always thought that the strongest people in life are the ones that are capable of caring and loving."

She looked up at him.

"Is there a difference?"

"Sure," Jim said, "but what it is I don't know right now. I do know one thing. They're very close."

Bev nodded.

"So what are you doing out here?"

"I was thinking about the future," he said, "and what it might hold. I had a dream that woke me up. It was pretty chaotic, all kinds of creatures warring with each other, and in the end, nothing being resolved—except the loss of the lives of a lot of people who couldn't defend themselves."

"What do you think it means?"

"When I left Idaho," Jim said, "it was just to get away. I was really lonely. Every person that mattered to me was gone. I had no real direction, just some vague idea to go east."

He paused, dropped the butt of the cigarette on the ground, and crushed it out with his boot very carefully.

"Now," he said, "I think about what's going on in this country, not only in an intellectual way but an emotional one, and I've really come to realize that if the Rejects come to rule it, civilization as we know it in America will be gone. But if the Believers win the day, it will also be gone. I think the chaos in the dream represents those things."

Jim paused, then continued. "I was also thinking about what would be best for us. And I realized that I'm really hoping that someone like Ben Raines comes along who can carve out something good and lasting from this mess. But I don't know. How many Ben Raineses come along in our lifetime?"

"What about you?"

"Are you kidding?"

"No, I'm not. Ben Raines himself saw something in you that he liked. Maybe the potential to lead. He had to be a quick study when it came to reading personality. I think great leaders can always evaluate people quickly."

"He actually gave me a note to introduce me to the Rebels. And he told me the locations of their supply depots for food, water, ammunition, and the like."

"Really? There you go."

Jim shook his head.

"Like I said, I'm not a warrior. This is a job for a soldier. And I don't want to be part of any war. I'll defend myself, and you and others, but I have no plan to fight for a new government, or be willing to neutralize the bad guys—unless they're trying to neutralize me. Like I said, I was really burned by war with my father and brother dying. And there were others, too. My dream is that at one point people can sit down and talk it all out.

"I remember once," Jim continued, "when a neighbor was in a dispute with another guy over grazing land, and the situation was getting hot and heavy, close to violence. And in Idaho that means guns, because everyone owns a gun. Anyway, somehow my grandfather got enlisted—he was a very wise man—to mediate it. And he succeeded in settling it."

"How?"

"By having the people compromise, give up land and certain water rights. They shook hands and that was that, even though neither was very happy when they left the bargaining table. My point is that people have to give ground, actually or . . . what's that word . . .?"

"Figuratively?"

"Yes. They have to do that or you're still in conflict. The best example I have of that is in World War I, when the Allies, after crushing Germany in the war, crushed them at the Treaty of Versailles. They left them with a big hole in their pocket and their national pride, so when they left the table they smiled but they were enraged. And one fine day, when Hitler came along, they expressed their anger through him."

"That's very true," Bev said, "but I still think that sit-downs can be very unrealistic if the people you're dealing with are psychotic, or won't bargain in good faith. The only way things are going to get better in America against people like this is to fight them and win the fight."

Jim thought a moment.

"You're absolutely right," he said.

Bev smiled, kissed him again.

"You know what I love about your mind?" she asked.

"I thought you only loved my body."

"That too," Bev said, "but you're capable of being objective, to admit you were wrong or modify your position if someone makes a stronger case than you. I mean you have an emotional investment in something, but not so much that you hide what your brain is telling you."

"I guess."

"I don't think any of us who want a good life is going to be able to avoid taking part in some sort of conflict. I mean, I'm the last one who wants war, or battles or anything like that. My life as a religious person has espoused the opposite of that. But like Ben Raines said in that SUSA manifesto, sometimes it's the only way."

Jim looked at her and kissed her on the mouth, but this time, though tender, there was some other urgency.

"Let's go back to the tent," he said. "I just can't keep my hands off you."

"You won't see any hands-off sign on me."

They both laughed, then started to walk arm in arm back to the tent when suddenly they heard a commotion back near the tent area. It was Rosen. He was screaming, and two people were assaulting him, or trying to get him under control.

Jim reached for his sidearm preparatory to advancing when, from the adjacent woods, somcone barked a guttural command.

"Keep your hand off your gun and raise your hands high, stretch. You too, beautiful."

Jim looked to his left. Someone—someone large—was partially obscured behind an oak tree, and he had some sort of guerilla-style weapon pointed at him. An AK-47. There was no way he could respond to that, and Bev, he had noticed, was unarmed. He raised his hands slowly and so did Bev, but as he did, his mind raced with tremendous speed though his face was calm. Who were these people? he wondered. It was logical to assume they were Rejects, but then again it wasn't, based on one of the escape unit troops getting back to their home compound, and assuming that they traveled by foot through the woods. The maps didn't show any roads going from east to west into the area. Bottom line: they wouldn't be here yet. They were forty miles away.

"Take two fingers of your hand and pick your gun up by the butt and place it on the ground," the voice said.

Maybe, Jim thought, he could whirl and perhaps take out the person behind the tree. A single shot in the middle of the head wouldn't be hard. That would drop him. Then what? If Jim got to squeeze that trigger, even as the man dropped he would let go a short burst and possibly get him and Bev both.

Then, of course, he would have to deal with the guys grabbing Rosen. They might kill him before they turned their attention—Jim assumed automatic weapons—toward Jim and Bev.

But whom were they up against? Jim could see, now, that two people had control of Rosen, but who knew how many were in the woods? No, he wasn't going to do anything. Couldn't do anything. Not yet. Not until he knew the terrain. To commit to some course of action without knowing what you were getting into was insane—and stupid.

He picked the gun from his waistband with two fingers and laid it on the ground.

"You and your ladyfriend move toward the tents," the man in the woods said.

Jim did as he was told. He was well aware that he still had his knife—in a sheath on his right side—on him, but that would only be good in close quarters. If he threw it at someone, that would be only good enough to take out one person.

Then it struck him. He was not alone. Bev was with him, and he was sure that she would act with a ferocity that would be a big surprise. It didn't get any tougher than those two Rejects back at the church. If she could, she would try to do something. Still, even if he could do something he might be in trouble because the plain fact was that he didn't know how many more people he would be dealing with, and instinct told him that there were more people in the woods.

Very true, because just as he and Bev came into the tent area, three more people filtered out of the woods. None had Reject or Believer uniforms on. All were dressed differently but all carried automatic weapons, bandoleers of cartridges, and grenades hanging off their belts. They looked like real badasses. Jim had no idea who they were.

One of the men, thirtyish, with a shaved head and tattoos all over muscular forearms, looked first at Rosen.

"You own this HumVee?" he said to Rosen. He had, Jim thought, a distinct accent, perhaps Irish or British.

"No. I'm just sleeping in it," Rosen said.

"How about you, stretch?" he said to Jim. "Yours?"

"Yes."

"Where'd you get it?" he said. His eyes had narrowed.

Jim had not sensed any particular anger in the man. Now he did.

"It was given to me by a man named Ben Raines."

"Who, the general?"

"Yes."

"Where?"

"Back in Nevada. He gave it to me before he died of the plague."

"He died?" The voice was low, sad. Jim sensed, in fact, sadness settle over all of the men.

"Yes. Like I said, of the plague."

"Why did he give it to you?"

"I met him by chance. And some people attacked

us while he lay dying. I helped him defend against them. He said he liked the way I handled things, and wanted to give it to me, that he had no further use for it."

"Did you leave before he died?" This came from one of the other men. He was as tall as Jim and looked like a full-blooded Indian in his mid-sixties.

"Hell no. I wouldn't do that. I buried him and said a few prayers, and then I left."

All of the men just stood there, each with his own thoughts. Ben Raines had meant something to them, though Jim did not know yet exactly what. Then a man who Jim would guess was the youngest of the group suddenly had tears running down his face.

"Christ," said a tall, dark-haired, creepy-looking guy.

"What a way for the general to go," he said. "He should have a holiday named after him but instead he dies of the fucking plague in some little place somewhere. He should have died a hundred times before that, and he didn't."

"He didn't die," Bev said.

Abruptly, there was total silence. All the men, including Jim, looked at her.

"What do you mean?" the British-sounding guy said.

"The lessons of his life for the world will never die."

The truth of the statement hit like a silent bomb. And subtly, without an announcement, the situation had changed from Jim and Bev and Rosen being captured to a conversation. The guns had lowered.

"And by the way, who are you all?" Bev asked.

"We served under him," the Indian said. We're part of what's left of the Rebel army.

"I'm Duke Kindhand," he continued. "That man who drew down on you is Kevin Shaw, from across the pond, and the other guy here is Frank Langone." He pointed to the tall, creepy-looking guy.

"And Jim Watson, and Slobodan Granic, or Bo as we call him."

In turn, Jim shook hands with each of the men and introduced Bev and Morty Rosen.

"I also have a note from the general," Jim said, "to introduce myself."

"Where?" Kindhand said.

"Right here."

Jim reached in his back pocket, took out a wallet, picked the note out of it, and handed it to Kindhand. He read it while the other Rebels read it over his shoulder.

"He also gave me all thc locations of your supply depots."

"You have something on that?"

"In my head. He told me to memorize and then tear up the paper. I did. You want 'em?"

"No," Kindhand said. "I know where they are too."

Jim nodded.

"Where are you headed now?" he asked.

"We're on our way to meet up with more Rebels in a town on the Wyoming-Montana border named Billerica."

"I know of it," Jim said.

"How are you getting through to them?" Rosen asked.

"Cell phone," Kindhand said, "and radio. But the connections are spotty at best."

"Where are you headed?" Kindhand asked Jim.

"Right now just north. Ultimately east, maybe."

"What's there?"

"Nothing, but it isn't here," Jim said. "What are you guys meeting for?"

"You know about the SUSA?" Kindhand asked.

"Sure."

"We're going to try to establish a new one up here in the Northwest and go from there."

"There are going to be folks in your way. You're going to need a big army," Jim said. "How many Rebels are left?"

"There are thousands. They're scattered all over the country, but the phones and the radio communications are so spotty that Rebels are networking rather than all of them being directly communicated with. Whatever, we're just trying to get a force together that's big enough before the Rejects, who have vastly superior forces—and well-trained ones, I might add—take us out. Fortunately, we're not a priority. They have the Believers to contend with."

"I've dealt with both groups," Jim said.

"Yeah," Kevin Shaw chimed in. "They're all cut from the same bolt of cloth, except the Rejects kill you."

"But so will the Believers," Jim said. "Or at least drive you out if you don't believe in their philosophy."

"Yes," Kindhand said, "exclusionary thinking leads to that, the fanatical belief that what you're doing is the way, the truth, and the light and that people who don't think that way are nonbelievers and may someday be perceived as a dangerous enemy—with violent consequences."

"I agree with that," Jim said, "one hundred percent," and Bev nodded.

"Now," Jim said, "I have to tell you something that should affect your plans."

"What's that?" Kindhand asked.

"There's an outside possibility an elite unit of the Rejects may be heading this way."

"Why?" Kindhand asked.

"Why don't you tell him, Morty?" Jim said.

Rosen laid out the story of his undercover work, his escape—and its implications.

"How big is this escape unit?" Kindhand asked.

"Twenty-five."

"I don't know what the other guys feel," Kindhand said, "but I'd say our best bet is to wait a day and see if they show up, then give them a reception they don't expect. We haven't engaged any Reject forces yet, and at one point it's inevitable we do. It might as well be now."

The other men nodded. They did not seem upset by facing a force four times as large as theirs.

"You have only a half dozen men," Rosen said, as if to remind Kindhand of something he didn't know.

Surprisingly, Jim, instead of Kindhand or any of the others, responded.

"Surprise is worth everything," he said. "In battles it's a force unto itself. I mean history is just full of how surprise won battles against superior forces. Troy was probably the best example, but I think ordinary people know that if they're in a fight with someone and throw the first punch the chances of winning the fight increase geometrically."

"That's right," Kindhand said. "Ten or fifteen of these guys will be standing in front of God"—and he chuckled—"before they know it. They'll be surprised to be dead—and surprised that there is a God!"

Everyone laughed.

"What kind of firepower you got?" Jim asked.

"I'll show you," Kindhand said.

For the next fifteen minutes, Kindhand showed Jim, Bev, and Rosen their firepower inventory, stored in two camouflage-painted HumVees parked a couple hundred yards from where Jim's was. Among the items were a variety of machine guns, pistols, rifles, and shotguns, but also mortars and explosive devices, including Semtex and booby traps and a supply of ammonium nitrate fertilizer, diesel fuel, and dynamite.

Jim knew just how powerful ammonium nitrite was—he used it to fertilize fields and was very careful with it—but Bev didn't.

"Why fertilizer?" Bev asked.

"Makes a big bomb," Langone said, "which is my speciality."

He paused.

"We weren't even born when this happened, but in one city, Texas City, Texas, it showed the world just how powerful it was. A freighter was in the harbor with its hold full of the stuff and it went off. They found the anchor two miles away. That blast—actually a series of blasts—killed a lot of people. Destroyed the town itself."

All Bev could do was shake her head.

"And you've heard of the bombing of the Murrah Building in Oklahoma City years ago by terrorists?"

"I saw a film on it," Bev said.

"Ammonium nitrate is what they used."

"By the way," Kindhand said after they were finished examining the weaponry in the HumVees, "did you know that the vehicle you're driving is armor-plated?"

"No," Jim said, "I didn't. All I knew that it was a good solid vehicle."

"I'll say," Kindhand said. "It's also got a windscreen that's made of one-and-a-quarter-inch Lexan and side windows that are an inch thick."

"That's good," Jim said. "As you saw, I travel with cans of gas."

Kindhand nodded.

"Now," he said, "we'd like to debrief Mr. Rosen a little more on this escape unit, and maybe some other things."

"No problem," Rosen said.

"Also," he said to Rosen, "when you get through—I assume you're having difficulty too—"

"Yes," Rosen said.

"We'd like you to sit on what you know for now."

Rosen looked as if he had been stabbed in the heart.

"Why?" he asked.

"There are pockets of Rejects all over the country," Kindhand said. "We also know a lot, but we don't want them to know what we know."

"Surprise," Jim said, "remember?"

"I don't like it," Rosen said. "Countries are dependent on a free press—for freedom."

"I understand that," Kindhand said, "but you've also heard of the press sitting on a story for a little while if it's in the national interest, haven't you?"

"Yeah, sure, but—"

Kindhand interrupted him.

"We're just asking you to hold on to what you know for a little while. Anyway, there's no way you have to get the information back to New York right now."

Rosen still did not seem convinced, but on the other hand he knew that he really had no choice.

"There's another reason," Jim said, "if you think this through. If *Rolling Stone* publishes the story, this may give the Rejects a military advantage in some cases—and may influence the course of whatever conflict there is. And if it helps them achieve victory, you, me, and the *Rolling Stone* are going to be no more."

"That's it in a nutshell," Kindhand said.

Rosen nodded and threw up his hands and walked away. Both men, as well as Bev, were watching Rosen's reaction, and got the distinct feeling that he had not been convinced.

14

The debriefing by Kindhand and the other Rebels of Morty Rosen took a half hour. Jim attended the questioning, but the interesting thing was that the way Kindhand conducted it, it seemed more like a conversation than a debriefing or an interrogation, which, about one-third of the way through Kindhand's gentle, conversational style, complete with laughs and anecdotes, he realized it was. The result was that Rosen was very relaxed, and Jim was sure that he would remember more details and come forth with more information because he was more relaxed than he might have been had Kindhand come on hard.

Rosen told the Rebels all the salient details on the escape unit, the bloodhounds without larynxes, how they were lightly armed so they could travel rapidly, and how all were in excellent physical condition so they could cover a lot of terrain quickly. In fact, they wore light, ridged shoes that could negotiate the forest floor quickly and light clothing that would not impede their progress.

"They don't train like other troops," Rosen told Kindhand at one point, "because they're not engaged in assaults on other forces or towns. Their only job is to run down escapees."

"But you don't have someone try to escape every day, do you, Morty?" Kindhand asked.

"I have nothing to do with it," Morty said with a laugh, and Kindhand laughed at the ambiguity of the question.

"So what does the unit do while they're not running after other people?"

"They work around the compound, keeping weaponry shipshape, working on vehicles and other equipment, doing odd jobs for the premier. But they definitely don't work as hard as other troops."

"Why?"

"Because they are special. They've been selected from the force at large to become part of the escape unit. It's the equivalent of someone being selected to be a SEAL—you remember them?"

"Sure. And their leader is a guy named Krill?"

"Yeah."

"What kind of guy is he?"

"He's a stickler for training and rules. He'll train you until your butt drops off on the road."

"Do you know his background?"

"Just that he was a mercenary. You can tell by the way he conducts himself that he's been in the military a long time."

"And what about our friend Alex Szabo?"

"A lot," Jim piped in. "Do you think you could show Duke the report from the psychologist on Szabo?"

Jim had made his comment in a very low-key way, and Rosen immediately went and got the doctor's devastating report from his backpack on the persona of Alex Szabo. Kindhand read it quickly and handed it around for the other Rebels to read.

"Well," Kindhand said when everyone was finished

reading the document, "the Apache have a name to describe his personality."

"What's that?" Jim asked.

"Lakuna da freede."

"What does that mean?" Jim asked.

"He's three quarts low."

Everyone, including Rosen, laughed.

Rosen, using the excellent Rebel maps, showed them where Compound W was, and estimated that it was forty-three and a half miles away. Kindhand, therefore, did not expect them to arrive for a number of hours. How many was hard to say because Rosen was not able to say what their rate would be. But it was understood that they would certainly arrive more quickly than troops not as highly trained.

Once the briefing was over, Kindhand—obviously the leader—started to set up a reception for them. Joining him in the discussion were the other Rebels, and Jim volunteered some ideas as well. Where they came from, Jim thought, he had no idea. It was just that he seemed able to visualize the enemy, their possible approaches, and to volunteer some ideas for neutralizing them. And the beginning of a trap started to form in his mind.

"You shouldn't have any trouble," Jim said, "if you can keep can keep surprise on your side."

"Are you planning on trapping them all, capturing them?" Rosen asked. "Or driving them away, or what?"

"No, our plan is to kill every single one," Kindhand said.

Bev, who had been listening, asked: "What about the dogs?"

"They have to go too," Kindhand said. "When we're finished we want every single entity of this escape unit gone, so they will not be able to hunt someone down another day soon. I love dogs, and it pains me to have to handle them this way, but the dogs are at the core of that unit. They have to go."

Jim nodded.

"It's funny" Jim said, "in the brief time I knew Ben Raines I got a sense of what he was like. And I think he would be doing exactly what you're doing. I had a brother who once told me, 'War is not tiddlywinks.'"

"Absolutely," Kindhand said. "I think our best bet is to stay here. We could try to rendezvous with the Rebels up north, but we might be attacked before we meet them. Better that we make our fight in a place that's familiar . . . and hopefully have surprise on our side."

"I agree with that," Jim said, and the other Rebels nodded.

Kindhand also asked Rosen if he wanted to help.

"Sure," he said, "I'd like to help. But as a journalist I don't think I can. I'd rather observe."

"You better hope we win," Frank Langone said. It was a simple statement, but filled with peril. Rosen was very well aware that if the Rebels did not stop the escape unit, he was a dead man. It was that simple. Indeed, Rosen could feel the color go out of his face, then he walked off.

The first thing Kindhand did was set up a picket about a hundred yards from where the rest of the small force was. Kevin Shaw was chosen first. He was, surely, good at all aspects of warfare. He had been a mercenary in Bosnia, Africa, and later for America before it had become the swamp of self-interest and depravity, as it had after the Great War.

Kindhand also assigned Jim and Bev as pickets. He knew they were in love, and wanted to station them together so that they could keep an eye on each other.

He also was aware of Jim's background as a mountain man, and it certainly didn't hurt to have someone with his acute senses waiting to sound the clarion call that the enemy was coming.

Kindhand suggested that Bev use the AK-47, and he gave her some additional instruction on how to use it.

"Just make believe you're pointing your finger at someone and pull the trigger. Aim for the chest. Even if they have body armor on you'll knock them down, you then can go for a head shot."

He also instructed Bev and Jim in how to use grenades, how to pull the pin and throw the grenade stiff-armed.

"Actually," Kindhand said, "you shouldn't have to use one, but in case you do you'll know how."

Kindhand also broke out a pleasant surprise for them: bulletproof jackets made of Kevlar.

"They won't help you if you take a shot in the head or the leg, but if you take one in the torso it's likely you'll end up with a bruise or two. Once the unit is spotted, Shaw will lead you guys back to us so you can take firing position with us."

The other Rebels would be a fluid force, ready to take up wherever needed. As usual, the Rebels were armed with everything but the kitchen sink, including antipersonnel grenades and AK-47s with each man carrying four or five extra bandoliers of thirty cartridge banana clips, 9mm sidearms, and knives. Also, each of the AK-47s would be equipped with silencers and bayonets in case there was hand-to-hand fighting, an unlikely scenario if the Rebels executed their plan well.

Ben Raines had structured his Rebel army to fight the way Kindhand was setting them up, like any well-oiled guerilla army, which was to say by ambush. Quick, deadly strikes that lasted only a few minutes with everyone dead or dying by the time the smoke cleared. Exactly what Jim had opted for.

Kindhand remembered one young Rebel soldier, observing the way Ben Raines set his forces up for an ambush for the first time.

"It doesn't seem very fair," he had said.

"That's exactly the way we want it, young man."

Bev had, of course, agreed to fight, but Jim wanted to make sure that she wasn't doing it just for him. He took a short walk with her after Kindhand had briefed them all, and waited to speak until they were outside hearing distance of any of the other people.

"Are you sure," he said when they had stopped, "you want to play things this way?"

"What do you mean?"

"To fight."

Her brow crinkled.

"Of course," she said. "I don't see anything wrong with fighting in this situation. I really do view it as a holy war, which, of course, is a terrible kind of war. But like the SUSA says—and not to play the record to death—if you want to have liberties you must sometimes fight for them, and sometimes blood will be shed."

Jim nodded.

"What do you think your father would have done?"

"I don't think, I know," Bev said.

"What do you mean?"

"He was in the second Iraqi war as a chaplain, and once the group of soldiers he was with were ambushed by Saddam Hussein's special guards. The Americans were outmanned and outgunned by the Iraqis, so my father took up a gun and fired back."

"Good," Jim said, giving her a long hug.

"I was thinking one day that with my ninja background and willingness to fight I was probably more like an Israeli female fighter than an American."

Jim nodded.

"I think the Rebels are like the Israelis," Jim said. "I don't think the escape unit troops have a chance."

"Absolutely," Bev said.

Jim paused.

"It looks like Duke Kindhand is the main man here. Let's go over and see where he wants to situate you when we get off the picket line."

"Okay."

They went up to Kindhand, who was busy screwing a baffle type of silencer on his AK-47.

"We'll be setting up positions in a few minutes."

"How would it be if you could get all these Rejects in one spot?" Jim asked.

"What do you mean," Kindhand asked, "one spot?"

"All close together within a radius of, say, twenty-five yards."

"That would be ideal. Like shooting fish in a barrel. You think you can do that?" Kindhand asked.

"Yes, I do."

"Let me hear what you got."

"Well, first, let me ask you a question."

"Go ahead."

"Do you have any household bleach?"

"You mean like Clorox?"

"That's exactly what I mean."

"Yeah," Kindhand said, "I think we do."

A couple of the other Rebels were standing nearby.

"What are you going to do," one of them said, "blind them?"

Jim smiled. He thought the remark funny too.

15

Otto Krill, the leader of the escape unit, insisted on all personnel in the unit being in top physical shape, which was why now the unit had covered a tremendous amount of ground and figured that they would be delivering an unpleasant surprise to the little bastard reporter very shortly.

As they went, threading their way through evergreen forest, lodgepole pine, and patches of sagebrush, they had to be very careful to make sure that they did not receive a surprise from the Believers. They believed in God, Krill thought, and he knew, like other Rejects, that they could act like the devil. More than once the armies of the Rejects had been run into a Believer trap, with the resulting loss of many lives. The Believers fought with the same ferocity as the Rejects.

Krill had almost lost his life. Once, he and a force of some two hundred men had gone through a natural tunnel in Utah and were caught in a withering cross fire from the Believers with the loss of all lives except for himself and five other people. They were saved because another Reject force happened to be in the area—just by chance—and had heard the gunfire and come to investigate and quickly crushed the Believer force. The only positive thing about that whole raid was that it was then decided to nail all survivors to crosses, and Krill had been able to personally crucify twelve of the forty-five men captured. It was hilarious, and ironic, and thoroughly satisfying.

The premier had had a great idea: to take photos of those who had been crucified, and send them to the head of the believers, McAulliffe. He included a tape of "Onward Christian Soldiers" to be played while viewing the photos, and a little note that suggested that McAulliffe might want to change the lyrics of the song from "onward Christian Soldiers" to "upward Christian Soldiers."

As it happened, it was said that when Father McAulliffe got the package he became livid.

Recalling that now, as he trotted behind the bloodhounds and handlers, Krill smiled. It was one of the more satisfying moments of the campaign.

This was going to be satisfying, too, because it was one of the most important missions of his time with the Rejects. He knew he would succeed. It was just a question of when.

It all depended, of course, on the effectiveness, first, of the bloodhounds, and they seemed to be doing just fine, loping along, noses close to the ground.

These bloodhounds performed very well. As soon as their collars and leashes were put on, which was a signal to them to go on scent, they did.

It was, Krill thought, the training that kept these dogs so good. They were tested once a year to make sure their skill level was high, and trained three to four hours a week.

Krill had also trained these dogs to detect explosives. So, if someone wanted to set a trap for the unit with an explosive, the dog would be trained to detect black powder, TNT, Flex-C, C-4 plastic, and a Gl explosive.

These dogs were ideal for such detection. They were calm and of an even temperament, a good way to be around explosives. If they found anything suspect, they were trained to sit still, not go sniffing around it—and possibly set off some hair-trigger timer.

He was as proud of his dogs as he was of his men. He smiled. But men could not be motivated by the same things as dogs. Because when he had first started to train them he rewarded them with praise and a favorite fetch toy, a ball or a towel.

And they could do much more, including building searches and hard tracks, following a scent along a concrete surface.

Krill knew they were still on the scent, the route that Rosen had traveled as obvious to them as if the path had been marked with neon lights.

They had stopped twice. When he had first started doing escape-unit work, Krill had driven his forces to near exhaustion, and that was the problem. Men didn't perform as well as they ordinarily would when they were tired.

So, as every good commander did, he had modified his strategy, and would stop his crew for two half-hour snack breaks plus a rest. The result was that they were now loping along with the same energy as the bloodhounds, who, of course, had also gotten breaks.

Now it was just a matter of time before they tracked Rosen down. There was no way he could escape them.

Krill knew that Rosen had a .45 with him, but he did not expect him to fire at the dogs. Krill could have trained German shepherds or other dogs for tracking like this, but no canine beat the bloodhound. If he had the shepherd, it could have been trained to attack the shooter, even in the face of being fired at. The bloodhound wouldn't do that. On balance, though, the bloodhound was best. Its scenting ability was far superior to that of a shepherd.

About two hours after the break, Krill was at the back of the escape unit, when abruptly the unit came to a stop. Krill wondered why. He was the only one who could halt the unit. Why had they stopped?

He trotted up to the front lines, and as he approached his second in command, Lieutenant Balter held up his hand so as to caution him to go slowly and be quiet. The dogs were of, course, quiet, but they seemed very excited. Had they found Rosen's body?

He trotted up and Balter pointed to a low sagebrush. Impaled on it was a small piece of gray cloth, and there was only one way it could have gotten on the branch—it had been torn off during Rosen's flight.

Meanwhile, it was obvious that the dogs were on to something. All were straining to the right, or northern direction. A couple of times they started to head straight ahead, west, but stopped, as if by an invisible wall.

"Let's go," Krill said. He ran to the head of the unit.

Krill was elated by the find. It just sort of symbolized the kind of crap that Rosen was going through, running along and abruptly, getting speared by a bush—covered with thorns—and part of his pants ripped off.

Great!

The unit, too, was encouraged by the find, and they quickly followed. Very quickly. All, that is, except one young soldier, barely nineteen years old, who had felt an urge to go to the bathroom. Indeed, he was, as someone said, "crowning." It was stop and go now or crap in his pants.

He was very gratified when he saw that Krill, who had been running next to him, had assumed the leadership of the unit.

He hoped that Krill would not hold it against him. If it had been the premier leading the pack he would have risked going in his pants. But Krill would understand, and the young man, whose name was Otis Williams, was sure that he would not fall so far behind the pack that he would lose them.

If he lost them he would just desert, because that's the way he knew he would be treated.

He gradually drifted away from the unit, and then looked around for some cover. This patch, in particular, was open, covered with sagebrush and rough terrain. In fact, the unit had disappeared behind a hill.

He quickly found some cover in the fringe of woods that bordered the open area, ran back into it, then pulled down his pants and underwear and squatted. The relief was such that at that moment he didn't even care if the premier had appeared.

Now, about one hundred yards away, Krill and his unit kept pace with the silent bloodhounds, who would have been shattering the sky apart with their baying had they not had their voice boxes removed.

Krill knew they were close. That's the way the dogs acted when they were close.

He raised his hand, the signal for the unit to draw their sidearms, though he was sure that they wouldn't need them against the little shit they were chasing.

Krill's thoughts were filled with days of glory. He knew the premier looked on him in a special way.

This was going to make him more special and, hopefully, get him a promotion to captain. It was easily the most important assignment of his career. They had to get this little punk.

They had been running through an area with some woods, but now the dogs broke out into a clearing. The land was much rougher underfoot than the forest, and particularly beautiful. Gradually, the dogs were following Rosen's scent into a sort of arroyo, at one side of which was a cliff and a small waterfall.

Then the unit was stopped again, this time by Krill. The dogs had come across another piece of cloth, this time snagged in a bush. Krill was puzzled. He was a good soldier, and had the instincts of a good soldier, which is to say that he sensed when something was too good to be true, and therefore it was too good to be true.

The word *trap* occurred to him just as he heard the first *pfft* sound, like someone spitting hard, and at the same moment he recognized that it was the sound of a silencer, the side of the head of the soldier standing next to him came off as if someone had sheared it off with an ax. Bright red blood splashed and sprayed on him, and then he felt a hit, a searing pain in his back, and his mind was functioning amid a cacophony of *pfft* sounds, so many it was like one long sound, and all the soldiers falling around him, some screaming in agony, others not screaming because their heads were blown half off, their gray uniforms dark with crimson blood, and then the desperate sound of real gunfire, the sound of men shooting their .45s at, really, nothing. And the last thing Krill was aware of before he died was being on the ground with many other men of the unit and falling over the body of a dog who had been hit multiple times.

Then Krill realized that he wanted to die, but as some sort of blackness oozed around him, blocking out his consciousness, he had a thought that he hadn't had since he was a little boy: he was going to meet God because, indeed, there was a God.

The firefight, such as it was, had taken all of two minutes.

When everyone was on the ground, Jim, Bev, Kindhand, and the other Rebels came down from their perch on the top of the cliff from where they had launched the ambush.

It only took them a minute, and then they were walking among them. The escape unit had been shredded with at least a thousand bullets, but miraculously three of the men were still alive.

Jim went over to first one, and then the other, and then the third, jamming his SEAL knife into the carotid artery of each, changing them from barely alive to very dead.

"Good work, Jim," Kindhand said.

Jim just nodded. Then he said: "What do you want to do with the bodies?"

"They'll probably come looking for them," Kindhand said. "Maybe we'll wait until they come this way, then arrange another greeting party."

"I'm not sure I like that," Jim said. "That gives them the advantage."

He paused.

"I have another idea," he said.

"That trick with the bleach to throw the dogs off was great," Kindhand said.

"You can also do that with oregano," Jim said.

"How?"

"Just sprinkle it on. It masks the scent."

Kindhand nodded. "I like your ideas," he said. "Tell me what you have in mind."

Otis Williams was just tightening his belt when he heard the random *pffi* sounds. He quickly headed in their direction but, well trained as he was, he approached with caution, his body always shielded from the shots. It was a good thing he did. When he came to a little hill and peered over, it looked like something out of a movie. The entire escape unit had been slaughtered—including dogs—and were lying in a bleeding heap and jumbled together, all dead . . . or he thought they were all dead. And then he watched in burgeoning horror as their ambushers had come down from the nearby cliff and one of them had finished off those left alive with knife thrusts.

But that was not all he saw. He saw Rosen standing there—and Beverly Harper, the religious bitch whose coworker had been hung!

Williams immediately pulled back down the hill. He knew that he had to go back and alert the premier. But the premier would ask him: Why didn't you get ambushed too?

Otis would have a simple explanation: "Because I was able to get away." It was that simple. "They chased me for a while, and I got away."

He was sure the premier would listen to him, particularly with the kind of intel he had to report.

No, Otis thought. He was not sure of that at all. He was not sure of anything when it came to the premier. There was only one thing for sure when you dealt with him. You never knew what he was going to do.

16

"Listen, Duke," Jim said to Kindhand, "my idea is really simple. Let's just keep going. We'll meet up with your colleagues and just keep going. Or maybe, depending on how many troops show up, you might want to launch an attack on the Rejects. But if we stop and make a fight now, who knows how many troops they'll have? We could be overwhelmed."

Kindhand nodded.

"Also, there's no way that the Rejects can find us—unless they get lucky. They don't have spotter planes, choppers, and the like. They're on foot, just like we are."

Jim paused, then continued. "Now, if you didn't want to engage them now and wanted to establish a real secure base you could go on into Montana and I'll show you where I think you might be best off. Isn't your basic goal right now to put together a good-sized army?"

"Sure," Kindhand said. "Where do these ideas come from? I mean they're militarily sound. You don't have military experience."

"I don't know. I see what the problem is and somehow the solution presents itself."

"Well," Kindhand said, "your solutions are good. Now, what do you think we should do with the bodies? I'm for hiding them, but that's going to take hours."

"I agree we should hide them. But I have a place where it shouldn't take hours."

"Where?"

"There's a natural cave behind the waterfall that's not observable from outside."

Kindhand looked. The waterfall Jim was referring to was a solid sheet of water. It would hide the bodies very effectively, and at the same time keep animals away from them. Also, they could get them out of the way quickly.

"Okay, Jim," Kindhand said. "Let's get it rolling."

"I would also suggest that we take their weapons. Not only because they're good for us to use, but it means one less bunch of weapons they can use on someone else."

"Absolutely," Kindhand said, and his look lingered on Jim LaDoux. He had the feeling that if he had come up with a better idea on anything, LaDoux would have accepted it without a moment's hesitation, just like he would and did. It was the idea that ruled the day, not the ego. Small wonder that Ben had given him the HumVee and had such faith in him.

Kindhand gave the signal, and the men started to carry the Rejects behind the waterfall, first stripping all arms from them.

Williams waited a full hour before starting away from the area, because he was more than a little worried about what the premier might do. There was no way to predict what he was going to do. He might strangle him to death, then abruptly change his mind. But it would be too late for Williams.

Every now and then he would risk a peek to see what was happening, but on one occasion a steel fist grabbed his innards and squeezed. One of the ambushers had looked his way, and for a moment he thought he was spotted, and quickly decided that it was better to be safe than sorry. He lit out, being as quiet as he could, but taking a zigzag route through the forest. He was well aware that the ambushers didn't have any dogs to track him, so as long as he was able to put a lot of space between them and him he would be okay.

Two things he had on his side were his strength and speed. He was twenty-two years old and had a good lead. No one was likely to catch him, let alone see him.

One other good thing: it made any indecision he had about telling the premier what had happened final. He was going back to base camp and telling him.

In fact, Williams had been seen, or a movement spotted that indicated that someone was there.

It was the Rebel Frank Langone. But he did not overreact. He knew that if he had seen anyone any sudden movements would make him bolt, and he had a good lead and the forest was nearby. He'd be gone in a flash. And, of course, it might be a sniper. The next thing he knew might be the last thing.

But Langone did take action. He meandered over to Duke Kindhand, who was with Jim LaDoux.

"Don't look that way," Langone said, "but I think I spotted someone due south looking over a hill and observing us."

"Okay," Kindhand said, "we've got to get someone to sneak up there and see who it is."

"I'll do a fade to the other side of the cliff and then work my way back to the hill," Kevin Shea said.

"Good."

With that, Shaw drifted away casually. Once he calculated that he was out of the line of sight of anyone hiding behind a hill, he burst into a run, drawing his .45 as he went.

It took him about five minutes to work his way to the hill, and there was no one there. He did a brief search of the edge of the nearby forest, then went back over to the hill and raised his arms in a signal that said: whoever was here is gone.

Kindhand, Langone, and LaDoux immediately left the ambush sight and within minutes they were with Shaw.

"I only saw one thing," Shaw said when the others joined him, "a pile of animal crap."

"Where?" Jim said.

"Just inside the woods."

"Can you show me?"

"Sure."

LaDoux followed Shaw to the site.

"I have no idea what kind of animal made that. But it's a large one judging by the size of the turds."

"It's a human animal," LaDoux said. "And fresh. It's highly likely that the same person who was peering over the hill did this."

"How are we going to find out?"

"I'm more concerned if it was made by a straggler Reject," Kindhand said.

"So am I," Jim said.

They went back to the ambush site.

"Where's Rosen?" Jim asked one of the Rebels who

was busy with another Rebel carrying a body behind the falls.

"He's behind the hill."

Jim, accompanied by Kindhand and Shaw, went over to him. He was sitting down, writing something into a narrow notebook. He had listened in on the conversation Jim had with Kindhand, so he was probably making notes on this. But Jim wasn't sure. The bottom line was that he didn't know.

Rosen looked up almost in alarm when he saw the three heavy hitters approach.

"No problem," Jim said. "I just want to double-check the number of soldiers in the escape unit. You said twenty-five?"

"Yes," Rosen said. "Just a second."

He took another thin notebook from his breast pocket and flipped through the pages.

"Twenty-five," he said. "Each unit has twenty-five specialists in it."

"Could there be any deviation?"

"I seriously doubt it," Rosen said. "The premier was a stickler for organization and knowing exactly what strength he had."

There was silence for a moment.

"I counted twenty-four bodies," Kindhand said.

"So did I," Jim said.

"Which means that the guy I spotted on the hill was a Reject from this special unit," Langone said.

"And which also means that he's probably on his way back to his unit," Kindhand said.

"We're pushing on through."

"But what if they catch up to us?" Rosen asked. "They found you the first time."

"Well," Jim said, "we can cover our tracks."

Rosen looked like he was not convinced that the

strategy was a good one. And, in fact, he wasn't. He had great faith in the Rejects' tenacity and cleverness.

No one saw it, but abruptly Jim's eyes had gone cold. Rosen's attitude was the last straw. He had another idea, and Rosen was not going to like it.

17

The Rebel convoy had mounted up. Jim, Bev, and Duke Kindhand were standing near Jim's HumVee. Jim was watching, rolling a cigarette, but mainly looking at Rosen, who had gone off into the woods, for what, Jim didn't know. Kindhand looked at Jim and saw something in his eyes.

"Do you like reporters?" Jim asked Kindhand.

"Not really," Kindhand said.

Jim licked the paper closed and stuck the completed cigarette in his lips.

"Why?"

"Well, for one thing," Kindhand said, "they're ruthless. In particular I remember how when the priest pedophile scandals hit, reporters went on a rampage, implying that every religious person in town was a pervert. It was viscious and untrue—but their stories sold papers so they kept it up."

"But without a free press . . ." Bev said.

"I understand that," Kindhand said. "And I support that."

"What do you think of Rosen?"

"Something sneaky about him," Kindhand said.

"Sneaky?" Jim asked.

"Yes."

"I think that's a good word to describe what I sense," Jim said.

"Me too," Bev said.

"He told you why he took off, right?" Jim said.

"Yes."

"What I truly don't understand," Jim said, "is why he really left the Rejects' compound. I know he said that he sensed that the gig was up, but I don't accept that totally. I mean he's a reporter for *Rolling Stone.* Those guys are famed for their chutzpah. I don't know if he would have taken off just because of a feeling."

Kindhand nodded.

"The bottom line is if he's not telling the truth about that, what is he telling the truth about? A liar can be a dangerous person."

Both Kindhand and Bev nodded.

"I have an idea," Jim said.

"What?" Kindhand asked.

"I—"

Just then, Rosen came out of the trees.

"Okay," Kindhand said, "ready to roll."

Rosen was about to get into the HumVee when Jim said, "Wait."

"Aren't we going?" Rosen asked.

"First," Jim said, "I want to see your .45."

"Why?"

"It's a secret," Jim said, smiling.

Rosen hesitated, then drew his gun out of his pocket and handed it to Jim. Jim shoved it into his waistband.

"I wanted your gun, Morty," he said, "because I don't want any problems resulting from what I'm about to ask you."

"What do you mean?"

"I want to know, and Bev and Duke want to know, what's really going on here. Why did you leave the Rejects' base camp? It sounded to me like a bunch of baloney. And relatively shortly after you left they came after you. It doesn't add up to me."

"You mean that my sensing that I was going to be uncovered is not enough to have me take a powder."

"Exactly," Bev said.

"Well, I—" Rosen started to say.

"Okay, Morty," Jim said, "get ready to start walking."

"What do you mean?" Rosen asked.

"You're on your own. Here's your gun." Expertly, Jim ejected the clip in the handle and the single shot in the chamber, then handed the gun to Rosen and threw the clip on the ground where it was retrievable, but would take a little time to get to.

"Wait a minute," Rosen said. "I'll be on my own out here. I'm a city slicker. I'm not going to last. And they're going to come again—with more dogs. They'll track me down."

"You have a tremendous head start."

Rosen looked as if he had caten a goldfish.

"Nothing will do here, Morty," Jim said, "except the truth."

Bev got in the HumVee and fired up the engine. Kindhand said nothing. But he was watching the scene intently.

"Wait," Rosen said, "wait. I'll tell you the truth."

Bev turned the engine off.

"You're right," Rosen said, "it was more than my sense that I was going to be uncovered."

Bev, Kindhand, and Jim were silent.

"Every week," he said, "the slave women do your laundry, and I did something very stupid. I got mixed up, and allowed one to take away a pair of pants that had my ID card as a reporter for *Rolling*

Stone sewed into it. I never wore them. I just left them in a closet. I figured that one day if I got captured by the Believers—who are savages themselves—I would show my ID. It was my insurance policy."

"Why didn't you tell us that?" Bev asked.

"Because . . ." Rosen said, hesitating. "I thought maybe you wouldn't take me with you because you feared them. You would know for sure that they were going to come after to me. They have to."

Rosen laid it out some more.

"I was undercover for two months. I got enough in my head about them specifically and in general to create big image problems. And if the Believers get a hold of what I have, it will amount to important tactical information."

"Will you be willing to tell us what you've got?" Kindhand asked.

"Sure," Rosen said.

"Pick up your clip," Jim said.

Rosen went over and picked it up. Then he came back to Jim, who handed him the .45.

"Okay, Duke?" Jim asked, meaning, did he accept Rosen's explanation?

Kindhand nodded yes. Then: "Okay," he said, "let's go."

Then, Rosen, Bev, and Jim got into the HumVee and the vehicle started to roll. It was, Jim thought, a situation similar to someone cheating on a spouse. There is a reunion highlighted by people speaking the truth to one another, and the problem is settled and they get back together. But their relationship has changed forever, because what has not changed is the cheater's capacity to do it again.

And that was exactly the way Jim felt about Morty Rosen.

18

Otis Williams stopped to relieve himself again about two miles outside Compound W. That was the last thing he needed: to be in the middle of telling the premier all about the slaughter of the unit and then have to ask permission to excuse himself because he had to go to the bathroom.

Thinking about that made him feel like he could go in his pants.

Williams made it back to the camp in under fourteen hours. When he arrived at around midnight, he was very tired, but he knew where his duty lay. The die was cast. He went into the compound and immediately asked to see the premier. Williams was nervous enough because, technically, he was guilty of dereliction of duty—if the premier found out—and there was no telling what he might do. But he was not going to give all the gory details. He was not going to tell him about taking a crap. All he'd say was that he was part of the firefight and was lucky to get away. Period. Keep it simple. Of course, he told himself, he could have just deserted, and it would have been reasonable for the premier to assume that he had been killed like the others, just that his body could not be found. But this way, if he pulled it off, he would be in line for a promotion. In a way, he did not see how he could not get away with it. The premier was more than a little crazy, but there was no way that he could blame Williams for anything.

Five minutes after he arrived, the premier came out of his compound. He was fully dressed but sleepy looking. This surprised Williams. It was a hint of the premier's being human, and it was hard to imagine him as being that way. Usually he was conferring on some military matter, supervising an execution, or screwing one of the slaves, sometimes two at the same time, and of different ages. Williams had never seen anyone as hungry for sex. He acted more like a fifteen-year-old boy who has just discovered masturbation than a forty-year-old man, which was the age Williams guessed he was.

"What's up, private?" he said as he approached Williams. "What's so important that you have to get me out of bed? Where's the rest of the unit?"

Williams told him, starting with the phrase "we were ambushed," and as he did, the premier's face changed from sleepiness to savagery, pure rage.

The premier wanted all the details, such as how far the bodies were from base camp, and how many enemy there were.

"I saw six soldiers—"

"Did you see Rosen?"

"Yes, sir, he was there, and I saw someone else. That religious bitch Harper, the one that got away."

For a moment, Szabo just looked straight ahead, and then he spoke. His voice was low, but somehow terrifying.

"You're sure it was her?"

"One hundred percent."

"What were you doing during all this?"

As nochalently as he could, Williams explained

that he was on the perimeter of the firefight and was able to kill a few of the enemy before he had to retreat. Here, Williams thought, he had played it very cool. On the way back to the compound he had thrown away all but one clip for the .45 and had fired the gun once. It would not be good to have to explain to the premier why his gun was unfired and full of ammunition!

"Okay," Szabo said, "good work. I'm glad you got out."

"Thank you, sir."

Williams breathed a sigh of relief. He felt he had dodged a bullet. And, indeed, that was probably close to the truth. A bullet or a spike.

Szabo summoned Duyvill to the war room.

"I don't know who the attackers were," Szabo said, "but that little bastard was among them—and our friend Beverly. Whoever they are, they are professional soldiers, not beginners."

"What do you suggest, sir?"

"Well, I was looking at the map. We can go most of the way by jeep, and then filter through the countryside."

"How big a force?" Duyvill asked.

"At least a hundred men."

"When?" Duyvill asked.

"I think we can start out by 0200. This will get us there in daylight, and we can launch the offensive immediately."

"Sounds good," Duyvill said.

"When we attack, they won't know what hit them. And trust me, they'll never know how we found them."

"Take prisoners?"

"Absolutely," the premier said. And then he

added, "It's important to take some of these people alive. I want to find out what Rosen told them and who knows what. They might have contacted others by radio or phone and told them. Every last potential source of this information must be neutralized."

He paused, his eyes with a faraway glint.

"Oh," he said, "wouldn't I like to take this little bastard alive! If I do I'll disassemble him cell by cell."

"Sounds like a plan," Duyvill said.

19

It was nighttime. Rosen lay in his tent, and his mind was working overtime. Every sound he heard—and there were many in the Wyoming night, of course—he interpreted not as the sound of nature, but of Rejects coming either to nail him to the cross, make him sit on a stake, or merely give him some mercy—shoot him in the head!

The ambush was, after all, because of him. If he hadn't been undercover, if he hadn't escaped, there would be no need to send a doomed escape unit after him.

Oh no, the Rejects would be coming, coming primarily for him.

What was more, what about his story? If he ever got it published, he knew for sure that it would be in the running for a Pulitzer—if they even had such contests anymore. But if he stayed with these Rebels he would likely not get it published, or wouldn't be around to read it!

Maybe. Maybe he was panicking. Maybe nothing would happen at all. He would join the Rebels and travel north and get away and live happily ever after.

Maybe. Or Maybe he would be getting a colonoscopy with a stake.

He blinked, thought harder. How do you make a decision in something like this?

He took some deep breaths, tried to relax. And he started to think back to the other times he went UC. What did he rely on then?

And he had been in three different situations where he had to make some life-or-death decisions.

He remembered one. The Wolverine MC Club in Brooklyn. He had worked his way inside that over a year's period, and what had guided him was his fear. He now remembered reading a great book by a guy named Gavin DeBecker called *The Gift of Fear,* how if your gut told you there was something to be afraid of, then by all means be afraid. It had been the thing that had made him walk away from the MC Club. His gut told him to move his ass toward the door.

And later, after his piece came out and ten indictments were handed up on MC members, and they were tried and sent away for long stretches upstate, it came out that the consiglieri of the club had very great suspicions about Morty and they were within hours of grabbing him and torturing him to find out what the truth was.

His acknowledging his fear had saved him.

So, what about now? The Rebels were a force to reckon with. No question. They had hoodwinked the escape unit and wiped them out. LaDoux was going to lead them out of the area and into the safety, most likely, of the north. How the could Szabo and his force find him? There was no way. No way . . .

No way obvious. But Morty had seen Szabo in action. This guy had a way of getting the job done.

Everything pointed to him to continue to travel with the Rebels. They would meet up with a stronger force and then Mr. Szabo.

The only thing telling him now to go was the fear in the pit of his belly. That told him to hightail his skinny ass out of there. And he did have a very good head start.

But where could he go?

He couldn't go back east, he wasn't going north, and he had no idea what was down south. What about west?

Then it struck him. An idea. He could go west and . . .

Yes, go west, young man. That was the way to go. And he would leave—now.

He sat up and looked around. The camp was quiet, but he knew there were pickets around. The Rebels didn't want any unpleasant surprises from the Rejects. And they wouldn't stop him. They had almost released him on his own as it was.

A half hour later, Rosen had packed everything that he thought he needed: a supply of food, his tape recorder, notebooks, pens, and a .45. He also packed a blanket and some clothing.

He did not plan to say good-bye to anyone, just leave. But as he was trudging out of the camp he abruptly heard the voice of Jim LaDoux.

"Where are you going, Rosen?"

"I'm leaving."

"Why?"

"The Rejects are going to come after me. I want to live."

"You'll have a better chance with us," LaDoux said.

"Why? You got six men and a woman and yourself. They have hundreds."

"We're going to be gathering more, building up our strength."

"I'll take my chances alone."

"You look like you're heading east."

"So what?" Rosen said. He kept his tone of voice down, his expression quizzical. No way did he want LaDoux to know where he was headed, because in fact he had something else in mind besides just heading west.

"They'll come up with more dogs," LaDoux said. "No question."

"I'll take my chances."

"Okay," LaDoux said, "have it your way."

"I will," Rosen said.

Rosen could feel LaDoux's eyes burning into his back. He would be glad when he could put this dude far behind him.

20

After losing sight of LaDoux, Rosen headed due east for about a mile. During the last quarter of a mile he looked back frequently to make sure that he wasn't being followed by LaDoux. The moon was up so he could see pretty well through the trees, and once or twice stopped and looked back. There was no one behind him. It was safe, he thought. Then he started heading back west, glad to be going in the opposite direction that the Rejects would be coming from.

His route was not straight west. He walked at an angle so he would not retrace his steps. The last thing he needed was to run into LaDoux. No, that was the second worst thing. The worst thing would be running into a Reject force coming west.

He had walked about two miles south and west before he started to feel comfortable. Of course there was always wildlife to worry about, but he was starting to get used to that. It seemed that if you didn't bother them, you didn't get bothered by them.

He knew that what he was about to do was morally wrong. A reporter's job was to report, not get involved in the internal politics of something. But he also had to be concerned about saving his ass. And that's why he had decided to hook up with the Believers. And he knew that what he was about to do was going to lead to a battle—a big one.

He pictured, as he walked quickly through the woods, him having to explain all this to John Wagner, his editor in chief at *Rolling Stone*. He would come into his office, a surprisingly threadbare affair given that he was editor of *Rolling Stone*, one of the most influential magazines in America, and would tell him what he had in mind. And Wagner would say: "Christ, Morty, you can't do that. You're a writer, not a purveyor of public policy! As far as danger goes, that comes with the territory."

He would say that before the event took place. But if it came to pass in the way Morty hoped it would, he knew that Wagner would have an entirely different reaction, because he would have gotten what could be one of the best stories of the last couple of decades—and an exclusive. Then he would say something like: "Morty, you shouldn't have done that." Bad boy.

But around Christmastime Morty would find a bonus check that would be the largest in his ten-year career at the *Stone*.

Actually, Morty thought, and he didn't think he was rationalizing things, he was involved in the conflict. And why wouldn't he be? He had heard from his mother and father that many years ago during World War II many relatives had been executed by the Nazis. And what was the difference between the Rejects and the Nazis? Nada. They were the same savages with different names.

Thinking that, Morty felt better. Yes, indeed, he was more than a reporter in this conflict. He was a soldier trying to do the right thing.

He stopped by a creek at one point, got himself a

long drink of water, rested for a moment—and relaxed as much as he could. There was no way, he thought, that the Rejects were going to get to him. If they were going to go after anyone, it would be Jim LaDoux and the Rebels. But they also would be long gone into the wilderness by the time the Rejects came across their slain brethren. Hopefully. Of course the dogs would have his scent, if there were dogs. The only ones Morty had ever seen were those attached to the escape unit. Maybe there were no dogs. Great.

He did not, Rosen thought, know quite as much about his destination, the Believers, as he did the Rejects, or the Rebels for that matter. He knew the Believers were fanatics, but they weren't Nazis.

He had done research on them before going UC. Numerically, they were probably superior to the Rejects' forces, but they weren't as well trained. Still, in head-to-head confrontations in maybe forty towns across the U.S. they had fared pretty well.

While they weren't fascists, Morty thought, they were still nutcases, and many of the people who were part of the Believers had gone over to them in desperation. They were so rocked by the horrific things that had happened in America that they had joined the Believers and their bedrock adoration of Jesus Christ.

One of the things that made them fanatics, maybe the only thing, was the rules they lived by. They didn't believe in the Ten Commandments, they believed in what they called the Fifteen Commandments—ten plus five. As a Believer a sexual affair before marriage was forbidden, you were required to attend services three times a week, there would be no marriage between races, homosexuals were not allowed in their ranks, nor were Jews. And there were maybe four or five other restrictions and rules.

But while nuts, they weren't—at least not yet—killers. If you did not accept their way of life, or their religion, you were not allowed in or banished.

They also saw themselves as "Soldiers of Christ," and had taken up arms against the Rejects, whom they characterized as "godless hordes," because they threatened their way of life, just as "infidels" threatened the church and its way of life during medieval times. Hence, soldiers of Christ went out and kicked some ass. This was a holy war.

The head of the Believers, Rosen thought, rising to his feet, his break over, was Jay a.k.a. Father McAulliffe, a born-again believer who had been a drug dealer in the south Bronx. Wasn't that always thc case? Rosen thought. Born-again believers were among the most fanatical people on earth. Of course there were some very good born-again Christians, and being born again was certainly not *ipso facto* bad. He had seen many people come back from the brink because God came into their lives, or they believed He had.

Rosen was walking more rapidly than he had before. His eyes scanned for bears or unfriendly people.

He knew that he had at least two immediate problems with the Believers. One was that he was Jewish. The other was that he had the tattoo on his forearm saying that God is Dead. He would have to explain that.

On the other hand, he had a good explanation for the tattoo, and based on what he had to offer the Believers, they would believe him.

The Jewish problem—and Morty laughed at the

irony of that phrase—was easily handled: he would tell the truth about his heritage because he had no interest in joining the Believers. He assumed the Believers dealt with Jews, that when he came on to the scene they wouldn't run from the room. And he didn't think they'd try to throw him out of the country.

Rosen did not know exactly where the Believers were located. No one, apparently, except other Believers, had seen their main base camp. But he knew that they were located in western Wyoming.

He just hoped that they would not spot him, think he was hostile, and send him to his eternal reward without speaking. Well, he had nothing that was colored gray on him. No way could they mistake him for a Reject. He was just a guy trekking through the woods wearing a backpack and carrying a .45.

He stopped once to have lunch. More peanut butter and jelly sandwiches, cold coffee—and then continued on. At first light, he came upon a small, dirt-packed road that generally ran west. He could either stick to the woods or follow the road. He decided to follow the road.

He walked along ever conscious that at any moment it might be a good idea to jump into the woods and haul ass. It was funny, the more time you spent in the woods, the more you felt like an animal.

He had gone maybe a hundred yards on the open road when he heard some people talking, very faintly. At first, he didn't know where they were coming from and then he did. Down the road.

He stepped into the woods. Maybe, he thought, they were coming his way. But after hiding for a few minutes he decided they weren't.

He continued up the road, and as he did the voices got louder.

He climbed the final portion of the rise in the road by threading his way through the woods, and finally he could see.

It was, he thought, a group of Believers—he recognized them by their khaki uniforms and beards and medallions. They had the road barricaded.

He thought for a moment: should he or should he not go forward? There was no reason not to. He stepped out into the road, now fully exposed, and started walking toward them.

Within five yards he was spotted, and two of the Believers, both huge guys, trotted toward him, long guns at port arms.

Rosen kept walking toward them.

"Hold up, stranger," one of them said, holding up a hand. "Who are you?"

"My name is Rosen. Morty Rosen. I'm a writer with *Rolling Stone.*"

Morty paused.

"I wanted to make contact with you guys."

"Why?"

The two men came closer.

"Can you prove that?" one of them asked.

"Yes, I can. But I have to speak with your top guy to show him what I have."

The men looked at each other. They were not sure which way to go.

"Look," Rosen said, "I have something on me that will enable you to drive the Rejects from the land."

They looked at each other again. They turned away from Rosen and whispered to one another, obviously discussing what to do. Then they turned back and the first one who had spoken said, "Wait here."

With that, he ran back toward the barricade where there were three other men. Rosen watched him talking with a short man and then pointing toward Rosen. After ten seconds or so he ran back down toward Rosen. "Come with us, we'll take you to see our major."

"No," Rosen said, "I don't want to see a major. I want to see the top guy—the one known as Father McAulliffe."

"Come with us. But first, we must search you. Do you have any weapons on you?"

"A .45 in my right-hand pocket."

They went over to Rosen and patted him down, one of them removing the .45 from his pocket. They also searched his pack. What they did not search was his boot, which was going to help Rosen establish his identity—and much more.

21

The vehicle carrying Rosen and his guards went down the road that the barricade was on, and five minutes after they started they turned off onto another road, this one through the forest and so small that the vehicles looked as if they could barely get through. A couple of times branches brushed against the car, and Rosen then knew why the windows on the vehicle were kept closed.

They traveled slowly through this narrow, occasionally bumpy road. Then after another five minutes it looked like they would break out of the road into an open area.

When they did, Rosen blinked. The sight was, in a way, spectacular. Directly ahead, across an open field maybe a hundred yards wide, was what looked like a church. It was a large white building with straight edges and roughly shaped like a mountain. On the top of it was a massive white cross. It was one of the most awe-inspiring sights that Rosen had ever seen.

There was something written beneath the cross that Rosen was able to read only when he got to within fifty yards of it. It was written in script, and it said BELIEVE.

Rosen immediately thought of Ernest Hemingway, a writer who had died many years ago and who exhorted people to write with economy, because that equaled power. Rosen didn't know if the writer of this word read Hemingway, but it sure had power.

The vehicle stopped about twenty-five yards from the entrance to the building in a packed-dirt parking lot, and then the driver parked the car next to a space where there were some twenty others. Then Morty was motioned to get out—in a nonhostile way—and, flanked by his two guards, walked toward a portal at the front of the buildings.

It was only when he got out of the vehicle that Rosen realized that the building was surrounded on all sides by mountains that were rough, covered with evergreens, craggy, and high—typical Rocky Mountains—and served as quite a dramatic backdrop to a totally dramatic building.

"This is some place," Rosen said to no one in particular.

One of the people who was walking beside him said, "It was built to show our devotion to Jesus Christ." And as he said the name he and the others nodded.

Rosen thought: *Well, you showed it, buddy.*

The doorway was flanked by two other guards, and as they went by they greeted each other with the term "brother."

The inside of the building was as impressive as the outside. It was a church, but a very impressive one. There were the usual pews, but there were also many paintings on the walls, most of Christ. The most dramatic thing he could see was a crucifix over the altar: the figure of Christ hanging from it was the bloodiest and most realistic he had ever seen. This Christ looked like he had really gone through agony, which, of course, He had. Another thought: and all because of the Jews . . . Jews like him.

The church was fairly crowded, maybe one-quarter full with both men and women, the women wearing hats of some sort, the men all Caucasian, as were the women. They ranged in age from very young to very old.

The feeling came through to Rosen like heat: this was one fanatical group of believers and adorers.

The guards walked him across the back of the church, then through a small door. To his left was a long corridor, which was far less lovely than the church, being made of cement blocks painted light blue.

Rosen walked along with them for perhaps fifty yards, then went through another hall and came to a large unpainted oak door on which there was one word: FATHER.

They knocked, and someone said, "Come in." A guard went in, was gone for a moment, and then the guards led Rosen in.

It was not exactly the word to describe the room they went into, but Rosen immediately thought of *spectacular.*

In fact, the room was filled with religious paintings as well as statuary on shelves on all the walls. Rosen got a sense that he had stepped into a store where they sold religious objects.

A desk near the middle of the room might have someone sitting at it but Rosen couldn't tell. The chair was turned around, and whoever was sitting in it couldn't be seen behind the back of the chair.

Then he turned, and Rosen was surprised. The premier of the Believers was an awesome physical specimen.

The man's features were plain, he wore glasses, his clothing was plain—a long-sleeved white shirt, undistinguished except for the medallion around his neck. And he wore a neatly trimmed gray beard. The only unusual thing was what was obviously a toupee—black—and a bad one: as bad, Rosen thought, as that any of TV preacher he had ever seen. What the fuck? Rosen thought. If you were going to be some kind of religious zealot, it seemed that you were required to wear a bad toupee.

The man smiled.

"You're Mr. Rosen," he said.

"Yes. What is your name?"

"I'm Father McAulliffe."

"You're the man I want to see."

McAulliffe nodded. His toupee, Rosen noted, stayed on.

McAulliffe said, "May I ask who you are? You told the guard that you were a member of the press. Also that you have learned that the plague is gone?"

"Yeah. But I don't want to be a member of your church."

Father McAulliffe smiled. Rosen noticed his eyes behind the glasses. They were small and blue and had a certain glint in them that said this guy was a total f'ing nutcase.

"First," Rosen said, "I should explain that I am a reporter for *Rolling Stone* magazine, and for two months I went undercover in the Rejects organization in Compound W."

McAulliffe looked over his glasses at him. His eyes had darkened. Rosen had no question that he was dealing with a very smart, very cunning, very dangerous man.

"How did you do that?"

"Using the same methods I used in going undercover in a Brooklyn, New York, motorcycle gang and other places."

"What were those?"

"Mainly you had to wait to be discovered. They had to find you, you couldn't find them."

McAulliffe nodded.

"Are you doing something like that here?"

"What do you mean?"

"Going UC for the Rejects."

"You're kidding, right?"

McAulliffe was silent.

"I have two things to show you," Rosen said. "First is a tattoo. Reason: I don't want you to think that I got this willingly. It was part of my UC persona."

With that, Rosen opened up his shirtsleeve on his left arm, revealing the Reject tattoo.

McAulliffe didn't react, except to say: "What's the other thing?"

"The main reason I'm here," Rosen said.

McAulliffe looked at him.

Rosen said, "I was trying to think of the value of what I'm about to show you, and I came across a couple of quotes that might do that. From Sun Tzu in his *Art of War.* You know of Sun Tzu?

"Yes," McAulliffe said.

"He said: 'A hundred ounces of silver spent for information may save the thousands spent on war,'" Rosen said.

"That's true."

"And the other one I like is from Napoleon. It's real clear and straightforward: 'One good spy is worth twenty thousand soldiers,'" Rosen said.

McAulliffe nodded.

"Well, I didn't start out being a spy," Rosen said,

"but I gathered a spy's know-how because I figured that one day it might be valuable to someone."

"Mr. Rosen, what exactly do you have?"

"I have the Rejects' orders of battle in the entire United States, which is, of course, the strength, command, structure, and disposition of personnel, units, and equipment, plus the locations of all Reject compounds. In other words, I have intel that will enable the Believers to drive the scourge of the Rejects off the face of the earth."

"Where is this information?"

"In my left shoe."

"What's to prevent me from just taking it from you, assuming I think of it as valid, and not give you a reward? I assume you want a reward."

"Nothing. But I don't figure you'd do that. You're a man of God, right?"

"Yes, a soldier for Christ."

"I didn't figure you'd do it."

McAulliffe nodded and said, "And how do I know that what you're giving me is valid, correct? How do I know you're not a fabricator, as they say in spy circles, providing false information?"

"I think that would be pretty simple," Rosen said. "I assume you have some valid intel about the Rejects, stuff gathered by your own people. All you have to do is take those random samples and see if they jibe with the intel you've gathered."

McAulliffe looked at him.

"Fair enough."

He paused. Then: "Let me ask you this. Why are you giving us this information? What do you want?"

"Simple, I want to live," Rosen said, "both in the short and the long term."

"What do you mean?"

"I'm sure the Rejects are going to be looking for me. I hooked up with what's left of the Rebels . . ."

"Ben Raines's army?"

"Yes, but he's dead. Yeah, died of the plague."

McAulliffe nodded.

"Anyway," Rosen said, "I made a mistake while in the Rejects' camp and they found out I was UC for *Rolling Stone*. They sent the escape unit after me, but the Rebels killed them all. But they'll be coming again. They know that if I'm able to get a story in the magazine about them it's not going to do them a lot of good.

"Also," Rosen continued, "if you don't win the war with them we are all going to die anyway. I had to set aside my reportorial objectivity and go for one side or another. I just want to be embedded in your army, not only to protect myself, but to have a front-row seat on the battles."

"Why don't you convert to Christianity and join us?"

Rosen laughed hard.

"Are you kidding? I'm beyond repair."

"No one's beyond repair."

Rosen was about to say: how about Premier Szabo? But that might have pissed off the Father.

The Father nodded.

"Can I see what you have?"

Rosen loosened the shoelaces, then reached down the side of his boot and extracted a folded-up glassine envelope that contained a folded sheaf of papers.

"Some of these notes were written when it was pretty dark outside, so some of it may require translating," he said.

Rosen handed the sheaf of papers to McAulliffe, then retied his laces. McAulliffe opened up the papers very carefully—this was one deliberate dude, Rosen thought. Fifteen seconds later a tall man came into the room. Like all the other believers he sported a beard, this one gray, like McAulliffe's.

McAulliffe glanced up.

"This is Morton Rosen," McAulliffe said.

The man, who had large, dark, even scary eyes, looked and nodded. "And this is Jeffrey Weaver."

Weaver looked away, and then down at the papers that Rosen had supplied for McAulliffe.

"Why don't you wait outside, Mr. Rosen?" McAulliffe said. "We'll call you back in after we discuss what you've provided."

"No problem," Rosen said, and one of the guards escorted him down the hall a ways.

I hope, he thought, *that I have made the right decision.* You never knew when you were dealing with fanatics. Of course these guys, Rosen thought, weren't the Rejects, but they were, in their own way, fanatics: it was their way or the highway.

Ten minutes later the guard came for Rosen.

"Father McAulliffe would like to see you."

Rosen nodded. He could not help but feel a little flutter in the pit of his belly.

He was led into the room. Both McAulliffe and Weaver were looking down at the orders of battle.

McAulliffe looked up.

"This is some valuable information you've brought us," he said, and Weaver nodded. "The single-most important piece of military intel since we started warring with the Rejects a couple of years ago. We thank you, and congratulate you. You're a brave man."

"I just like to do my job," Rosen said.

"Good."

"When the plan is coordinated and the attack sequences decided, you will be there, fully embedded. And two of our soldiers will be assigned to guard you."

"Thank you," Rosen said. But inside he was shouting hallelujah, and he was looking forward to a night of sleep uncluttered by fear that someone was going to make sure he took a permanent nap.

22

All day, Jim LaDoux, Beverly Harper, Duke Kindhand, and the rest of the Rebels were traveling north toward Montana, and by dusk they were ready to stop.

They made themselves dinner from a deer that Kindhand shot and the venison was quite delicious, and not just because they hadn't had something like it in a long time.

After dinner they were sitting around a fire, this because they weren't concerned about the Rejects catching up with them, simply because they had no way of finding them, and they had traveled quite far north during the day.

"So, Jim," Kindhand said, "what are your plans?"

"I don't know. They're still up in the air. But I expect they'll be to settle in Montana for a while until things straighten out, then head east."

"What, you going to live alone?"

"I hope not," Jim said, his eyes flicking to Bev, who was pointedly looking at him. "I might find some ugly old goat who wants to live with me for a while."

Abruptly, Jim had to dodge a towel, this thrown by Bev, and Kindhand and the other Rebels got a laugh out of it.

Kindhand looked into the fire. The light flickered off the deep crevices in his face, his eyes glittering.

"I don't think things will ever straighten out," he said. "One way or the other we're going to have to fight for whatever we get. That's the way it was with the SUSA, and that's the way it's going to be with anything else we form."

"You going to try to do that?" Jim asked.

"Absolutely. My philosophy and that of the other Rebels hasn't changed just because Ben is dead. In fact, we want to realize the dream that was always his."

"It seems that you guys have been fighting all your lives," Jim said.

"It seems that way because it is that way!" Kindhand said to appreciative laughter from the other Rebels.

"But how are you going to fight anyone with just a handful of men?"

"We aren't," Kindhand said. "I don't know if you know it but I sent a message out in code on the CB, if any Rebels are within listening distance. I told them what road we're traveling, where we are, and before long I expect we'll be meeting some people. I just know there are thousands of Rebels still alive, it's just that they're scattered."

"Is it safe?"

"What, the code?"

"Yes."

"It's pure Indian wind-talker stuff. The Axis couldn't figure it out in World War II and couldn't figure it out now."

"Somebody said the Jamaicans were the same way," Jim said, "the posse gangs. Spoke in their own special pig English and the U.S. Drug Enforcement Agency couldn't figure out what they were saying."

"I had heard that too," Kindhand said. "I don't doubt it for a minute."

There was silence for a moment, everyone sipping hot coffee, a moment like so many moments so long before the wars and the plague started. Just brothers-in-arms, enjoying each other, the calm before the storm: the storm, they knew, that some of them wouldn't make it through.

"So," Kindhand said, "you're just going up to Montana and live there?"

"Yeah," Jim said, "I got mountain man in my blood."

Kindhand took a long sip of his coffee. Then he looked levelly at Jim.

"You know you won't be able to do that until this world straightens itself out."

"Maybe," Jim said, "but I'm going to try. At least we have a good chance to avoid conflicts with the Rejects. They won't be able to find us, not in the country we're heading for."

Kindhand looked at Jim.

"Do you have a minute, Jim?"

"Sure."

"There's something I want to show you."

Kindhand got up—he was remarkably agile for his age—and Jim followed him to his HumVee. He reached in and took an envelope out.

"This," Kindhand said, taking some papers out of the envelopes, "is a memo from Ben Raines that contains some valuable info on fighting war."

"Why are you showing it to me?"

"Because I think that someday, Jim, you might find some of these tips valuable. In fact, if I should get killed I have told my men that you would make a good leader."

"I told you," Jim said, "I have no intention of fighting a war."

"Well, like I said, maybe someday you'll have to."

Jim just looked at him.

"Why don't you just look them over and see what you think? Some of them apply to full-scale war where artillery is used, but there are some ideas that are very useful no matter what the mode of warfare."

Jim hesitated but then said: "Okay. I'll take a look."

Kindhand nodded, turned, and walked back toward the fire. Jim read the memo by moonlight.

CONFIDENTIAL
To: Field Commanders
Subject: Most Effective Combat Procedures and Principles of Command
From: Ben Raines, Gen.

Over the years that we have fought as brothers in arms, a number of things have come to my attention that need to be addressed relative to combat procedures and administrative principles. For some of you, this information will be old hat, but some of your are new and are relatively unfamiliar with the information or simply have gotten blasé about its execution. Upon reading these tenets, some may seem academic, even boring. But it is absolutely crucial that these principles be followed. If anyone reading this does not understand anything contained, please communicate with me or the chief of staff at once.

GENERAL POINTS

• Leadership. It is expected that anyone who is put in command of any unit should lead that unit personally, should lead in person. Any commander who fails to obtain his objective, and who is not dead or severely wounded, has not done his full duty.

• Visit Front Daily. In the event that combat involves the maintenance of a front, rather than a guerilla-style action, each chief of the general staff sections—Signal, Ordnance, Engineering, and Quartermaster section—should visit the front daily. The commanding general or his chief of staff—but never both at once—should also visit. To avoid duplication of duties, the chief of staff will designate which sectors are to be visited by whom.

When visiting the front, remember that the function of the visiting officers is to observe, not interfere in any way. This does exclude, however, them reporting anything of military importance no matter where it comes from. Remember that praise is militarily more valuable than assigning blame. And remember that as a commander you have objectives in visiting the front: to gather relevant intel and have your men meet you at the front.

• Execution. The promulgation of an order involves only ten percent of your responsibility. The other ninety percent must be devoted to making sure, by vigorous and proper supervision, that the order is carried out.

• Staff Meetings. Frequent meetings among staff commanders is required to ensure that all relevant information in a particular campaign is fully circulated and acted upon. Attendance at these meetings is required. If information is discovered that is of an urgent character, it must be distributed quickly.

• Rest. Any personnel, whether line or commanding, will not survive without proper rest. All sections are required to run a duty roster and enforce compliance. Different sections require different rest time, and this should be calculated as time goes by. Of course, in some situations we all must work all the time, but such emergencies are not frequent. The central point is that men who are not exhausted work better when pressure is high.

• Command Post Location. All command posts must be strategically located, following the central idea that the closer to their front the command post is the less time is wasted in driving to and from the front. Ideally, the Chief Command Post (CCP) post should be more than a half-hour's drive away from the front and the command posts (COs) of field units closer to the line. The closer the COs are to the CCP's saves much time. Command posts should be set up so that there is a minimum amount of radio traffic.

COMBAT: RULES OF ENGAGEMENT

• Maps. Some of us think that we acquire merit because we read maps in the safety of a CCP or CO. This is in error.

Maps exist to allow us to plan overall strategy and give us a panoramic view of battles.

Very importantly, maps also exist to allow us to see where critical situations are or may develop, and the commander should be aware of these. In the higher echelons, a layered map of the whole theater drawn to a reasonable scale, showing roads, railways, streams, and towns is better than a large-scale map clogged with ground forms and nonessential information.

• Plans. These should not be rigid, but flexible, ready to be changed as needed.

• Reconnaissance. The plain fact is that there is no such thing as too much reconnaissance. However you can get it, by whatever means, do so. The reports submitted must not be speculative or opinions, but facts, whether negative or positive.

If you intercept a message, be wary: sometimes intercepts are sent to be intercepted and provide false data. Cross-check them. And remember, information is like bread: the fresher it is the better it is.

• Orders. All commanders will receive written orders on battles and other relevant matters that are complete. That is, the overall goal of an operation will be made clear as will the mission to be accomplished by each major combat unit. The order should be short, and perfectly clear, accompanied by a sketch that will tell what to do, not how to do it.

• Fragmentary Orders in the Field. Commanders will get many orders electronically. It is necessary to write them down and repeat what you hear.

Whenever possible, issue the order in person and always try to have the senior officer issue the order rather than the junior. Allow ample time, whenever possible, to allow the person to act on the order.

Keep troops informed, not only of what is going on, and is to go on, but also in detail of what they have achieved.

• Supplies. All units must anticipate supplies that they need and ask for them in time for them to be effective in combat. To aid this process, reconnaissance should be used as needed to help anticipate demands.

Remember: a rifle without bullets is just as useless as a gun truck without gas.

• Medical Care. There should be adequate care available—and quickly. If a field hospital is involved it should be close to the front.

All commanders should visit the wounded personally, not have a junior officer do it.

• Special Note: Decorations. These are very important to keep morale up and should be given whenever time allows. There should be one officer on the staff who will be able to write up the citation for proper consideration.

• Discipline. There is only one type of discipline—perfect. If you don't enforce and maintain discipline you are potential murders. You must set the example.

Discipline is based on mutual confidence and respect, meticulous attention to detail, and pride in being a soldier. Discipline must be as much a part of a soldier as his breathing, something that is stronger than the excitement of battle or fear if death.

Discipline is only possible when officers care deeply about their troops, and are imbued with their cause. These officers will not tolerate negligence; officers who fail to correct mistakes or compliment success are useless in peace and dangerous in war.

Officers must also be meticulous about their dress, their conduct—and demonstrate courage.

Discipline is also maintained by engaging in various activities, such as getting up at a certain time, standing at weapons inspection, keeping one's gear clean, firing at the range, saluting, and many other things that result in a mind that is sharp and ready to respond in war.

• Rumors. Any army has to deal with more than its fair share of rumors. Of particular concern are unsubstantiated statements received after dark. Also, stragglers and walking wounded. Such persons tend to justify themselves by painting alarming pictures.

Note that it is very difficult to respond to every call for help after dark. Note that units will not be wholly destroyed at night, usually because some can escape in the dark. If you must counterattack, launch this attack in daylight, but first check out the information you received via adequate recon.

• Physical Condition. It is important for troops to be in good physical condition. Fatigue can make cowards of us all. Men who are in good shape do not tire.

• Courage. As the poet once said, "Do not take counsel of your fears."

COMBAT PRINCIPLES: WHAT WORKS AND WHAT DOESN'T

In war, there is only one tactical principle that is immutable: to use any means at hand to inflict the maximum number of casualties that lead to the destruction of the enemy in minimal time.

In battle, casualties relate directly to how long you are in the line of fire.

Your own firepower will cut down on the enemy's firepower and the rapidity of the attack as well as will shorten your risk of exposure. As a famous general once said: "A pint of sweat will save a gallon of blood."

Battles are won by frightening your enemy, which is achieved by wounding and hurting—wounding and killing him in any way you can. Fire from the rear is three times as effective as fire from the front, but to get fire behind the enemy you must hold him with frontal fire while you work your way around a flank. If the enemies' positions are in place, direct assault on them should be avoided if possible.

Battles are won by hitting the enemy with the maximum force you can muster before the enemy can assemble any force of his own. If he has one division, you want two. If he has two regiments, you want to overrun him with four. Make your force as strong as humanly possible as long as the gathering of that force does not unduly delay the attack.

Battles are won by never yielding ground. It is much better to hold what you have won than to take back what you have lost. At night, never move your troops to the rear to rest or reform. In the daytime this may be done, but only when absolutely necessary.

The danger of retreat is that it may produce a panic. There are numerous instances of men—brave men—fleeing in panic when this is done.

Battles are won by using your firepower. Mortars and artillery are great weapons, but just scrap metal when not used! Keep them firing.

• Tactical Ops. Whenever you can use roads to travel on, they are fastest. Use the fields to fight in. However, when you get closer to an enemy you may find the roads demolished, or mined. But stay on the roads until you are shot at.

If you are in broken country where there may be tanks, use leapfrog tactics and keep the antitank guns well up.

If you are fighting in the mountains, first secure the high ground. The best way to do this is daytime recon followed by attacking with a platoon at night, which can be reinforced with troops at dawn.

If you are trying to get to high ground on mountains or hills, don't take the obvious road. It is almost certain to be defended. Rather, look for other pathways; hills almost always have them. If you try to go up an obvious path in hostile territory you will be engaging in something very simple—suicide.

Don't be deeply concerned about land mines. Indeed, the impact of mines is largely mental. In war, not more than 10 percent of all casualties are caused by mines. When you come across them, you must go around or through them. But do remember that there are not enough mines in the universe to cover the whole country. It is less time-consuming to go around them than to search for them. However, while the other troops are making this detour the engineers should be engaged in clearing a straight path. Make sure that all troops have mine detectors and know how to use them. Above all you must—absolutely must—get through.

Never allow a unit to dig in until the objective is reached. When it is, dig, wire, and mine.

Dig slit trenches within ten yards of artillery. Do not place them under trees, as these create shrapnel showers. Also, set up camouflage nets so that if and when they catch fire they can be pulled off instantly.

Take the time to prepare for an attack.

Small forces, such as platoons or companies, are capable of three actions: go forward, stop, or run. It is a bad mistake to run, because then they are even easier targets of artillery fire. If caught under fire, advance out of it, never retreat from it. Artillery batteries can seldom shorten their range.

All security detachments must advance farther into enemy lines than anyone else. Radio transmissions from such positions can be vital. Also, all security detachments must be deployed at night for transmission of intel.

• Training. Physical condition is vital. All soldiers and officers should be able to run a mile in ten minutes with a combat pack on, and march eight miles in two hours. During battles, it is impossible to maintain top physical condition, but if physical condition is optimum before the battle it will not lower significantly during the battle.

It is important to be able to mount and dismount machine guns more rapidly than at present. Training should include so many repetitions of these procedures that they can be done in the dark.

Attacking in the dark, as opposed to in daylight needs to be improved greatly.

Digging and entrenching tools such as axes and shovels must be sharpened and kept in excellent condition.

Battles are won or lost mostly by small contingents of men—platoons and squads. Training here should be constant, enable the men to take the good solution now, which is much better than a perfect solution ten minutes after it is needed.

• Tips for Commanders. It is vital that officers have self-confidence, and that men have confidence in them. One of the best ways to do this is for men to observe them at the front lines during battles.

A close watch must be kept on materials, men wounded and lost, replacements—anything and everything required to win the battle.

Most people do not repeat oral orders in the field. This is the royal road to defeat.

All orders must be repeated back to the issuer.

When issuing orders, language must be clear and concise. General U.S. Grant was a great general, in great part because his orders were so clearly written that no one in the field misunderstood them.

• Prisoners. When interrogating prisoners, remember that the older the prisoner the more likely he is to talk. Prisoners over forty are usually ideal; as the age drops, so does the willingness to talk.

Make sure that the interrogation of a prisoner is done out of sight and hearing of other prisoners. There can be no hint that the prisoner is in any way cooperative.

• Miscellaneous. When heavy weapons, cannons, and machine guns are used, remember that it is the firing of light machine guns and rifles that enables the heavier ones to move forward.

Very few men are killed when bayonets are used, but most troops are afraid of the bayonet. The Rebels use these weapons better than any force in the world. Make sure that if you have to use them they are sharp.

If flat trajectory force is being used against enemy machine-gun emplacements, then it's best to deliver it near and parallel to the axis of the fire. This will pin the enemy down and let other troops get behind them to throw grenades and use other weapons to neutralize these guns.

Night attacks are often very effective. On nights when there is no moon, little light, attacks should start two and a half hours before dawn; on moonlit nights, by the light of the moon. All attacks should be preceded by day recon. Objectives must be recognizable in the dark.

• Caring for Your Men. Officers are responsible for their men not only in terms of how they are performing in battle, but for their health and well-being when not fighting. Officers should be last out of battle or march, and make sure their men are cared for.

An officer should know his men so well that he recognizes the first sign of nervous strain or sickness and take action as needed.

Officers must check, in particular, his men's feet to make sure that their shoes and socks are in good condition. The officer must anticipate changes in weather so footgear can be changed.

Medical facilities must be kept as close to the front as possible. The shorter the distance the greater the chance of survival.

Medical facilities must be in the open and clearly marked as such so that the enemy will not attack them.

Finally, remember: there are no bad troops—only bad leaders!

Jim finished reading the document. He found it very useful, and he agreed with 99 percent of it, realizing at the same time that he had no basis, no experience with which to make such an observation. Still, he did. For a moment, he pictured Ben Raines and then Duke Kindhand. These guys had been out in the field a long, long time. They had seen men live, and they had seen men die, and they had seen great warriors and not so great ones. And they picked him. If nothing else, it was a hell of a compliment.

23

There was an unspoken truth that Jim, Bev, and the Rebels shared as they stopped in early afternoon. Namely, that the threat of them encountering the Rejects had diminished, if not faded completely. The reason was simple. They had gone quite a few miles and so far had not seen any hostile forces. In fact they had only seen relatively few people, but fortunately all the people were alive. And they had not seen a single body claimed by the plague, an all-too-frequent occurrence farther south.

There was also an unspoken truth existing between Jim and Bev, something that showed itself quite clearly the last time they had stopped and Jim had made a joke about an old goat coming to live with him. She had tossed a towel at him, and everyone had had a good laugh, but the truth was plain to see: Jim had assumed that she would come to live with him, and indeed she would. The truth was very clear: they had fallen in love and wanted to be with each other always.

Despite being sure that Bev loved him, there was something he had to ask her, and something he needed to do. Because he had been doing some thinking about them—and their lives together. On the ride to the rest stop, Jim had thought about the best time to broach these things; it was easy to decide that bouncing along in a HumVee while you were alert to possibly being ambushed by the Rejects was not exactly the best time.

He knew he got his chance when the Rebels stopped, and he knew that it was a good time. And he also found that he was very nervous, something that assuredly was not helped when he looked into her gorgeous, stomach-squeezing eyes and said: "You want to take a walk? I need to talk to you about a couple of things."

"Sure," she said. "What do you have in mind?"

"We'll talk about it."

"I hope we're also going to do something that doesn't require talking."

Jim laughed. But he had to be careful. She was capable of getting him very excited very, very quickly. She was spectacularly sexy.

"I saw a lake a ways back," he said. "Why don't we walk down there?"

"You got it."

They exited the HumVee, and then Jim went over to Kindhand, who with the other Rebel soldiers had also exited his vehicle.

"Hey, Duke," he said, "I'm going to take a stroll down to that lake we saw coming in. When do you expect to mount up again?"

"At least an hour."

Kindhand's eyes had dropped down to Jim's waistband.

"I see you're taking your Glock with you."

"Well," Jim said with a straight face, "you know how it is. She doesn't seem dangerous, but one never knows."

Kindhand laughed, and then Jim went back to Bev.

And they started walking in the direction of the lake, which was through a stand of pine.

As they walked, Jim took her hand in his, and again the electricity started to flow into him.

"Wow," he said, "every time I touch you it's like plugging myself into a wall socket."

Bev looked up at him and smiled.

"There are better things than a wall socket," she said, and they both laughed.

They continued to walk through the forest and gradually the lake appeared. After ten or fifteen yards, they stopped and just looked toward the lake, which was as shiny and flat a mirror, and was rimmed by low, rolling brown hills.

"You know," she said, "it looks false. Like you could step out onto it and walk across."

Jim laughed.

"Only one person I ever heard of could do that."

Bev laughed, turned, and kissed him again.

"Please don't do that for a while," Jim said. "You're distracting me."

Bev kept looking at him, a little smile playing around her luscious lips.

"Okay."

For a moment, transfixed by her beauty, Jim forgot why he had come with her, but now as he did the ideas returned, and with it anxiety. He loved this woman so much. But he had to ask her.

"I wanted to ask you a question."

"Sure," Bev answered.

"Have you ever lived in the wild?"

"No, I haven't. Why?"

"I was thinking that maybe I wouldn't head east. Maybe I'd just go into the mountains, the mountains of Montana, at least for a while, and I was thinking that maybe you'd want to come along, and if you did whether or not it would be a problem for you."

He had gotten all of it out in one breath.

"Not really. I'm with you. I think people create the environment they're in, whether it be in the middle of the Mojave Desert or the mountains of Montana."

"Well," Jim said, "let me tell you there is nothing happening in those mountains in the conventional sense. You might get bored. And it gets bitterly cold in the winter. There's no TV, we use a generator for lights at night, and also in the winter the snow gets as high as a mountain itself.

"There's also no such thing as medical care, unless you want to go into the nearest town, which will be some miles from where I have a general idea I might want to live."

"No problem yet," Bev said. "Keep going."

"Well, getting back to medical care. I'll have to teach you some things."

"Oh, goody. Going to medical school in the mountains of Montana."

"Well, some things are essential. I was taught CPR, the Heimlich maneuver, a bunch of other things. My father saved my grandfather one night from choking to death."

"Really?"

"Yeah, my grandfather was at the dinner table one night and he held up his hand to his throat, which is the way you're supposed to indicate that you're choking. My father had been trained in the Heimlich maneuver and he tried to clear he blockage—later we found out that he had gotten a piece of steak lodged in his windpipe, but Dad tried and tried and couldn't do it, so he had to go into a backup procedure, which was to actually do a tracheotomy on my grandfather with a sharp kitchen knife. And he did."

"Wow," Bev said, "I'm impressed."

"Yeah, but that's the kind of thing you have to contend with."

Bev reached down and petted Reb.

"Well, there are some good things too, right? I mean other than you and I making love and being together all the time?"

"Sure," Jim said. "I love it for many reasons. But one surely is that you get so close to nature that you see the miracle of it all. You haven't really experienced life until you see an animal give birth. I've been seeing horses and countless other animals give birth since I was a little boy and it's terrific."

"There's a question I have for you," Bev said. "How are we going to get by?"

Jim paused. He was not naturally a humorous man, but whenever he was with Bev it seemed to bring the humor out in him as never before.

"Do you like marmot?" he asked with a straight face.

"What's that?"

"A small rodentlike creature very common in the Northwest. They can be prepared ten different ways. And it's good for breakfast, lunch, and supper."

Bev laughed out loud.

"Hey," she said, "I also like grizzly bear. We can have a couple of sides of that every now and then." She laughed hard, Jim joining her.

"I'll find a way to support us," he said.

"You have great confidence in yourself, don't you?"

"I really do think it's a trait everyone develops who grows up in the mountains."

Abruptly, Bev became silent. "I have two other questions."

"Shoot."

"Hey, don't say that around here."

They both laughed, and when the laughter subsided Bev asked: "Do you love me?"

"Absolutely."

"Okay. But," Bev said, "before we live together, I need for us to get married. Do you have a problem with that?"

"Absolutely not. That's the way I want it too. That's what you do when you're in love, right?"

She leaned over and kissed him softly on the neck. "Yes," she said, "that's what you do when you're in love."

"Absolutely."

"The other thing is that I'd like to continue my missionary work, at least to some degree."

"I don't know how many people you'd find where we might be living."

"There's always some," Bev said.

"I'm pretty sure of that," Jim said.

Jim started to lead her away from the lake. He stopped.

"Oh," he said, "I almost forgot. There's something I want to give you."

"Okay," Bev said, "give away."

"No," Jim said, "if you don't mind I'd like to go down to the edge of the lake for this."

Bev looked at him with a deadpan face.

"I know what it is. Swimming lessons."

Jim laughed, but then he said, "How did you know?"

Bev laughed hard. And she was nervous too. In fact, she knew that if Jim had told her that he was going to enroll them both in a course on advanced calculus she would have responded buoyantly and brightly. She knew why. That's what love did to you. Love, she had always known, would turn life into something more wonderful than it had ever been before. Now that had been confirmed.

"So," she said, her face serious, "what is it that you want to give me?"

"Well," he said, "it's a ring. An engagement ring."

Bev was silent as Jim reached into a breast pocket of the denim jacket he was wearing. With two fingers he took out a solid gold ring.

"This is the only one I have available," he said, "and I think you're going to have to wear it on your thumb for it to stay on."

Jim showed her the ring, turned it a little so she could see it better. Then he handed it to her and she looked longingly, and lovingly, at it.

"It's beautiful," she said. "Where'd you get it?"

"My grandfather gave it to me, but my brother had it before me. It has a history."

"Please tell me."

"The ring is about a hundred years old. As I mentioned, I'm Irish and Cajun extraction, and my great-great-grandfather was the first owner of it. He was from county Cork, Ireland, and came to America around 1850. He got it from his mother the night before he left for America. Things were terrible in Ireland in the 1850s. They had the potato famine, of course, this at a time when, believe it or not, the diet of the average Irish peasant—and they were all peasants—was fourteen pounds of potatoes a day and a little buttermilk—women ate ten pounds a day—but it was also because they were horribly treated by the English, who ruled things in those days."

"I read about some of it," Bev said.

"Yeah," Jim said, his eyes narrowing, glinting, getting that feral look that his eyes sometimes got, "but I think it's one thing to read it in a history book and quite another to hear the stories from someone who experienced it, or heard them from someone who experienced it. In fact, the Irish in Ireland were treated worse than the blacks were treated by plantation owners before the Civil War. They had no rights and lived like animals in hovels and, literally, caves. That's why they came in droves in the middle of the nineteenth century to America."

"Oh."

"But once they left Ireland, very, very few would return."

"Why?"

"Ship passage for one thing. It was an arduous, two-or-three-month journey by sailing ship. Greedy ship owners crowded them together in packed and unsanitary conditions, a perfect breeding ground for disease. Plus, quite simply, it often took people's life savings to afford the passage."

Jim paused. Sadness crossed his face.

"I get the feeling that you were almost there," Bev said.

"Sometimes I think I was, because I can imagine what it was like for my great-great-grandfather. He was only in his late teens at the time, and the night before he was to leave they all had a party, almost like an Irish wake. And there was drinking and reveling and Irish dancing, but beneath it all was sadness. Because the next morning his mother knew that Michael would be leaving for America, and she would never see him again. When she kissed him good-bye, that was it. In a way, it was like he was dying."

Bev wiped her eyes.

"God," she said, "that's sad."

"Yes," Jim said, "it is. But it's also about love. A love for a mother and father for their child. They wanted Michael to have a better life, and they endured that—this ultimate pain of his loss—to make sure that he did."

"Wow," Bev said.

"And the ring that she gave him—the ring you're holding—was to be a reminder of her everlasting love."

"God," Bev said, tears streaming down her face, "you're killing me."

He kissed her wet cheek and then took the ring and slipped it over her left thumb. It was a snug fit.

Bev's eyes brimmed with tears.

"Oh, Jim," she said, "I love you so, so much."

"You took the words right out of my mouth. You know," he said, "when I started on this trip I was filled with loneliness and emptiness. Everyone in my family was gone, and I left the only home I've ever known. And then I traveled down through all this death and destruction and it only got worse, and I was starting to think that it would never get better and then you came along in all your glory—"

"Needing a bath."

". . . And my life has changed. All—all—that emptiness inside me has been filled, and I'm looking forward to a long and beautiful life together. And we will have it."

"So am I, so am I."

They kissed softly and passionately.

"Okay," Jim said, when they pulled apart slightly and he looked down into their eyes. "I want to take you someplace now."

"Where?" she asked coyly. She had felt him becoming very aroused.

"On our prehoneymoon."

Bev smiled.

"Where?"

"C'mon, I'll show you."

They walked arm in arm along the edge of the lake, and then Jim finally stopped and led her by the hand into a secluded section of the forest, a small clearing surrounded by dense trees, walled off like a room. There was a pine needle mat at least four inches thick.

"Welcome to the Hotel Wyoming," he said.

Bev laughed.

She looked up at him, her eyes smoldering with desire and love.

"Make love to me, Jim. Make love to me."

"Oh," he said, his voice husky, "twist my arm."

They returned to the camp site just as the Rebels were starting to get ready to mount up.

"Hey, Duke," Bev called out. "Look at this."

She held out her hand, displaying her ring.

"We just got engaged."

"Congratulations," Kindhand said. "You deserve each other." And with that the other Rebels clustered around Jim and Bev and also offered their congratulations.

Finally, just before he mounted his own HumVee, Kindhand looked at Jim and Bev and said: "It's nice to be reminded that despite all this chaos, life goes on, that good things happen too. Godspeed to both of you."

Two minutes later, the Rebel convoy was on its way.

24

Just ten miles up the road the Rebels and Jim and Bev got a surprise—this one pleasant. Parked outside an unlikely diner was an unusual scene: six camouflage-painted HumVees, three of them gun trucks.

Kindhand was excited. They belonged to Rebels . . . probably.

As Kindhand and his Rebels approached a little guardedly, the door to the diner opened and Rebels virtually poured out as if the diner were on fire, laughing, happy, and waving. There were, Jim estimated, about thirty Rebel soldiers—in dark green fatigues, the regular Rebel field uniform—and when they saw Kindhand they really whooped it up. Kindhand's Rebels jumped out of their trucks and embraced their comrades, and started animated conversations. Reb, who had gotten out of the HumVee with Bev and Jim, was happy too, wagging his tail furiously.

Jim and Bev watched the happy melee, for a short while. Then Jim said "This has been one heck of a day."

"A wonderful day," Bev said. "I think we're all going to make it."

"I think you're right," Jim said.

All the Rebels and Jim and Bev and Reb went into the diner. The Rebels from the diner went back to their food, but at the same time conversed with their buddies.

When the group settled down somewhat, Kindhand brought Jim and Bev over to meet a short man, perhaps forty, with a square jaw and hard eyes. Kindhand had been talking with him and a couple of times he had pointed to Jim.

"This is Major Matt Garrett," Kindhand said. "Jim LaDoux and . . . his fiancée, Beverly Harper."

Bev and Jim smiled broadly,

"Matt is going to join us heading north to meet up with the main Rebel force."

"Great. And glad to meet you," Garrett said, extending his hand. "Duke has some good things to say about you, Jim."

Jim nodded.

"I understand you were with the general when he died."

"Yes, I sure was. Heck of a guy."

Garrett smiled.

"They don't come any better. I'm very sorry that he's gone, but we're going to continue on without him. He would have wanted that."

Jim nodded.

"We were lucky to meet you," Kindhand said. "How did you know we were on this road?"

"Sometimes the radio would work, and sometimes it wouldn't. We did catch a transmission that you guys were around here," Garrett said.

"You were in the Chicago area, right?" Kindhand said.

"That's right. DesPlaines, so we just headed this way."

"How was the trip?"

"A bit hectic," Garrett said. "We had a couple of

skirmishes, one with a group of Rejects and another time a freelance band of marauders."

"Lose anyone?" Kindhand asked.

Garrett's eyes darkened.

"Yeah, we lost one trooper in battle. Art Mannion. Great loss."

"I'm sorry to hear that," Kindhand said. "I knew Mannion."

"I was sort of aware of that," Garrett said.

"Yeah, we went back a long way."

"I know."

There was a pause.

"A lot of Rebels died from the plague," Garrett said.

"Any from your unit?" Kindhand asked.

"Fifty-eight."

"That's still below the average," Jim said. "You were lucky, if that could be said. Maybe it's gone. We had a guy here for a while a reporter for *Rolling Stone* magazine. He said the plague is gone."

"That's great if it's true," Garrett said. "It's bad for everyone but I think the average grunt really feels frustrated that he can't fight it. It's an enemy that doesn't carry arms, but it surely is devastating."

They all nodded.

"How are you doing with equipment?" Kindhand asked.

"Well, certainly we look better than you guys," Garrett said, laughing, and Jim and Kindhand joined in.

Indeed, the uniforms that the men in Kindhand's unit wore were very worn versions of their original uniforms, and some articles had been replaced with others. Garrett's men obviously had found replacement uniforms, because they were still the rich green that were the standard Rebel issue now.

"How are your supplies?" Kindhand asked. "I got the general's list of where the Reb supply depots are."

"We don't need 'em right now. Got plenty of guns and ammunition and explosives and the like."

"Everything working well?" Kindhand asked.

This was a standard question, and one that Ben Raines had encouraged his men to ask. If equipment went bad, it was important that the information be shared with all the units. In some cases, individual units would be able to tell others how to correct the problem, if it was correctable. Or, if it wasn't, everyone should know that, too.

"Well," Garrett said, "we had trouble with the MIK-19. It was failing in critical spots. So a couple of the men had to tear down and reassemble the thing, and the other .50-caliber gunners did the same. But it didn't take long before they knew the cause of the problem. It was the fragile linkage system that held together the belts of 40mm grenades that the gun fired. The solution was simply to replace the can of rounds with a new one and the weapon was ready to go."

"Listen," Kindhand said, "do you have any spare helmets? My guys, as you can see, aren't wearing any."

"Yes," Garrett said, "we do, and one for Jim and the lady."

"Great," Kindhand said, "just great."

Bev and Jim also thanked him.

"And let me ask you something," Garrett said.

"Sure," Kindhand said.

"Do you have any candy?"

"No, I don't think so."

Garrett smiled for the first time since Jim and Bev had met him.

"That seems to be rarer than hen's teeth. These guys are ready to kill for a Hershey bar!"

They all laughed.

"Have you heard anything about the Rejects and the Believers?" Kindhand asked.

"Well, I did hear something but it's in the category of rumor."

"What's that?"

"That things have heated up to the point where only a major assault is going to solve them—by the Believers."

"Where did the intel come from?"

"We ran into a couple of Believers who had dropped out of that life and they said that the word was that the Believers were, in the not-too-distant future, to come at the Rejects with everything they have."

Over the next ten minutes, helmets were found for Jim and Bev, who put them right on. Fifteen minutes later, Kindhand—who automatically, because of his rank, which Jim and Bev found out for the first time was a general—took over and gave instructions for the force to mount up. It was a happy, heady group. Most of them got the feeling that nothing could stop them now.

Kindhand put his arm around Garrett. Jim was nearby and could hear him. For the first time since they had met him, Kindhand showed the depth of his emotion.

"The dream," he said to Garrett, "is still alive."

"Believe it," Garrett said.

25

Alex Szabo had not gotten to be premier of all the Rejects in the United States by virtue only of his ability to terrorize others because of the bottomless cruelty he seemed capable of. He was also smart and innovative. Or, as one opponent termed it, "cunning."

The adoption—or the way he used it—of the Universal Global Positioning System, an outgrowth of the GPS developed years earlier, was one of his major triumphs, something that occurred when he was only third in command of the Reject force, at the time when a man named Owen Foster was premier and his next in line was James Harold. But one day Harold, who was to succeed Foster if he died, had been found impaled on some sharp rocks at the bottom of a cliff, and word was that he had fallen off the cliff, an accidental death. Still, investigators who probed the accident said that the circumstances of his death seemed "suspect," meaning Harold might have had a little help getting off the cliff, but no one was charged with any crime. But like so many other things in life, the common man, in this case the troopers, knew what happened. As one of them said: "V offed his ass."

No doubt was cast on whether or not Szabo "offed"

Harold when Foster also passed away, this from a strange, apparently natural malady that acted very much like arsenic ingestion. But when an autopsy was done by a small commission investigating Foster's death, nothing criminal could be found. Alex Szabo was anointed premier, and not surprisingly no one complained about his ascendancy.

Once he become premier, Szabo solidified the reputation he had known among his troops, his "warriors from hell" as he put it—known for his savagery, his leadership, and his cleverness in developing things that would win him battles. His clever addition to the problem of escaping prisoners was to buttress this reputation. Over the past six months prior to his tenure in office, seventeen prisoners had escaped. And then he told the Rejects about the UGPS, or Universal Global Positioning System, and how it could be used in cutting back on escapes.

He had explained it to them one day in the compound that the UGPS consisted essentially of twenty-four earth-orbiting satellites that allowed any person who owned a UGPS receiver to determine his or her precise longitude, latitude, and altitude anywhere on the planet.

For example, Szabo pointed out that he once knew an ex-helicopter pilot who used a GPS receiver on his boat to navigate his way home in foggy weather. The same machine could be taken the next day to calculate his progress and distance to a particular destination. And then he could use the same technology on his car.

In the years that had followed its invention, UGPS technology had developed, like most technology, by getting smaller. So small, in fact, that it was no larger than a dime, and could be sewn into the lining of a prison uniform, or in the sole of a shoe, a procedure that Szabo suggested be done with "profile" prisoners, such as scientists or military people they had captured, particularly attractive women that were used as sexual slaves.

And it was a short step, he explained, for Reject soldiers to install the sending mechanism into their own gun belts and holsters. Then, if they got lost, it was relatively simple for base command to locate them and give them instructions on how to find their way back to base camp, or wherever. And it also served as a way for base camp to know where they were in case they had been attacked and killed or were otherwise incapable of communication.

And this, too: it enabled them to know where the enemy was if they stole their guns. And the fact was that every single one of the escape unit soldiers had a transmitter built into and hidden in his equipment. If just one soldier's equipment had been taken, that would have been enough to track them. But after the Rebel firefight with the escape unit the weapons of twenty members of the unit had been taken by the Rebels and, undiscovered, all had had transmitters built into their equipment and were transmitting locations back to Alex Szabo. The plain fact was that they could have been in China and he would have been able to locate them. His only regret was that Rosen had not taken something with a transmitter in it.

Now he was assembling a force with which to track them down. According to Otis Williams, there were only eight people, six soldiers, Rosen, and Beverly Harper, who shouldn't be a problem. To be on the safe side, he was assembling a force of some hundred men, the very best he had.

From his command post inside the compound, he had been able to pick up their location immediately. It was apparent that they were traveling along back-country roads, heading north through Wyoming. It was apparent to Szabo that they could get close to the Rebel location by vehicle, and then make the final assault on foot. In other words, they did not have to make any cross-country journey to intercept them. They could cut considerable time off their arrival time.

Based on the time, it was not clear whether or not they would launch the attack in daylight or darkness. It didn't matter to Szabo. His night-vision equipment was, if not the best in the world, close to it. In fact, he had loved the example used by the supplier who sold it to him.

"Imagine," he had said, "a situation where a Norwegian rat is in some warehouse area, hunched down, gnawing on bread covered with peanut butter, courtesy of one of the area's workers who dropped it there. Things couldn't get much better for the rat—peanut butter is five-star cuisine—except when it's having intercourse on one of its regular 750 times a year!

"But what the rat doesn't know is that crouched in a doorway across the street about thirty yards away is a big orange tomcat. One would assume that the cat couldn't see the rat very well. After all, the night is starless, maroon, a rainy sky. But its eyes, normally slits, are dilated to the size of dimes, and it's using all available light to see the rat, though in black and white rather than color.

"That's the way our equipment works. It magnifies the ability to see at night twenty times what you'd normally be able to see."

"Sounds good," Szabo had said, "and what would happen between the cat and the rat?"

"Well," the salesman said, "at one point the cat bursts across the street and the rat takes off for a hole in a doorway ten yards away, but he doesn't make it. The cat ends up eating the rat."

Szabo had howled. "And who ate the rest of the peanut butter sandwich?"

The salesman felt lucky to make the sale, but even luckier to make it out alive. That Szabo guy was a real fruitcake.

Szabo didn't care. Day or night, it would be like shooting fish in a barrel. Or rats.

26

If the Believers could read his mind, Rosen thought, they would probably nail him to the cross. In the few days that he had spent among them, he had noted that their quintessence was fanaticism. And for this reason, when they launched an attack against the Rejects they would be difficult to defeat. People who would be willing to die for a cause, Rosen thought, were far more dangerous than those men who would think twice before giving up their lives.

Rosen, who was sitting in the Believer mess hall drinking a cup of coffee, looked around him. The women were all dressed in white, the men in gray. And all had that long-gone look in their eyes. And everywhere you looked there were pictures of Jesus Christ and medallion symbols. What did they do when they had sex? Pray for a good orgasm?

Down through history there had always been fanatics like this. What came to Rosen's mind were the Japanese. He had once done a story that involved him looking at all aspects of Japanese life, getting to know the people well, and when he was finished he told his editor, "I wonder how come the Allies were able to beat the Japanese in World War II. This is one crazy bunch of dudes. Guys who take off in airplanes and crash on the deck of an aircraft carrier; a culture where if someone in a family is disgraced they have "'family suicides.'"

Rosen smiled. He could just see him suggesting a family suicide to someone in his family. Maybe his sister Jenna or brother Dave. "Sure, why not? You go first, Morty."

Rosen drained the last of his coffee and stood up. He was trying to be blasé, act as if it didn't matter, but it did: when were they going to fight this crazy war?

He took his empty cup, walked over, and dropped it in a trash receptacle and then went outside.

It had been three days since he had met with McAulliffe. Maybe, he thought, he had changed his mind. Maybe he wasn't going to invade.

No, Rosen thought, that didn't make any sense at all.

He went outside and then wandered into a sort of park, an area that had benches and, of course, a couple of statues of Christ.

He sat down and looked around. Nothing seemed any different than the previous three days.

He only wished that he would get through to the *Stone.* But so far that had been impossible. To file this story, he was going to have to hand-deliver it to Wagner.

Of course, he had asked McAulliffe for permission to "look over" the military part of the camp and had been politely denied. Of course.

Rosen briefly considered trying to find the section himself and looking at it, but decided against that. If he ever got caught, he could forget being embedded with the Believer army. Indeed, they might throw his ass in prison.

The other reason he decided not to try it was that

he felt that he knew he was being shadowed. Not all the time, but some of the time. And who knew what kind of surveillance equipment they had?

It was a risk he'd better not take.

He got up from the bench and was about to go back to the quarters they had assigned him, a little room in the main building, when he noticed something. Three Believers, far down at the end of the path, were walking together and they were carrying something unusual—machine guns of some sort.

A moment later, they were gone.

Rosen thought about it. Maybe, he thought, that was a sign. A sign that the invasion was getting close. He sure hoped so.

27

Szabo, sitting in the back of his command vehicle, watched the monitor of the portable receiver, the rhythmic blink of the red dot and blue dots on the electronic map of the northwestern section of Wyoming. He was getting closer and closer to the Rebel force. Indeed, he estimated that they were within twenty-five miles. He had an idea, but he wanted to check it with Duyvill and Dill.

He pulled his lead vehicle to a stop, and all of the others stopped behind him. He spoke into his radio, which was connected to all the vehicles in the convoy, but which he could selectively reach. He told Duyvill and Holland to come up to his command vehicle.

A minute later, both men were standing at the side of the vehicle.

"We're getting close. I had an idea for where to set up our ambush," he said, "and wanted to run it by you."

Szabo presented his plan.

"Good idea," Duyvill said.

"Very good," Dill said, nodding. "I can't think of a better way that we can do it."

"Good," Szabo said, his eyes twinkling. "And all of

our troops have descriptions of Rosen and the bitch, right?"

"Absolutely," Duyvill said.

"Repeat to them that under no circumstances are they to be terminated. And remember, if we don't get Rosen, we want to take prisoners until we find out if he told anyone what he knows and if this was spread around."

The officers nodded, and both said, "Yes, sir."

When they had left and remounted their vehicles, Szabo gave the command to proceed and the convoy started up again. The way things were going, he would arrive at the road well before the convoy carrying Rosen. Szabo smiled. He felt very pleased with himself. He was, he thought, a great general.

28

Kindhand's HumVee, flying the Rebel flag, led the convoy of Rebels as they tooled down the road, which at this point was flanked by lodgepole pines, some of them burned out from one of those spontaneous wildfires that sometimes occur. They had two gun trucks in the lead, two bringing up the rear, which included the HumVee Bev and Jim were in, and an FSB.

Just as the convoy had started, everyone abruptly heard the sound of "Satisfaction," an old Rolling Stones record that was still popular with the troops in the Vietnam War. Its lyrics expressed perfectly the lament of all soldiers for all time: "I can't get no satisfaction."

The convoy, Jim thought, represented a new mindset: when it was only him and Bev they were just hoping they could slide through undetected to Montana. It was amazing, he thought, what a few .50-caliber machine guns and a bunch of battle-hardened veteran troops did to change your point of view!

The Rebels couldn't know it, but a half hour before Kindhand had met Garrett and his troops, Szabo and his hundred-man Reject force had moved into position down the road about a mile. Szabo, who had climbed a spruce tree, looked down the road with a pair of binocs. He knew the enemy was coming because the UGPS monitor had told him so.

He did not like what he saw. He expected only a few Rebels. Now he saw seven vehicles, three with gun turrets, an FSB, and perhaps twenty-five troops. And he knew from the uniforms who they were: Rebels. This was not good.

Where the hell did they come from? he thought. *Should I care that much?* He made a quick calculation. He had over a hundred men, all well armed, all experienced. He had heard that the Rebels were very efficient, even great soldiers, but they were simply outgunned.

He picked up his walkie-talkie, which was connected to all the troops, positioned for the ambush at various points.

"Stand ready," he said. "Here they come. More than we expected."

Stupidly, as soon as Szabo spoke, a number of the Rejects ran across the road to get in position. Why they had not done this before was anyone's guess. But there was a problem: they did not get across undetected. The lead Rebel driver saw them. He told Kindhand, and he barked into the radio.

"We got company up ahead," he said, "flanking us. Put the hammer to the floor and get ready."

Within less than two minutes, the HumVees were rocking along at seventy miles an hour, and the first fire came from the right side of the woods and from troops who were foolish enough to step out from the cover and the trees and received for their mistake a spray from the lead MK-19, sending them off to, according to what they believed in, a godless universe.

Then the fire coming at them increased, a huge

amount of tracer fire, and then abruptly the woods were gone and they were in an open field, a place Szabo had picked because there was no place for them to hide, to get off the trucks and run into the woods. They were now sitting ducks and were being fired on not only from a berm to the left, but from windows of some sort of abandoned building on the right.

Kindhand sent a long, arcing stream of 400-mms from an MK-19 and they disappeared in a flash of impacts and dust, followed by a cacophony of fire from the following vehicles, and then the HumVees were parallel to the building and the Rebels abruptly, under the savagery of the firepower directed their way, turned to retreat at the onslaughts of 400mm fire and tried to hide down behind a culvert while 50mm tracer poured in after them without any letup. One round in five created absolute carnage, and then as the vehicle sped by the building the Rebels poured fire into the windows where muzzle flashes were evident.

But the Rejects were hardly free and clear. The road rose up and then down sharply and there was another berm swarming with Rebels, pouring out fire, including Jim and Bev, she with an Uzi that Kindhand had given her and Jim with an AK-47, operating it with one arm, blasting whoever appeared. And then, fairly close to the woods, rocket trails started to appear, whizzing back and forth across the highway, followed by mortar fire.

Then Kindhand got lucky. About thirty feet out from the woods a Reject popped from behind a berm, ready to send Kindhand heavenward, an RPG set to fire, Kindhand so close he could see the man's face and eyes—which were leveled at him in hatred.

But nothing happened and Kindhand knew that it had misfired, and then fired his own weapon and one third of the man's head went away to expose a mess of bloody gray matter. It all happened so fast—as all this was happening—that the Reject never even had a chance to express disappointment in the misfire.

A hundred yards from the woods the speeding convoy was the subject of more rocket fire, in fact three rockets, one coming so close that Jim and Bev found out that it was a dull green color. It did not connect but two did, one with a sequoia tree and the other near a tire, and the powerful, concussive blast lifted the HumVee, perhaps loaded at this point with twelve to thirteen thousand pounds, up on two wheels, the tires screaming in protest. But it righted itself and Jim continued his mad dash down the road without missing a frenzied beat.

Then someone in the convoy fired a smoke grenade far ahead and the smoke blew back, obscuring much, but not so much that Rebel gunners, who had spotted positions of the Rejects, couldn't lay down .50-caliber rounds at a ferocious clip.

Part of Jim watched what he was seeing in awe. For some reason, the Rejects, who had a superior force, were missing the Rebels. When a muzzle flash appeared, .50-caliber fire was directed into it and the light went out, and Jim then realized why the Rebels, as well as he, were being more effective: they aimed, whereas the Rejects, who did not seem to have had much experience in firefights of this kind, sprayed their fire. Jim didn't know if they were hitting anyone, but it didn't look like it. And some part of him thanked his brother Ray. "Don't ever fire randomly," Ray had said. "Aim. If you have nothing to shoot at, don't shoot." And that applied, Jim thought, in hunting or war.

The smoke had thickened, and there seemed to be a corresponding decrease in the amount of fire coming from the Rejects. By the time the Rejects had burst through the smoke, it had ceased completely, and it was clear to Kindhand that the main reason that the firing had diminished was that many of the people manning the guns were dead.

The convoy slowed and drove a few miles until they hit a clearing, then pulled to a stop. Pickets were posted to make sure that they were not being followed, and then the damage was assessed, both to humans and equipment.

It was amazing.

No one had been killed, and not a single person had been seriously wounded.

The HumVees, however, had not been as fortunate

One seemed near death. The driver started to try to get it going without success. It was gushing oil from holes in the oil tank, there were three bullet holes in the driver's-side door, two in the passenger door, and from the punctures it looked as if the bullets had Rebel eyes. Every single one of them had penetrated exactly where human flesh was not located.

Jim and Bev had had a very close call. The bed of the HumVee they were in looked like a colander for draining spaghetti, the bullet holes innumerable, and fuel ran freely from the drums inside.

When Kindhand looked at it he said with a straight face to Jim and Bev: "Do you know why those gas drums didn't explode?"

"No, I don't," Jim said.

"Neither do I," Kindhand said, still with a straight face.

In the bed of one of the HumVees there was an even more bizarre story. Its driver discovered that one of the AT-4 antitank rocket tubes was empty, having gone off, this because the AT-4, which was secured crossways on the roll bar, had apparently been set off when hit by a machine gun bullet. Where the rocket had ended up was anyone's guess.

The machine gunner now found at least a theoretical examination why he was, as he put it, "knocked on my ass." There was so much incoming that no one had noticed that a rocket had been fired off one of the trucks!

Few of the vehicles had any windows left. Indeed, in the one the sergeant commanding the FSB was riding in an RPG tail fin had sheared off and was buried in the dashboard, fins out. The rest of the rocket had proceeded through the cab and out the window, taking what was left of it past the nose of the driver and out the partially open window, taking the glass with it.

A driver of one of the gun trucks narrowly escaped death. As it happened, a bullet had hit the glass in the rear door passenger window but instead of going through had caromed off. From its angle, Kindhand concluded that if it had gone through the glass it would have smashed into the driver's skull at around the base. In general, everything was just riddled. As one of the Rebels commented, and got a good laugh:

"We arrived at that section of road as American cheese and we left as Swiss!"

Ben Raines had been a great one to assign a battle-damage-assessment team to find out what went wrong—or right—when the Rebels battled, and

Kindhand and few other Rebels automatically did a BDA.

They didn't have much time to do it, figuring it was best to get on the road.

There was no way of telling whether there were more Reject forces in the area. Certainly, the defeat—though Kindhand did not know how many casualties they had inflicted—would eat into the gizzard of a guy like Szabo and he would want to come back at them.

Finally, Kindhand gathered his troops in front of him and, with Jim and Bev in attendance, said, "I don't know for sure why we succeeded. They clearly had a superior force in terms of numbers, but not in experience.

"It probably boils down to this," Kindhand continued. "Our experience. Though we haven't been engaged in many battles lately, we have been engaged in a whole bunch of these that involve coming in and hitting like a hawk—with total power—and pouring out fire. They weren't able to catch their breath. To put that another way, we were the pigeon but we reversed roles and became the hawk."

"I think that's true," Sergeant Ray McCafferty said. "Over and over—and over—again we've had failure drills and instinctive shooting. I got the feeling that we were firing at wide-eyed recruits. I mean, it's not that we're better than them essentially. We've all been on the range—or whatever serves as a range these days—firing thousands of rounds. You almost get used to getting fired at. These guys weren't. They may be great on tactical patrol, but this is combat."

"What do you think, Jim?" Kindhand asked.

"I think it's a matter of experience as well. I remember the first time I faced a charging grizzly. I was nervous, and my father had to bring it down.

"The second time," he continued, "I was much calmer. Because I had decided not to go into the woods anymore . . ." The Rebels laughed. "So there was no second time."

They laughed again.

Kindhand started to speak again to the men when Jim said: "My brother was in all kinds of battles and the like, in Vietnam and other places, but something has me puzzled."

"What's that, Jim?" Kindhand asked.

"How did the Rejects find us? We're in, as they say, the middle of nowhere, and not only do they find us, but wait in ambush ahead of us."

"Well," Kindhand said, "one thing I know for sure. No one from this outfit is telling them where we are."

"Right," Jim said. "Maybe it happened somehow when you sent the message out telling all the Rebels where you were. It was intercepted or something."

"Maybe," Kindhand said.

"Well as long as you don't send any more, we should be all right because we're moving our position."

Kindhand nodded.

"Unless," Jim added, "there's something we're not seeing—but I have no idea what that is."

Kindhand nodded again.

"Okay," he said, "mount up."

29

The clearing was totally quiet, except for the normal sounds one hears coming from the woods when darkness falls. This night it seemed especially quiet, just the wind and, appropriately enough, the sound of a lone wolf. It was about the way many of the Rejects—just forty-nine—who had survived the firefight with the Rebels felt. Lonely—and scared. The troops, who stood at attention in four lines, were stiff to the point of being frozen, and tenseness came off them like heat. The only light was from the moon.

Opposite them was Premier Szabo, who had gathered them together, he said, to speak to them—just to speak, they hoped.

"At ease," he said, and the soldiers came out of the attention position. At ease was another story.

"I have a couple of questions—and an observation," he said. "First, did anyone see that little pipsqueak we're looking for?"

They shook their heads.

"I didn't see him either," Szabo said. "And how about the bitch?"

Hands shot up. Szabo nodded to one of the soldiers at the end.

"I saw her in one of the HumVees," the soldier, a

tall, lean white guy, said. "She had a helmet on but it was her."

Szabo nodded.

"Yes," he said, "that confirms it. I saw her too. Now, let's talk about the battle."

He paused, and his eyes scanned the troops from left to right.

"There are a couple of things that we should have learned today," he said. "Does anyone here have any idea what they should be? They are important because we lost fifty-one men, including Colonel Duyvill. And Dill."

Smiling, he scanned the group again, his expression something that his soldiers either knew they should fear, or instinctively did. You never knew what was going on behind the smile, and almost always it was evil and violent.

No one answered.

"C'mon," he said, "this is very important to our efficiency as a force. Indeed, if any of you have any idea what went wrong today. . .

"Surely," he continued, "something did go wrong. We lost many good men. According to my observations, I didn't see a single Rebel trooper hit."

He paused and looked along the line.

"I need an answer to this question," he said, smiling, "or there are going to be consequences."

Still, no one had the temerity to offer a postmortem on the battle.

Szabo's face didn't change, but he walked toward the group and as he did they seemed to back up just a little, though none moved their feet.

He went up to one soldier. He looked like the others in the sense that he was in good condition. The trooper was maybe twenty-five, handsome, and had blue eyes and short blond hair.

"What's your name, soldier?"

"Johnson."

"Okay, Johnson," Szabo said, "are you able to tell me what went wrong with today's operation?"

Johnson looked up Szabo. Though Johnson's eyes were bright blue, even in moonlight they seemed brighter against his skin, which was almost glowing with redness. He was fighting to hold back starting to shake.

Johnson knew he had to give an answer.

He hesitated, but then spoke.

"I don't know, sir. I really have no idea, sir."

Szabo nodded and smiled but it was the wrong answer. He brought his hand around in a blinding arc of speed and what was in it—a box cutter—sliced the jugular vein of the soldier in half, and blood spouted from the wound like a jet spray onto Szabo, who did not seem to notice or mind it. In fact he liked it—because he was too busy making other killing cuts in the soldier's neck, increasing the flow, the only sound that of the soldier gurgling, desperately trying to stop the flow with his hands.

Szabo backed off as Johnson dropped to the earth, shitting his pants just as he did, and still gurgling, still trying to stop the flow, which was now a spurt rather than a spray, but shortly he started to lose strength and went unconscious and then Szabo watched him slowly exsanguinate on the ground, the blood spreading in a shiny bright pool that continued to increase its margins. The smell of the blood and methane rose upward from the soldier.

Szabo looked at the soldiers with glazed eyes. He was smiling. He made no attempt to wipe off the blood that had sprayed all over his chest, a few drops catching his chin.

"Now," he said, "let me ask the question again. What was wrong with today's firefight?"

A black trooper raised his hand.

"Yes?"

"Those motherfuckers got more experience. We're not used to it or something, because it seemed to me people were just firing all over the place but not aiming."

"That's correct! What else?"

The soldier shook his head, but then a tall muscular white soldier raised his hand.

"It seemed to me that we weren't standing our ground. We would fire, then retreat, which made us vulnerable."

"Exactly!" Szabo said. "Exactly."

He paused, looked around.

"And you know what?"

If anyone knew, they weren't making any suggestions.

"We learn from our mistakes, and next time we're going to make sure that the people who go on a mission like this are very experienced. You troops are fine when it comes to taking over a town, or fighting some of the Believer forces. But against a group like these Rebels the odds were stacked against you, even though you had superior numbers."

He paused again.

"But the other important lesson here is that when a commanding officer asks you a question, you must answer it directly and as clearly as possible. Nothing else will do," he said. "There is another issue here that needs to be resolved. Does anyone know what that is?"

No one spoke.

"Well, it's this: there is still a job to be done. We still don't have Rosen. And until we do we are all at great risk. Do you understand that?"

The troops nodded, assented, and in other ways indicated that they understood.

"What I need now," he said, "is two volunteers to go with me and continue the pursuit of Rosen. Anyone?"

The black guy raised his hand and Szabo bade him to come forward. Then from the back of the group a tall, thin trooper raised his hand.

"Come ahead," Szabo said.

The trooper came ahead.

"Your name."

"Atkins."

"And you?" he said to the black trooper.

"Wilson."

"Okay, good."

"And the rest of you are all sentenced to death."

But then he added quickly, "Just kidding," and laughed heartily, some of the troopers laughing along with him. He looked down at the body.

"Clear this away and bury it. I don't want to see a sign of it."

He walked off, leaving a couple of major questions never posed. Why didn't he take the responsibility for the failure of the battle? After all, he was the commander, the one who bore the ultimate responsibility. But no one would ever ask him that question. That is, no one who was desirous of keeping on living.

30

An hour after the firefight with the Rejects, Kindhand and Garrett's Rebels crossed over into Montana and hooked up with over two hundred Rebels, men who had come from all over the country. The occasion was just as festive as when Kindhand and company met the first group of Rebels at the diner, and the news was all good.

They decided to stop for the night. The Rejects would never risk an attack of so formidable a force and, anyway, the chances of finding them were very slight, though Jim, for one, was not too happy that they were still not able to come up with an explanation of how they had been found.

The leader of the large contingent was General Thomas Bradley, who, with his gray hair and handsome features looked like a fifties general from Hollywood Central Casting, confirmed what Kindhand had heard about the plague from Rosen. The plague was now history. Though Bradley had not heard anything about the Believers and the Rejects colliding in a big war, the idea did not surprise him.

"It's been coming," he said. "Doesn't surprise me at all."

Kindhand and Bradley, who as generals were at the same rank in the Rebel army, had much to discuss about the future government of the Rebels, though they certainly had a model: the principles employed by Ben Raines when he formed the SUSA.

Kindhand also introduced Jim and Bev to Bradley, who said: "I understand we'll be losing you, Jim."

"Yeah, Bev and I are going up north and from there who knows? Hopefully, there's a preacher somewhere who could marry us."

"Really?" he said. "How about if you could get married right now?"

"Are you kidding?" Bev asked.

"Not at all. One chief medical officer, Ray Lownbes, is a minister, and I'm sure he'd be glad to marry you. I do agree that it might be difficult finding someone up north."

Bev looked at Jim, and she at him. It was crunch time, and though both were deeply in love with each other the idea of getting married was still scary. It was a big step, something both had dreamed about their whole lives, and if they wanted to, they could get married.

There is, of course, only one thing stronger than fear, and that's love.

"Let's do it, Jim."

"Absolutely," he said. "It's an odd place and time to get married, but that's okay. Just as long as I get you out of circulation!"

Everyone laughed.

"Actually," Bradley said, "this is not the first time that Ray has performed the ceremony in circumstances like these. He's performed at least a half dozen in the ten years that I've known him."

"Good," Jim said.

"So," Bradley said, "do you have a ring?"

Bev stuck out the hand with the ring on her thumb.

"Good. Beautiful ring."

"Thank you."

"How about a best man?" Bradley asked.

Jim looked at Kindhand.

"How about you, Duke?" he said.

"Sure," Duke said. "Be happy and proud to."

"I guess we're going to have to live without a maid of honor. I think any of the troopers here would be reluctant to get into a dress, even if we had one."

"That's okay," Bev said. "I do have a dress for myself."

"You do?" Jim asked.

"Yes, and a white one."

"A white one? Where'd you get that?" Jim asked.

"At one of the houses we stopped at."

"What would ever possess you to take a white dress?"

"I'm optimistic," Bev said. And all the men laughed very hard and appreciatively, including Jim.

"How about you, Jim?" Bev asked. "Are you going to wear a tuxedo?"

"I doubt it. But I will put on clean clothes. How's that?"

"Perfect."

"I'll go get Reverend Lownbes," Bradley said.

"We going to do this right now?" Jim asked.

"No time like the present."

"I have to leave you for a little while," Kindhand said. "I have to get dressed too, and rustle up a band."

"A band?" Bev asked.

"Sure," Kindhand said. "What do you think, this

outfit is cheap? Only the best for our friends Jim and Bev."

Jim and Bev went back to their HumVee, which was parked in a sort of motor pool near the edge of the road.

"Okay," she said, "following tradition, this is the last time I can see you until we're married."

She was about to get up into the HumVee when Jim stepped over and grabbed her by the shoulders.

"May I say something to you?"

"Sure."

"I feel so, so lucky to have found you. I mean who could have predicted in this crazy world that one day I would look under a house and there you would be?"

Bev laughed and looked up at him.

"God," Jim said, "your eyes kill me. I just want to . . . uh, suck you down inside me."

"Suck away."

He leaned down and kissed her with an open mouth, and she responded in kind. Then she pulled away from him.

"Hey, we better stop. We'll never make it to our wedding."

"I wouldn't miss that for the world."

Jim and Bev took bags out of the back of the HumVee. Jim went off into the woods and Bev got into the cab. Reb wasn't there, having previously been taken out and released around where most of the troopers were clustered and who were having great fun with him.

Everything was ready within a half hour. Bradley had decided to become Bev's father for the event to "give her away," so he, too, put on a fresh uniform and wore just a few of the many medals he had been awarded by Ben Raines over the years.

Duke Kindhand followed suit, changing into a fresh uniform, and he did indeed round up a band, two guitarists and a banjo player, who, of course, had their instruments with them.

While all this was going on, there were an unlucky few: the troopers who had to act like pickets in case the Rejects somehow paid them another visit.

Then they were ready. Most of the Rebels had come out to experience this most unusual event. They formed a flanking path in the field, a path that Bev would follow, accompanied by General Bradley, to join Jim and Duke Kindhand.

Jim and Kindhand then waited by the preacher, Ray Lownbes, who had a book from which he would read the passages that would make Jim and Bev one. Lownbes was in religious garb, including a collar.

"How you feeling, Jim?" Kindhand asked, and then looked toward the trooper-flanked path down which Bev would come.

"When I was a little boy I adopted a piece of a blanket that I called my 'blankie,'" Jim said. "And I always held on to it as a security blanket. I wish I had that now."

Kindhand laughed, and before he could say anything else a kind of hush fell over the group and the music started, the two guitars and a banjo playing the familiar "Wedding March," and then Bev, Bradley holding her by her arm, appeared and started to walk toward Jim.

It wasn't a wedding dress, he thought, but it was surely a dress and the first time he had even seen her in one.

He felt his breath go away. He smiled inwardly.

Everyone, he knew, thought of him as a tough guy. It surely wouldn't do to faint!

As Bev approached, Jim saw that she had pinned some local flowers in her hair. That, plus the simple white dress—which had a plunging neckline—was just spectacular, and he thought that of all the beautiful sights he had seen in his life—the mountains and the froth-white rivers and the births of animals and all the rest—nothing could beat this, the image, the magic of this beautiful woman in a white dress, looking at him, in love with him, and he knew what the phrase the "luckiest man alive" meant.

She came up and, released by Bradley, was guided by the preacher to join Jim.

Then the familiar words that preachers and priests had uttered for time immemorial started to be said by the preacher. . . .

"Do you take this woman to be your lawfully wedded wife . . ."

And all the rest, and then it was over and they were kissing, kissing to the cheers of the Rebels, and they walked down the path, the guitars and banjo playing them out, and the battle-hardened veterans of the Rebels waving and wishing them luck, and some of the Rebels had tears in their eyes. They too had loved ones, and a ceremony like this was a cruel yet wonderful reminder of what once was, or still was, but they were not part of. Not now. It was a tremendously moving moment for all.

Later, a number of bottles of wine appeared, lots of dancing was done—including, to the great amusement of all, Rebels with Rebels, and many of the Rebels also danced with Bev. It had been a long, long time since many of them had been with a woman, and to be close like this was just wonderful.

Then tents were set up and the night petered out and Jim looked at Bev and said, "Well, while you were dancing with everyone I set up our honeymoon tent."

"Honeymoon tent?"

"Sure. You perhaps expected a condo?"

Bev laughed hard, the laughter going deep inside her.

"Actually," Jim said, "I set it up in a more private area of the forest so that, well, we could have more privacy."

"I like that," Bev said. "The idea of being alone with you has merit."

"Tell me about it."

Jim and Bev bade everyone good night. As arranged, they were to leave in the morning, just heading north. The troop was scheduled to get up at dawn and start to look for a base camp with Jim as their guide.

Jim had set the tent up perhaps seventy yards from the other Rebels so it would ensure plenty of privacy. For the occasion he had left all his weapons in the tent, and gathered up Bev's, which she had left in the HumVee before she left for the wedding ceremony.

Five minutes after they told everyone good night, they were in the tent, the flap fastened.

Inside, Bev didn't say a word. She was standing up, and then she said. "Undress me."

Jim kissed her softly on the mouth and then turned her around. The back of the dress was fastened by a few buttons on top, and he unfastened these, then reached down and grasped the dress by the hem and slowly peeled it off her.

"You smell wonderful," he said.

Bev did not respond.

Under the dress she had a brassiere and panties and he unlaced the back of the brassier, her breasts free, but so firm that they hardly sagged at all.

He needed to keep calm, but it was very difficult. Bev could hear his breathing coming in a slightly labored way. Then he reached down and peeled her panties off, his hands brushing against her buttocks as he did. His breathing got more labored.

Then she was nude.

"Now," she said, "let me undress you."

It was Jim's turn: he couldn't talk too well either.

Slowly, deliberately, she unbuttoned his shirt, then pulled down his pants and then his underwear.

He was already almost fully erect and when she touched his penis he instantly became as a hard as a rock.

Then, very carefully, they knelt and lay down, kissing and hugging and fondling, being very careful to satisfy each other in the way they approached and then engaged in intercourse.

After the first coupling had been completed, they rested, but they both knew that this was going to be a long, wonderful night.

They lay side by side silently for a while, and then Jim said: "Happy wedding day, Mrs. LaDoux."

"Oh, Jim, I so love the sound of that."

"So do I," Jim said. "So do I."

31

Szabo explained the plan to the two volunteers, Wilson, the black guy, and Atkins, as they sped down the highway in a black jeep. Wilson was driving.

"Obviously," he said, "this pipsqueak has taken off someplace. What we have to do is find out where that someplace is.

"What we have to do is grab one of the Rebels and, shall we say, persuade him to give us that information? It's my guess that everyone will know. Once we get the information, we will find him—then terminate him and anyone else who knows our inner working. And I got everything we need when we dropped back to the compound."

Wilson and the other soldier had questions about Szabo's plan, but they did not want to discuss it. They were worried that discussion might be translated by Szabo into criticism. That could be dangerous, not so much on the way to the job as coming back.

The main question, of course, was how he planned to, in effect, kidnap one of the Rebels with all the other Rebels around. And what were they going to do? Just drive into camp, grab someone, and take off?

The *how* was shortly to be answered.

As they drove, Szabo had the portable monitor on

his lap, and he watched it intently, watching the blue and red dots get closer and closer. It was a short drive, and Szabo had all the equipment he needed on board.

"We're getting close," he said. "I would say we're no more than five miles away. Go until I tell you to stop, then find a place where we can turn off into the woods."

"Yes, sir," said Wilson.

They sat in silence for the next mile, the only real sounds that of the jeep moving along the narrow asphalt road and the steady blinking of the monitor on the UGPS. Szabo checked his watch: 0300. They should have plenty of time to complete their mission before dawn.

Szabo kept close watch on the monitor, and gradually the transmitters's beacon and his location got to the point where they were almost merging. Now Szabo started to look for a spot in ernest.

"Slow down," he said. "I'm looking for a spot to pull in to. And douse the headlights; running lights only."

"Yes, sir."

The driver slowed the jeep to about twenty-five. Then up to the left they spotted what looked like an opening.

"In there," Szabo said, "in there."

Wilson pulled the jeep into an open area of the woods and parked.

"Lights out," Szabo said. He checked his watch: 0334.

He got out of the vehicle. The moon was three-quarters full, but if you stood in the woods it was, because of the canopy of tree branches above, like standing in a darkened room. It was only when you were in an open area that the moonlight was any good at helping you find your way. But there was no open area here, just dense woods, very little natural light.

But Szabo was prepared, in more ways than one.

"Okay," he said when the two soldiers had exited the jeep. "Take off your clothing."

He noticed a moment's hesitation.

"No," he said, a smile on his face, "I'm not a fag. I have uniforms for both of you. Rebel uniforms, or something approximating them, as well as for myself. We're going into the lion's den dressed not as lambs but lions."

"Great idea," Atkins said.

"That's not the only one I have," Szabo said.

Szabo went to the back of the jeep and extracted a suitcase. He opened it up and handed Wilson and Atkins uniforms then took out one for himself. He had thought of perhaps eliminating himself from the raid because of his distinctive physical appearance. Not many soldiers were of his size and musculature, and any of the Rebels seeing him would automatically question who he was.

But he had another thought. When a picket stopped him—and it was likely that one would—all he had to do was to say that he was coming in from another area to join the others. That might be questioned, but that was fine. All he needed was enough time to get close to the picket or pickets, and then he would have a chance to kill him—or them—quickly and silently. Now, he thought, he would show the volunteers how to kill, and with what. Silently, so as not to alert the other Rebels.

He reached down into a bag and withdrew three small spray containers.

"This is for close-quarter combat," he said, "such as for use on the picket. It's small enough to store in your jacket pocket. If we spot someone we want to terminate quickly and silently, you arm the can by taking it out and twisting the nozzle 180 degrees toward the front. To use it, just point it a short way from the picket's face and press the plunger. Its contents will spray out and kill the picket instantly."

"Why?" Wilson asked. "What's in it?"

"Cyanide spray. Very effective at close range. But be sure not to do it if the wind is blowing your way!"

Wilson and Atkins did not laugh.

"Ideally," Szabo said, "we will not have to kill the picket. In fact, we can take him with us. And this will allow us to do that."

To each, he handed a hypodermic needle.

"You've been trained to use these. Just jab and press. Unconsciousness comes almost instantly."

"Are we taking guns with us?" Wilson asked.

"Do bears defecate in the woods? Absolutely, AK-47s and stun grenades, which, if we're pursued by a force, will come in handy. Also take your sidearm."

With that, Szabo handed each of the men four stun grenades. Both men had been extensively trained in the use of grenades, and were happy to have them. They had proved their worth down through the years. While their detonation produced few offensive fragments, the flash, noise, and shrapnel tended to stun, blind, and generally bewilder the enemy. They had a tried-and-true track record in situations where the taking of prisoners was the objective, or in situations where hostages were involved. They were unparalleled for creating confusion and sheer terror.

Szabo was well aware that this assault assumed that Rosen had left the Rebel force for some reason.

Maybe he hadn't. Maybe he was still among them. Then what? Szabo didn't know. But he knew that he would figure out something. That's what great commanders did. They solved problems.

And what about the bitch? There was no way to get her. That would come on another day, and he had something very special planned for her. Something, in a way, worse than death.

Finally, Szabo distributed the night-vision equipment.

"Let's put it on now," he said.

The men put the night-vision equipment on their faces, which tended to make them look like aliens. But, abruptly, the world they were in was not one of darkness but of light. While not as good as a cat's eyes in darkness, they were very good.

"Okay," Szabo finally said, "everybody ready?"

"Yes, sir," they said together.

"Okay, let's go get ourselves a punk."

The three started out, Szabo leading the way, the trees easily avoided bumping into thanks to the illuminated green world created by the night-vision equipment.

Szabo also brought along the UGPS system, which he checked as he went. They were so close, he thought, that the blinking signals were almost coming as one.

32

Before she and Jim had gone to bed, they drank their own fair share of wine, and when she awakened with the call of nature, it was thanks to the wine. One of the reasons Jim had set up the tent beyond the pickets was anticipating such an event. It was one thing for him to get up and take a whiz in front of another guy; it was quite another for Bev to do it. She needed privacy. And, of course, they both needed privacy for their lovemaking.

When Bev felt the call of nature and checked the digital watch she was wearing she saw that it was a little after 3:30. She was a little tired, but before she went outside she knew that she had to get some clothing on, particularly shoes. Rattlesnakes didn't care if you were on your honeymoon. They would be happy to make it short-lived if you got in their way.

She was just wearing panties, so she put on a shirt and pulled on some denim pants and the lace-up boots she had found, but she made no attempt to lace them up. It was a little windy and, she knew, a little chilly outside—what night, she thought, in this section of the country wasn't a little chilly?—but she figured she knew she'd be back very quickly. Just find a spot where she could conceal herself from any picket who could possibly see her, slip her pants down, go to the bathroom, and return.

Dressed, she opened the flap of the tent. She did not know if Jim was awake—he had incredible hearing—but he didn't say anything to her as she slipped out of the opening. The wine, she thought, was probably having some sort of effect on him.

The tent was in the woods, but most of the trees in the area were a little on the narrow side. Bev wanted to find a fairly thick one. She walked fifteen to twenty yards and then found one. She slipped off her denims and squatted.

Szabo, Wilson, and Atkins had made their way very carefully through the forest, getting closer and closer to where Szabo now knew the Rebel camp was. It shouldn't be long, he thought, before he encountered a picket. Or, to put that another way, the picket encountered him.

Szabo felt totally alive, totally unafraid, like a lion or tiger or panther stalking prey. Never mind that the prey was just as well armed, in a sense, as Szabo was. To him someone he was stalking was prey and he felt all-powerful and absolutely sure that he would succeed.

As they went, the scanned the woods, the world continuing to have its green cast.

At one point, Szabo put the UGPS away. He knew where he was; he knew where the enemy was. The time of location was past. The time of confrontation was here.

He and the two soldiers walked slowly and carefully, trying not to make excessive noise. Szabo knew that the forest was never quiet, so he was not afraid of making some noise. If any of the Rebel pickets heard anything they would assume that it was made by some sort of animal. Szabo smiled. In a sense, it was.

There was a slight wind, and occasionally he and his team would hear a sound of something unidentifiable.

Then, quite abruptly, he felt a hand on his shoulder and looked. Wilson was pointing to his left.

Szabo turned his head. Not twenty yards away someone was making their way through the woods. The person was far too shapely to be a man. It wasn't. It was a woman.

The bitch. He could not believe how lucky he was.

Instantly, he formulated a plan. He would do the same thing that he had expected to do with the picket. He motioned to the other two to come with him.

He whispered in one of their ears, "She can't see me. She knows me. Talk to her as if you're two Rebels. Get close enough to stick her. Here. She cannot make a sound!" Szabo slipped behind a tree and watched. By this time, Bev was squatting, in the middle of taking a whiz.

"Sorry," Wilson said, "I didn't see you."

Bev was startled but did not make any untoward noise.

Wilson turned away, hiding his eyes, and so did Atkins.

"Oh," Bev said, "that's okay."

"We're looking for the main force of Rebels." They stood nearby, shielding her from their eyes. Then she was finished. She came up to them.

"Oh, down that way," she said, pointing.

Then, Wilson grabbed her by the mouth and

Atkins plunged the needle into her neck. A ninjutsu move flashed to her mind, she started to whirl, but only in her mind. Her body was not working. And then she was unconscious.

Szabo came out from behind the tree. Bev was being supported by Atkins and Wilson.

Szabo picked her up as if she weighed nothing and place her on one of his massive shoulders as if she were a sack of potatoes.

They went back to where the night-vision equipment was and donned it. Then they started to move quickly away. As they went, Szabo thought: *If she knows where Rosen is, we will too.*

33

Jim awakened about 5:00 A.M. and automatically reached across to feel for Bev.

She wasn't there.

He wondered where she was. Maybe gone to the same place he was about to go—to take a leak.

He went out of the tent and took a few steps and took a leak, the wine from the night before seeming to pour out of him endlessly.

He looked around. The first rays of light were starting to penetrate the forest.

Where could she be?

"Bev," he called, "where are you, honey?"

No answer.

That was very, very odd.

He called her name again. No response.

Now a tickle of fear started deep in his gut and, used to paying attention to such signals, he listened.

He went back into the tent and found a flashlight and played the light over the equipment in the tent. Her white dress was folded neatly and on a blanket, the same spot she had placed it the night before. Her boots were gone, and so were the denim pants she had worn before putting on the white wedding dress.

Then he saw something that disturbed him. Her brassiere. If she was getting fully dressed she would have that on. If she was just going outside to take a leak, she would have heard him when he called to her.

He went outside again, and this time used the flashlight to scan the area. As far as he could tell in the limited light, there was no sign that she was around.

He walked deeper into the woods, calling her name, the light probing the darkness.

But there was no answer, and by the time he returned to the tent there was sufficient light so that he could see much better, but Bev was still nowhere in sight, and there was no sign of her.

He realized that he had been looking for her for twenty minutes.

Could she have gone somewhere?

Where?

He trotted back to the base camp. It was a beehive of activity, many of the Rebels packing up their gear, loading the trucks. Duke Kindhand was one of them. Jim went over. Kindhand could see the concern in his face.

"What's up? Jim?" he asked.

"I can't find Bev."

"What happened?"

Jim explained how he had made a small search for her.

"You want me to get a team together to look for her?" Kindhand asked.

Jim was about to say yes when he realized that he might have an even better resource.

"Maybe I can use Reb," he said. "He's part German shepherd. Maybe—"

"Good idea," Kindhand said. "Let's do that.

Reb, as it happened, had already been fed and

walked by one of the Rebels, and he started wagging his tail furiously when he saw Jim. Jim leaned down and petted him.

"Hey, Reb," he said. "I need a favor. Okay, boy?"

Reb's tail continued to beat even more furiously. The Rebel who had walked Reb that morning came over and gave Jim his leash, and then Jim, accompanied by Kindhand, headed back to where Jim's tent was, Reb leading the way.

When they got to the tent, Jim went inside and brought out the bra. At this point he wasn't embarrassed. Whatever worked was best.

Reb sniffed the bra and immediately started to sniff around. He headed back into the tent, sniffed around, then burst out. Jim had to hold the leash tight or he would have pulled it out of his hand.

But he didn't stop there. He was, Jim could tell, on the scent—Bev's scent—and he moved rapidly across the forest floor. The farther they went from their tent, the worse it was, Jim thought. But he had to keep cool, think clearly. And maybe there was some reason why she had walked—or run—this way out of the forest.

Maybe, he thought, she encountered an animal, say a grizzly. She didn't know that the best way to handle that situation was to stand your ground, but avoid eye contact. Maybe she didn't . . . and then Jim thought of something that he remembered Ben Raines had said: "Do not take counsel of your own fears." Absolutely. Suspend the functioning of the imagination.

Reb had gone at least a half mile when he abruptly made a left and pulled Jim, Kindhand following, to the edge of the road, and then onto the road. And then Reb started to go around in circles. He seemed a little confused.

But Jim knew what was going on. He had lost the trail.

Jim looked down, trying to pick up a hint of what might have happened, and on the other side of the road he found something that enabled him to put together a likely scenario.

"She got into a vehicle here," he said, "and she was heading west. Look at the edge of the road. I'd say the vehicle backed up here, then headed east."

"Which means that she was taken," Kindhand said.

Jim fought the sadness and despair and fear. He had to stay outside it all. That was the best thing he could do.

"The question is, who?" Kindhand said.

"I know," Jim said. "I think you do too."

Kindhand nodded. "Szabo," he said quietly.

Jim nodded, and he thought: of all the people in the world, Szabo was the worst.

"Why? I wonder," Kindhand said.

"He was after her," Jim said. "She and her friend Ida were trying to start up some religion around here."

"Where's Ida?" Kindhand said.

"Dead," Jim said. "The Rejects caught and hung her."

"Well, I think there's a good chance we know where he's taken her."

Jim nodded.

He also knew it was their only chance.

34

Alex Szabo looked at himself in the mirror. His nose, normally thin and well formed, was a blob of red and purple. He knew it was broken, this thanks to the bitch in the other room. He had underestimated her, and so had Wilson and Atkins. They had not restrained her, and when she had regained consciousness, inside the compound, she had suddenly and abruptly become a whirling dervish, a person with consummate skill at karate or something, who gave Wilson a fractured skull, Atkins a crushed spleen, and Szabo a broken nose. Szabo had little doubt that if she had not been bent on escape she could have killed him with her bare hands.

Fortunately, she had bolted out of the room and made it through two other rooms when she was overwhelmed by guards—who also took some big hits.

Whatever, now he had her, and she would yield the information on Rosen. First, he had to soften her a bit. They had tied her facedown on a large table and spread her legs and arms, and then to get the torture going he and four other Rejects had sodomized her to the point of her bleeding, something that Szabo had very much enjoyed doing, and very much enjoyed watching, particularly before the fourth assault when alcohol had been poured on her—actually into her—and she had screamed in agony.

Now, Szabo thought, she was ready. If she didn't talk he was prepared to work on her with a stick two feet long.

What also worked with most people was threats. Threats to remove fingers, limbs, genitalia. That got people talking pretty quick.

He didn't know exactly what he would do. He would play it by ear. Maybe with her ear!

Whatever, he had to move pretty fast. The longer Rosen was free, the greater the danger. He had to be neutralized. Just had to.

Szabo walked into the room and heard her say something. A single word.

"Jim."

"Who's Jim?" Szabo asked.

Bev did not answer.

"I would assume," he said, "that you were asking that wonderful God of yours for help. Is this Jim greater than your God? If he is, I'd certainly like to meet him."

He went over and squeezed her behind.

"Boy, you got one of the best booties I've ever seen. But it looks like it's taken a turn for the worst."

He paused. He walked around and sat down in a chair so his face was close to hers. Her eyes were red from crying and her face was blotchy with red welts and black and blue marks where the guards had beaten her into submission.

"I want to know something from you," Szabo said, "but first I want to ask you again: where is this God you were trying to spread around? Where is He now that you need Him so much?"

Her lips moved, and then he managed to hear

something she said in a half whisper. "He's right here, right here in the room with me."

Szabo stood up. He wanted very much to kill her, but he needed to know the answer to the other question:

"Where is that little pipsqueak of a reporter for the *Rolling Stone?* Where did he go?"

"I don't know," Bev said.

"You did see him?"

"Yes. He was with us for a while. He told us the whole story of how he hoodwinked you."

Again, Szabo wanted to kill her right then and there. But that would be stupid.

"What happened to him?"

"One day he decided to leave," Bev said.

"Why?"

"He was afraid of you. Afraid you would catch up to him." She paused. "Why are you so afraid of him?"

"I'm not afraid of him. I want to kill him."

"No," Bev said, "you're afraid."

"You know?" he said. "You got a lot of grit in you, and I'm going to surprise you by saying, first, that I believe you. I don't think you know where Rosen is."

Bev said nothing.

"Isn't that surprising, that I believe you?"

She said nothing.

"But the second surprise is one you're really going to like."

Again, silence.

"I'm going to let you live," he said. "Isn't that surprising? After all, I had your pregnant friend hung from a tree, so this has to be a surprise."

"Thanks, Santa."

"The thing is, I want you to be a walking advertisement that belief in God means nothing. That God exists only in your head, and that He couldn't help you when you needed Him most."

Szabo stood up and as he walked away he said: "Yes, I want you to be a walking advertisement for that."

Inside her head, Bev thought of Jim, and then she thought of God. *Please, God,* she said, *give me the strength to endure this. Or—I'm so sorry, Jim—take me home, Jesus, take me home to your kingdom of light and love. Take me home, or let me endure.*

Szabo returned. He had some sort of brown bottle in his hand, filled with a liquid.

He must have pressed a button of some sort, because a bunch of soldiers came into the room.

"Turn this messenger of God over," he said, "so Jesus can see her lovely face."

Bev did not put up resistance as the bonds holding her arms and legs to the table were unfastened. She was turned over and retied.

"What I'm holding here is hydrochloric acid," he said. "Now I want you to be an ad for me, so to do this I have to, shall we say, modify you a bit? And there's nothing like hydrochloric acid for that."

He approached her. She turned her mind inward, to nestle herself like a little child in God's embrace. But God did not shut down her earthly senses, and the Rejects heard again a shriek of agony, and the premier felt his genitalia engorge with blood.

35

Kindhand and Jim, in the lead vehicle, raced east along the road, the road that they speculated Alex Szabo had earlier that morning traveled on and snatched Bev. Both men left unspoken that if Szabo had taken Bev, it might already be too late. He might have killed her. But the world was full of possibilities, and both men followed the brilliant philosophy uttered by a baseball player from long ago named Yogi Berra: "It ain't over till it's over."

Jim was filled with focused rage. Not only was he not taking counsel of his fears, but they were not a factor in what he was doing. There was no fear, just the burning need to produce results, to get Bev safely back in his arms.

If . . . if Szabo had taken her. If he hadn't, Jim didn't know what his next step would be. But, as someone once said, "Destiny plays by its own rules." And Jim was very shortly to find out how true that statement was.

36

Twenty-four hours earlier, and in some cases before that, Believers in the camps from all over the country, but mostly clustered in the Northwest, prepared for the invasion of the Rejects, an invasion made possible because of the intel supplied to them by Morty Rosen.

The hours since it had been decided to launch what for the Believers was their own D-day had been spent gathering men and materials. A number of the Reject camps were built into mountains where there were tunnels; against these the Believers planned to employ their own modern-day "tunnel rats." In other cases, compounds were totally aboveground and tunnel rats were not required. All this information Rosen had furnished.

But at all Believer installations, one thing was basically the same, as reflected in the headquarters base. In the middle of the night, a mass of men knelt in an open field and importuned Jesus Christ to, on this day, help them. Their leader, Father McAulliffe, stood on top of an SUV, his voice patched through to all other Believer forces.

"On this day," he said, "please to God let us banish from the land the infidels, the devil-worshipping hordes that have infested our lands. Let us cleanse them from our midst, and drive them to the hell from whence they came so our land is once again free and peaceful and we may make it a suitable place to worship you, dear Jesus.

"And grant, too, safety to the Christian soldiers who are now about to enter upon the field of battle and engage in this conflict in your name, dear Jesus. Let them return safe and sound from this battle this day. And to those who will not come back, to those who will die on the field of battle, let them enter through the gates of heaven and into your loving arms forever."

And he finished, his voice thrumming with emotion: "Dear Jesus, we ask this of you in your most holy name, who shed your blood so that we might live."

And then he paused and spoke softly to the men.

"And remember this, my dear soldiers in Christ, what we do this day will echo in eternity! Go with God!"

The soldiers, cheering wildly, stood and started to board their vehicles, making up, counting all the other vehicles and men in all the other Believer camps, the largest Believer force that had ever been assembled.

And, true to his promise, Father McAulliffe had agreed to allow Morty Rosen, in helmet and wearing body armor, and with bodyguards, to ride in the lead vehicle of the force, which was theoretically the most dangerous position, but which, Rosen knew, would give him the best possible view and, of course, draw in his readers with the emotion of it all. He was not reporting from the ass end of this convoy, but from the head.

Morty knew he was on his way to a Pulitzer, a slam dunk if there ever was one.

37

The Rebel convoy rounded the turn that, they knew, had to be close to where the Rejects were when they got a surprise—and almost engaged in a totally unscheduled firefight.

The woods were teeming with khaki-uniformed Believers, and they both leveled their guns at one another, but didn't fire. Jim had had the presence of mind to hold up his hand.

One of the Believers, a tall, muscular man with the characteristic beard, came over, gun still at the ready.

"Who are you?"

"We're a Rebel convoy," Kindhand said. "Where's you leader?"

The Believers didn't know quite what to do.

"Better get him," Jim said. "We got a volatile situation here. Don't set it off."

The Believer by this time was backed by innumerable other Believers, all positioned in the woods and with guns facing the Rebels. And by this time, too, all the Rebels had gotten off the long line of trucks and filtered into the woods. It was, indeed, a volatile situation. One shot could ignite a firestorm of bullets, blood, and death.

A group of the Believers went off to get someone.

A minute later, the leader of the Believers, Raymond Dawson, approached. And with him was none other than Morty Rosen.

"Hey, Jim," Rosen called out, "I heard you were in the neighborhood."

"What are you doing here?" Jim asked. But now he and Kindhand knew where Rosen had gone when he left the Rebel camp.

"I'm being a good reporter," Morty said. "This is D-day for the Believers—all across America."

How, Jim wondered, and why? Because, he thought, Rosen must have given the Believers some very valuable intel. Coincidence had its limits.

Raymond Dawson spoke.

"My name is Raymond Dawson. I'm commander in chief of military ops. Why are you here, sir?" he asked.

"Because," Kindhand said, "we suspect that the leader of the Rejects has kidnapped Jim's wife."

Dawson nodded.

"Are you Christians?"

"Sure," Kindhand said.

"Then perhaps you and your force would like to join us in wiping this scourge from the face of the earth."

Jim and Kindhand looked at each other.

"Yes," Kindhand said, "that would be fine."

Dawson nodded. He looked at Kindhand.

"You are the commander?"

"Yes."

"Let me show you our plan and how you can integrate your force into ours."

Kindhand took the walkie-talkie off his belt.

Jim thought that maybe, during the fight, he could somehow slip inside Compound W.

The walkie-talkie crackled.

"General Garrett?"

"Yes, sir."

"Can you come up to the command vehicle? Something I need you to see—and hear."

When Garrett arrived, Dawson explained his plan. He had formulated a two-pronged offensive against the Rejects. One, called Operation Under, would be directed at emplacements in the tunnels and caves, whereas the other would be an offense against the forces they had in the open. No prisoners were to be taken. It was to be a battle, on both sides, to the death.

Dawson made a suggestion: "I think your forces should work with mine on the above-land aspect of the invasion. Tunnel work requires very specialized training."

"We have people who have worked tunnels," Kindhand said, "but I understand where you're coming from. Fine."

The explanation took only fifteen minutes, in great part because Dawson realized that he was dealing with a very experienced force.

Then Dawson got what could only be described as a demented glint in his eyes and said into his radio, which would go directly to commanders set to strike at other Reject compounds: "Let's win one for Jesus!"

The Believers and Rebels filtered through the woods toward the mountain emplacements of the Rejects and then they were close enough—covering fire, including mortars and RPGs, was laid into the mountain to allow Operation Clean-out, the tunnel offensive.

Dawson, like Ben Raines, was another general who believed in preparation. As he once said, "It's good for preparing a house for painting and a battle." Two days earlier, recon teams, taking great care not to be exposed, had scoured the country to find shafts leading to tunnels. The shafts were usually marked by mounds of earth. Rosen's intel had said that the tunnels themselves were typically three feet high but could be much larger. The shafts that led down to them were as much as a hundred feet deep, but many were shorter than that.

Typically, too, Believer recon teams had learned that shaft entries were usually fifteen to twenty feet apart.

Now, simultaneously, the covering fire allowing it, Dawson, leading the assault on the mountain, as silently as possible approached the shaft entries, twenty-five in all, and first determined the depth of the shafts. This they did with mirrors, utilizing the sunlight to reflect light into the shaft so they could see what was there.

Then concussion grenades were dropped in to clear the area for the major explosive charges, which would follow. One after the other their muffled concussive blasts were followed by screaming, like people yelling underwater, and then the major charges, TCV-2.5 and TC-6.1 Italian antitank mines, were lowered to the bottom of the shaft. Then a second charge of high-explosive was lowered and the detonation cord linked to a standard hand-grenade fuse. The firing assembly would be locked in near the mouth of the shaft, a procedure that took only three minutes. When they were ready, the ring was pulled on the firing assembly, the troops first standing back seven or eight yards from the mouth of the shaft because when the charges went off, rocks and debris were blasted out of the hole at a velocity that could take your head off.

The effect was savage. Dawson, who was very knowledgeable about shafts and tunnels, knew that a double charge would work in concert like a left, right punch combination. The top charge went off a fraction of a second before the bottom charge. This resulted in the shaft being plugged with gases, and when the bottom charge went off the shock waves from them would push back down and against the sides of both shafts and tunnels, creating a deadly pressure between the two charges that Dawson knew was called the "stereophonic effect."

In a few cases, he ratcheted up this effect into something known as the "quadraphonic effect" by setting up charges in adjoining shafts for simultaneous exploding. When this was done even more pressure was created.

The explosions were universally followed by sounds that were music to Dawson's ears: screams of agony and faint, pitiful cries for help. But Dawson and his aides knew that anyone within reasonable proximity to the explosions was dead.

The next step was to enter the shafts, but before doing this a procedure was followed. First, the dust was allowed to settle so that they could see if it was safe for a team to enter. Any shaft could be rappelled down or entered by ladder depending on height. But first a nontoxic smoke pot was dropped into the shaft. If the smoke cleared, it meant that the ventilation system was working. Indeed, as the troops went down, Dawson received reports that the vent system was excellent, which meant that some tunnels were intact and that search teams could enter without masks. Dawson was also well aware that the methods he used would result in some people being buried alive. He didn't give it a second thought. As long as they were dead was all that mattered to him.

Dawson dispatched three- or four-man search teams. They were lowered into the shafts, and two of the men would search one way; the other two would make sure they were not ambushed from behind.

The lead searcher had a line tied to his leg. If he found enemy material, he tied the line to it and the others could drag it out—and up, perhaps. Also, if the lead was shot, the other team members could use the line to drag him out without being in harm's way themselves.

The searchers were equipped with entrenching tools, knives, grenades, pistols, and assault rifles—with flashlights taped to the fore stocks—the assault rifles were loaded with tracer ammunition.

As it happened, two of the searchers were shot, but neither fatally, and the Rejects who had shot them were shot back—fatally.

Dawson's experience showed. From his days working in tunnels of Bosnia, he had also used a weapon that he adopted for this assault using what Russians used during their war in Afghanistan. These were SM signal mines. He used these in eighteen of the twenty tunnels he had discovered, and it was basically a psychological weapon that would stun the Rejects temporarily and made them easy targets. The SM was essentially a Roman candle that fired a series of green, white, and red signals from five to twenty yards. Originally it was a booby trap with a trip-wire release, which let loose a sirenlike sound at the same time. Dawson had armed his troops with three to six signal mines taped together. They could be held by hand, ignited, and tossed into the tunnel. The result was screams of sirens, a brilliant flash of light, and a starburst of signal stars. The tunnel was filled with this cacophony of sound and light for nine seconds, the stars bouncing off walls like tracer bullets. In every case, when the smoke cleared, Believer searches found the felled Rejects covering their eyes with their hands, which made them proverbial ducks in a shooting gallery.

Dawson had not used flamethrowers that much and he thought them ideally suited for clearing tunnels without collapsing them as explosives would, but he found this, at first, a hazardous tactic.

They used a soviet-made RPO. A flamethrower, which had a maximum effective range of six hundred meters, a minimum of twenty.

At first, the flame was fired into the mouth of a shaft to clear anyone around it, but when the first Believer trooper stuck his head over the open shaft he was greeted by someone shooting an AK-47 wherein the bullet went through his forehead and exited at the rear, taking a half-dollar-size circle of brain and bone matter with it, splattering his fellow troopers.

To counter this, grenades were thrown down the shaft, clearing it, and then an aide to Dawson came up with a quick, clever way to use the flamethrower.

First, the RPO-A flamethrower was locked and loaded with a thermo-baric round, then two lines were tied to it and it was lowered into the shaft until it reached the tunnel, with another line tied to the trigger mechanism. When the Believers were sure the flamethrower was pointing toward the tunnel, the trigger was pulled. This was done in four tunnels and in each the correct direction was indicated by the screams of agony that ensued.

Dawson calculated that the chaos created in the tunnels would make some of the Rejects go deeper into the tunnels—some went on for miles—but most would make a mass and quick exodus out the main entrance of the tunnel. And, he told his troops, they would be waiting, but they were not to fire until the commanding officer gave them the signal, this because they wanted to make sure that the maximum number was exposed to fire before they fired.

Almost all the Rebel troops as well as a mass of Believers waited by the entrance—and Dawson was right. Over six hundred Reject troops poured out of the mouth of the cave and when it looked like the maximum had emerged the signal was given and they were cut down in a withering cross fire of assault rifle fire, grenades, and RPGs.

Some Rejects returned fire but it was ineffectual. Within minutes, the gray-uniformed six hundred, their uniforms bathed in blood, were lying dead or dying, and then a Believer death squad roamed among them, using .45s to shoot in the head any of the soldiers who showed any signs of life. Said one of the Believer troopers: "I was too young to be at Little Big Horn. But I know how Custer must have felt."

The aboveground assault, Operation Over, was led by Raymond Dawson's twin, Brian. Like his brother, Brian was a small, wiry man with intense blue eyes and as hard as nails (Someone once said of him he was small like a finishing nail but as hard as a railroad spike). With his brother, he had devised plans for making the aboveground assault, and it was decided, after extensive recon, that the key to the operation was snipers. As recon revealed, many of the Rejects were dug in on the mountainside and manned both mortars and machine guns. Also, anyone trying to get through the valley to their base camp, which was usually in it, would have great difficulty, because not only did they have mortar and machine-gun emplacements but their troops were free-ranging, with access to the natural cover of the mountains. Any troops trying to overrun them would be reduced, in short order, to hamburger meat.

Brian Dawson knew that his specific background was going to serve him very well. Two years earlier, he had started to select from the ranks sharpshooters, people who could qualify as snipers, individuals with eyes likes hawks and capable of great concentration.

He was certainly qualified as a teacher. In Iraq, at the turn of the century, he had made an unconfirmed kill, a chest shot, of the driver of an enemy resupply truck. If it had been confirmed, which it had not though it had occurred, it would be a new record for the longest shot made by a military sniper in combat, which was 2,500 yards or about 2,250 meters, held by Sergeant Carlos Hathcock, a marine, a feared sniper in Vietnam near Duck Pho, South Vietnam, in January 1967, with a Browning .50 HMG mounting an eight-power telescopic sight. Dawson's shot had been made with a Canadian-made McMillan .50 sniper rifle with a twenty-power compact spotting scope.

But, he discovered, it was not that easy to assemble a team. It was one thing to kill someone in the course of combat. It was quite another to lie six hundred yards away but bring a man's head so close by adjusting the scope that you could see the hair in his ears, and then squeeze off a shot and watch the head explode in a welter of bright red.

Four of the candidates for sniper quit before they got deeply into it after hearing Dawson describe what it was like.

"You may be far away from your target," he said, "but the scope brings you up close."

Some of the people disliked the idea of going up a mountain on foot after the enemy, while others felt heroic, being a doer, not a watcher. And by the time you graduated from Dawson's sniper school you could, as he said, "hole a target at seven hundred meters."

Dawson told them worrying about targets was a "terminal disease" for a sniper. "In one day," he said, "in Iraq Two, I killed seven of Hussein's private guards and also turned my scope on a lovely young woman—who was holding an AK-47. I watched her face go away in the scope.

"On the other hand, here is a chance to make a visible difference in the war between the Rejects and Believers. Every time you kill a Reject you know that that's one Reject who won't be able to end the life of a Believer.

"You can't care," he said. "Caring is for your brother."

In the two years he had been doing it he'd trained over a hundred snipers and organized them into a deadly fighting machine. Now they were ready.

The fight on the ground was much fiercer than the fight in the tunnels, but eventually they were neutralized, all killed, mostly because of the work of the snipers, who neutralized all Reject mortar and machine-gun emplacements.

Some of the Rejects gave up, exiting their foxholes and bunkers with hands raised. Snipers cut them down as they did. The order of the day was no survivors, and they followed it.

Some Rejects deserted, and they were not pursued.

Finally, just one hour after the battle started, the

Dawson brothers looked out on a landscape filled with bodies, puffs of smoke drifting across the beautiful wilderness.

They had won. Dawson contacted the other attack forces, listened intently, and then announced to the troops who were standing around, "Here is a message from Father McAulliffe. Victory is ours. This day Jesus Christ our Lord and Savior has seen fit to give us a victory. All the Rejects are being driven from the land."

The Believers cheered and shouted hysterically, pumping their weapons toward the sky.

Many of the Rebels were happy too, but some were not, because they knew why they were here. To try to save the life of a brother's wife.

Kindhand, who was standing around among a group of Rebels, asked: "Where's Jim?"

No one seemed to know.

Then a familiar voice came from the back of the group and Morty Rosen pushed his way through.

"I saw him," he said. "All through this he looked like he wanted to get into the compound. But I just saw him again. He was alone. He was heading into the mouth of the tunnel."

He paused, puzzled, then asked, "Did they nail Szabo?"

"I don't know," Kindhand said. "There's a lot of dead in the tunnels."

Then Kindhand left the group, and a couple of the Rebels went with him. He headed for the cave. There were few times in his life that he wanted something as badly as this, and that was that Bev LaDoux would be still alive.

38

Jim entered the Reject compound. He was armed with his SEAL knife and a Glock, fully loaded, and he was carrying it but he was beyond caring for this own personal safety. At some point in his life, he had come to realize that there were some things worth dying for, and once you accepted that, then, though you might be afraid to die, you were not so crippled with fear that you couldn't proceed.

He did not really expect to encounter anyone. They were likely long gone through the tunnels. And Szabo. Where could he be? He could be dead, but every instinct in Jim said that he wouldn't be. People like Szabo live. Other people die.

Jim really only cared about one thing. Finding Bev. He did not want to face it, but he knew he had to: it was highly likely she was dead. Szabo had killed her friend Ida. Why not her?

But if there was a chance that she was alive, even half alive, he did not want to let that go.

He thought about Bev. Oh, she was beautiful all right, and she had a figure like a movie star, but how beautiful was she inside? Exquisite. Like her father, who had died, she had put aside her fears and tried to be a missionary in this land that had become so unholy. No, Jim had never been religious, but he recognized how beautiful spirituality could be.

Now he stopped and uttered a prayer, a prayer to the God that she believed in to help him find her.

Please, God, he uttered to himself, *please, God, let me find your beautiful child.*

There were three doors leading out of the larger area. He was about to try each in turn when something occurred to him.

He called out her name: "Bev. Bev! Where are you?"

No answer.

He started for one of the doors when he heard something that raised the gooseflesh on his arms.

It was a sound, a sound like someone who was drunk trying to say his name.

It was coming from the middle door. He ran over and tried it. It was locked.

Again, the sound.

This time he opened it with his foot, crashing the lock off the doorjamb with one vicious kick. The door swung open.

Bev was lying on a table, faceup, her arms and legs bound. She seemed okay . . . and then she turned toward him and he almost stopped dead.

The entire left side of her face looked like it had been eaten away. It was one red mass of flesh, her eye gone, and when he took a few steps and got close to her he was sure that one of her beautiful breasts was mutilated. . . .

He walked up to her and looked down.

He could not talk. All he could do was cry.

He cut her free, touched her face.

"Oh, my darling. Oh, my darling."

She spoke. It was hard to understand her words, but he did.

"Cover me, Jim. Cover me."

He took off his shirt and placed it over her torso . . . and then he saw it, lying on the floor. A brown bottle.

He went over and picked it up, sniffed it. He recognized the smell. They had used it on the farm. Hydrochloric acid. Szabo had worked on her with hydrochloric acid.

He went back to her, put his hand on her face.

"He told me that I would walk around, proof that God did not exist."

Jim wiped his eyes and kissed her on the forehead.

"But God is here. He didn't take you away from me."

A tear rolled out of the single good eye.

"How could you want me like this?"

"Oh, baby," Jim said, tears rolling down his cheeks. "How could I not?"

Abruptly, there was a noise behind him, and Jim whirled, Glock in hand.

But it was Kindhand and others.

Jim looked at Kindhand, his eyes still full of tears.

"Szabo," he said, "hydrochloric acid."

Kindhand's face collapsed in grief, the profound grief that only an Indian face formed by years of pain and outrage could express so well.

"I'm sorry, Jim."

"But I still have her," Jim said. "I still have her."

Kindhand looked at Jim, and he realized that everything that Ben Raines had seen inside this man he was seeing now. Men, people didn't come any better than this guy, he thought.

"We need a doctor."

Kindhand did not need to ask any of the Rebels who came with him to get a doctor. They were out the door.

Jim leaned down toward Bev.

"Where did he go?" he asked.

"Out that way," Bev said, pointing to a far door.

"I'll be back, my love. Duke is getting a doctor, okay."

"Okay."

"Boy, you are one tough son of a beehive."

"I wanted to live, Jim. I wanted to live for God—and you."

Jim wanted to say, "I'll be back," but he couldn't talk. Then he opened the door where she said Szabo had exited. It was a tunnel, very dark. Jim vanished into the darkness, the only light the fire in his eyes.

39

It was dark where Jim entered the tunnel, but he could see ahead that it was light in some spots, where there were shafts.

It stunk, the smell a blend of explosive gas and methane. He hadn't gone twenty yards when he came across, near a shaft, his first body—or part of a body. It was a headless torso and, bizarrely, had no blood on the uniform. It was as if the Reject's head had been blown off cleanly.

He had the Glock out, though he knew his chances of finding Szabo were very small. He was probably long gone by now. But you never knew.

Jim stopped and listened. This reminded him of when he was a little boy, though that was a lifetime away, when he stood in the forest in the dark and listened for the sound of animals, something that he had gotten very good at.

He heard nothing. He moved on.

The tunnel at this point was about seven feet high, though Jim knew, according to what had filtered back to the aboveground force, that some of them were a lot shorter—only three feet high. He hoped that didn't happen soon.

Farther down were more bodies, these obviously killed with a flamethrower, their bodies charred black, their hands and arms in the classic boxer's pose that the body assumes when it is burned alive.

He kept walking and then he came, as it were, to a fork in the tunnel. Straight ahead the tunnel's height dropped dramatically, while to the right it was quite large.

If he were Szabo, what would he do? Would he go into the shorter tunnel?

No, he wouldn't. Szabo was a huge man. He would want to make sure that he could fit.

On the other hand, it would be a great way to throw off anyone pursuing him. Still, going into the short tunnel would mean he couldn't travel quickly. Jim decided to take the tunnel where he could walk upright.

He stopped, listened again.

So far, he thought, he had seen no sign of Szabo. Nor any wildlife, such as rats.

He walked on. He tried to avoid imagining what Bev looked like, tried to control the bottomless rage he felt toward Szabo. He had to focus. If he found him, he would kill him, but walking through a tunnel enraged was not the way to be.

He walked on, and then he noticed something strange. Up ahead, on the ground in relatively good light, because it was directly under a shaft, was another body, but the body of a Believer. He could tell because the uniform was khaki colored and there was a large medallion.

He came over and looked at it. It was faceup. It was a young man, just a kid, small, maybe seventeen or eighteen, with blond hair. He looked good, almost as if he were not dead.

Jim knelt down and felt for a pulse on his neck.

There was none, but the body felt warm. Jim lifted an arm. It was still limber, no sign of rigor mortis.

It was as if he had just died or been killed.

Then Jim noticed it. On the neck, a bruise. He pushed the chin back a bit. More bruises.

Szabo had killed this kid, strangled him to death, and not long ago.

Jim got up and started to walk rapidly down the tunnel, occasionally stopping to try to listen, to try to see if Szabo was running ahead of him.

Nothing.

Jim kept walking, in and out of fields of light and near darkness. Then he saw up ahead that the tunnel turned sharply, and as he turned he felt as if someone had hit his wrist with a baseball bat, because the Glock was knocked from his hand. Before he could resist, fight back, do anything, Alex Szabo had knocked him to the ground and was straddling him, his hands clamped around his neck, gradually squeezing the life out of him.

Jim's natural instinct was to grab those hands and try to pry them off his neck, but he could not, no more than he could pry a steel clamp off his neck.

He focused. He was not yet losing consciousness. He knew what he had to do. Szabo didn't seem to care that Jim had his hands free.

Szabo looked down, smiling, his eyes glinting.

Jim wrapped his hand, which still had feeling despite the whack it took, around the handle of his SEAL knife. Now he could stab him, maybe take him out, but he might be wearing body armor. . . .

Jim felt the first wave of unconsciousness. He gathered his strength and then brought the knife across Szabo's hand, just at the point where it met the wrist, and felt it go completely through the wrist and partly into the other hand.

Szabo recoiled in horror, realizing that one of his hands had been severed from his body. He got up, as if the action would somehow save him, but blood was spurting out of the stump at a high rate.

"You cut off my fucking hand!"

Now Jim, coughing, fighting to speak, stood up.

"I'm Bev's husband, Mr. Szabo."

Szabo was looking down at his hand, pressing it against his chest, trying to stop the flow of blood.

"Hey," Jim was able to say, "don't feel bad. Now you only have to buy one glove."

Szabo fell to his knees, and Jim took a stride over and said: "You're going to find out there is a God, Szabo. And you're going to meet Him right now."

And then Jim drove the SEAL knife all the way up to the hilt into the right side of Szabo's muscular neck.

40

Jim came up to Kindhand, who was standing by a large white tent, a medical facility that had been established. Jim knew Bev was inside.

"I caught up with Szabo," he said.

"Where is he?"

"I killed him. He's in one of the tunnels. I'll show you later."

"Okay, Jim."

Jim nodded and went into the tent. Bev was lying on a stationary gurney. A small bald guy who was obviously a doctor was just leaving.

"Hi," he said. His face was a mask of compassion.

"How's she doing?" Jim asked. "I'm her husband."

"She'll survive," the doctor said. "She's one tough lady."

"I know. Thanks."

Jim went over to Bev.

She looked at him with her one eye. The other was covered with bandages, as was the rest of the left side of her face and her upper chest.

"Szabo's dead," Jim said. "He won't be hurting anybody anymore."

"Good."

Jim leaned down and kissed her very gently on the lips, which were also damaged by the acid.

"Those were some beautiful things you said to me back there, Jim," Bev said. "You know I won't hold you to them."

Jim looked at her and said, "You goddamn well better."

"Look at me," she said.

"I am."

"I'm not all here," she said, half laughing and half crying.

"Listen," he said. "The important thing to me is that you didn't lose the most important thing in my life."

"What's that?"

Jim leaned down and whispered in her ear, "Your butt."

"Okay, Jim," she said, her eye tearing.

"Now you just shut up. We're going to get you back to health, and then we're going to live in the mountains, and I think we're going to be very happy . . . but with your approval, not right now."

"What do you mean?"

"I've been fighting against being a soldier, but sometimes doing what you don't want to do is the only way to do things right. Am I making sense?"

"Yes, you are."

"So what do you think?"

"I think that you're going to make a great soldier, and one day we will settle down. But I know one thing for sure."

"What's that?"

"You're not going to be lonely for me."

"Why not?"

"Because I'm going with you."

"You mean a female in the army?"

Bev kept a straight face.

"Ever hear of female Israeli soldiers?"

"I think I did."

"They didn't do too badly, did they?"

"I guess they didn't."

Then they both broke out laughing.

"Oh, Jim," she said, "I love you so much."

"And why not?" he asked, and kissed her gently on the lips.

THE ASHES SERIES BY WILLIAM W. JOHNSTONE

__America Reborn	0-7860-0490-8	$5.99US/$7.50CAN
__Out of the Ashes	0-7860-0289-1	$4.99US/$5.99CAN
__Fire In The Ashes	0-7860-0335-9	$5.99US/$7.50CAN
__Anarchy In The Ashes	0-7860-0419-3	$5.99US/$7.50CAN
__Blood In The Ashes	0-7860-0446-0	$5.99US/$7.50CAN
__Alone In The Ashes	0-7860-0458-4	$5.99US/$7.50CAN
__Wind In The Ashes	0-7860-0478-9	$5.99US/$7.50CAN
__Smoke From The Ashes	0-7860-0498-3	$5.99US/$7.50CAN
__Danger In The Ashes	0-7860-0516-5	$5.99US/$7.50CAN
__Valor In The Ashes	0-7860-0526-2	$5.99US/$7.50CAN
__Trapped In The Ashes	0-7860-0562-9	$5.99US/$7.50CAN
__Death In The Ashes	0-7860-0587-4	$5.99US/$7.50CAN
__Survival In The Ashes	0-7860-0613-7	$5.99US/$7.50CAN
__Fury In The Ashes	0-7860-0635-8	$5.99US/$7.50CAN
__Courage In The Ashes	0-7860-0651-X	$5.99US/$7.50CAN
__Terror In The Ashes	0-7860-0661-7	$5.99US/$7.50CAN
__Vengeance In The Ashes	0-7860-1013-4	$5.99US/$7.50CAN
__Battle In The Ashes	0-7860-1028-2	$5.99US/$7.99CAN
__Flames From The Ashes	0-7860-1038-X	$5.99US/$7.99CAN
__Treason In The Ashes	0-7860-1087-8	$5.99US/$7.99CAN
__D-Day In The Ashes	0-7860-1089-4	$5.99US/$7.99CAN
__Betrayal In The Ashes	0-8217-5265-0	$4.99US/$6.50CAN
__Chaos In The Ashes	0-7860-0341-3	$5.99US/$7.50CAN
__Slaughter In The Ashes	0-7860-0380-4	$5.99US/$6.50CAN
__Judgment In The Ashes	0-7860-0438-X	$5.99US/$7.50CAN
__Ambush In The Ashes	0-7860-0481-9	$5.99US/$7.50CAN
__Triumph In The Ashes	0-7860-0581-5	$5.99US/$7.50CAN
__Hatred In The Ashes	0-7860-0616-1	$5.99US/$7.50CAN
__Standoff In The Ashes	0-7860-1015-0	$5.99US/$7.99CAN
__Crises In The Ashes	0-7860-1053-3	$5.99US/$7.99CAN
__Tyranny In The Ashes	0-7860-1146-7	$5.99US/$7.99CAN
__Warriors From The Ashes	0-7860-1190-4	$5.99US/$7.99CAN
__Destiny In The Ashes	0-7860-1332-X	$5.99US/$7.99CAN
__Enemy In The Ashes	0-7860-1333-8	$5.99US/$7.99CAN

Available Wherever Books Are Sold!

Visit our website at **www.kensingtonbooks.com**

BOOK YOUR PLACE ON OUR WEBSITE AND MAKE THE READING CONNECTION!

We've created a customized website just for our very special readers, where you can get the inside scoop on everything that's going on with Zebra, Pinnacle and Kensington books.

When you come online, you'll have the exciting opportunity to:

- View covers of upcoming books
- Read sample chapters
- Learn about our future publishing schedule (listed by publication month *and author*)
- Find out when your favorite authors will be visiting a city near you
- Search for and order backlist books from our online catalog
- Check out author bios and background information
- Send e-mail to your favorite authors
- Meet the Kensington staff online
- Join us in weekly chats with authors, readers and other guests
- Get writing guidelines
- AND MUCH MORE!

Visit our website at
http://www.kensingtonbooks.com